Withou t
all the stor e
and war.

There are smaller dragon stories, no less epic in subject, that make the fabric of Krynn. You might find dragons in caves, freeing trapped soldiers; in the ocean, terrorizing the other creatures that call the water home; in the forest, defending it from evil gods; in a village, apologizing for accidentally terrorizing the inhabitants. There are dragons everywhere you might think to look, and some you have to look very closely indeed to see.

Their stories are told here.

Other DRAGONLANCE Anthologies

The Search for Power:
Dragons from the War of Souls

Dagons in the Archives:
The Best of Weis & Hickman

The Players of Gilean:
Tales from the War of Souls

The Dragons of Krynn

The Dragons at War

Relics and Omens:
Tales of the Fifth Age

Heroes and Fools:
Tales of the Fifth Age

Rebels and Tyrants:
Tales of the Fifth Age

Dragons of Time

EDITED BY

Margaret Weis

DRAGONS OF TIME

Printed in the U.S.A.

Cover art by Nilson Hamm
First Printing: April 2007

9 8 7 6 5 4 3 2 1

ISBN: 978-0-7869-4295-4
620-95961740-001-EN

U.S., CANADA,
ASIA, PACIFIC, & LATIN AMERICA
Wizards of the Coast, Inc.
P.O. Box 707
Renton, WA 98057-0707
+1-800-324-6496

EUROPEAN HEADQUARTERS
Hasbro UK Ltd
Caswell Way
Newport, Gwent NP9 0YH
GREAT BRITAIN
Save this address for your records.

Visit our web site at www.wizards.com

TABLE OF CONTENTS

Introduction

Dragons, dragons everywhere, and not a drop to drink. (Oops, I forgot that flaming dragon specialty of the house in one of our tales!) These stories feature dragons (naturally) and everything to do with dragons, including dragon drinks, dragon newspapers, dragon artifacts, and draconians. There are tales about old dragons and young dragons, evil dragons and good dragons, and the occasional mixed-up dragon, all coming to us from various points of time.

Writing about dragons are some of our favorite Dragonlance authors, including Mary Herbert with a Linsha tale; Richard A. Knaak; Miranda Horner, who joins with me to write a story; Kevin Stein, with another of his popular Wülfbunde stories; Paul B. Thompson; Jean Rabe; Douglas W. Clark; and Lucien Soulban.

In addition, we are proud to introduce you to several authors who are being published in Dragonlance for the first time: Jake Bell, Cam Banks, Rachel Gobar, and my very own daughter, Lizz Weis.

So, enjoy our dragon tales!

(Goes best with dwarf spirits and a bowl of gully dwarf stew!)

—Margaret Weis

Homecoming

Lizz Weis

Lizz Weis is a former Wizards of the Coast novels editor who currently works in the financial industry. Lizz and her mother, Margaret Weis, have recently finished writing a romance novel called *Warrior Angel,* which will be published by Harper Collins in the spring of 2007. She lives in Milwaukee, Wisconsin, with her pet rabbit, Terry.

Homecoming

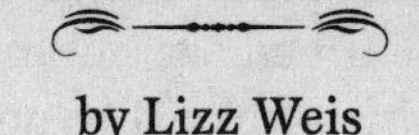

by Lizz Weis

Age of Despair, Summer, 352 AC

My father held me by the shoulders as the returning soldiers walked by our house. We stood on our front stoop, my mother, my father, and I, though I had wanted to run out into the street, to the edge of town, to look for Darden. He'd been away at war for four years, and he was coming home. I just knew he was. But my father, Erwyn, made me wait and watch.

I had been the first one to see the young men trickling down the road toward our town that morning. I recognized the first one in the shambling line: Camron, Cam for short. He was not much older than my brother, and we all used to play together before the war, before they both went away, though Camron played with Darden more than he had with me.

Before the war we had some happy times together

in our little town of Alban.

"You're too little, Em. Go play with the other little girls. Leave us alone, Noodlehead," Darden used to say because I was little and scrawny back then. But if Darden and Camron were hard up for a playmate, sometimes I'd get to join in. Sometimes I got to be their guard dog or be a sentry on duty while they skulked around pretending to be enemies attacking. Noodlehead was my nickname; at least that was what Darden called me back in those days. It had two meanings: one was my long blonde hair, which looked like noodles when it was dirty, and the other was I didn't have any brains—my head was full of noodles. It could be worse, my mother, Zoral, told me. The boys teased her when she was young, calling her Goldbug for reasons she couldn't remember.

Now that I'm older, fourteen years old, in fact, my hair doesn't look like noodles anymore. And to my relief, my childhood nickname faded away once Darden left Alban. Nobody has called me Noodlehead for years.

How different Camron looked! He was taller, all dirty, and he looked very tired. I saw him first from the window and wanted to rush outside to greet him and the others, saying hello to each and every one of them until I found my brother.

"Now, Emberlynn," my father had said, catching me by the arm and sitting me down next to him on the bench near the fireplace. "I know you're excited to see your brother and say hello, but some of the boys who left Alban may not be coming home today. We all watched as they left to fight the forces of darkness and now we will all be watching as they come home. And I'm sure everyone will want to run out and celebrate, like you do. But what if some boys don't come home and Darden does? How would their mothers feel, watching our celebration?"

My father looked at me.

"Bad, I know." I stared at the floor, thinking how bad I would feel if Darden weren't among the ones returning. My father's face was sad, his voice weary. Did he have the same worry?

"So what we're going to do is, we're going to go outside and quietly watch the boys arrive, and we'll do our celebrating indoors when your brother finally gets here. Do you understand?"

"Yes," I whispered. The truth was, we didn't know if he was alive or not. We hadn't heard anything of him since the day he left.

So we stood there and waited. First you could see their heads appear over the crest of the road. I checked the hair color, then the eyes, then the swagger of each one. Darden was bowlegged and had an unmistakable manner of walk that I would know anywhere. It wasn't long before, even far off, I recognized the walk of one of the young men tramping home to Alban.

I turned to my parents and whispered. "It's him." I was sure of it.

He looked different than when he'd left us years ago, but he was just about my age then, and I was only a little girl. He looked thin and hard and older, toughened up by war.

He had left us to squire for a Solamnic Knight. My father was a merchant, not a particularly successful merchant, who sold household tools and wares to the townspeople. The war had taken its toll on the regular supply of goods, and his shelves had grown bare. In essence, then, I suppose he decided to sell my brother.

At fourteen Darden had become bored and reckless, and he was getting into trouble—lots of trouble. My father was always busy trying to shore up his business, and my mother had trouble keeping track of him, especially in the evenings. Darden's repertoire of offenses grew daily. Food was scarce and Darden was caught many times stealing chickens or small items to sell, becoming, I suppose, a kind of small businessman like my father.

But he was a terrible thief, always getting caught red-handed while roasting a chicken he'd stolen. My mother and he had some pitched battles. I would play outside and try to get as far out of earshot as possible. Eventually my father would come home, my mother would be crying and stirring our dinner at the same time, and Darden would be reading a book on his bed, waiting for the punishment he knew was coming.

"Darden, come down here, please. I want to speak with you."

One night the severity of the punishment caught him by surprise, I know. Darden stomped down the stairs intent on pleading his case, but my father began to talk even before his foot touched the last step.

"Enough!" My father shouted. "Enough is enough. Darden, this time you will listen to me." His voice grew quieter.

I thought at that point my father had never looked so tired in his life as he did that day.

Darden's jaw dropped. Usually he was given a chance to try out some excuse he had imagined. He sure looked uneasy now. This time was different, though. Father didn't usually raise his voice. Darden quietly took a seat on the bench near the fire.

"There is a man, a knight. Lives out by Lake Shadrin. He's going off to fight in the war, and he needs a squire. Tomorrow he is going to come by here, and you're going to leave with him. He's a good man, and he's going to take good care of you. He has money and food, and the work will keep you out of trouble, I hope."

Tears fell from my brother's eyes, as well as my own.

I looked at my mother; she was still crying and stirring the pot on the stove. She didn't seem surprised by what Father was saying, so I figured they had worked it out beforehand. I wondered if she agreed with sending Darden away. I sniffed.

A look of surprising strength and resolve fell over Darden's face. He brushed the tears from his cheeks.

"You're right, Father. Hey, I need to see the world. I've been clinging to Mom's skirts for too long. I'll just go and pack my things."

And that was that, so long ago now it almost seemed a dream.

There he was now, walking toward our house. My mother stood on the stoop, quivering in anticipation. My father was steely, though, and kept his grip on me.

"Mother, Father, Em, it's good to see you." Darden spoke to us formally, as though we were strangers, and I suppose we were, in a way. Wordlessly, my mother ushered him inside the house.

But once inside with the door closed, we fell on him with hugs and kisses and lots of fuss. Darden hugged me the hardest and the longest, until my father broke us up. He gave Darden a rueful smile, shook my brother's hand, and welcomed him home.

"Zoral, please start supper if you would. Darden is tired. Let's let him rest and get his bearings 'fore we start asking him about where he's been and what he's seen."

I was shocked by how different he looked close up in the privacy of our house. He was taller, his hair was long and dirty. Everything on him was dirty. His clothes, his shoes, his every possession was coated in dust or caked mud. Yet he was handsome too. There were lines around his eyes. His face was dark from the sun, and looked more weathered.

It was all I could do not to stare at him while I helped Mother, peeling the potatoes, minding not to peel the skin from my hands.

"Father, I'd like to clean up some before dinner."

"I'll go with him!" I shouted.

Darden stood and headed for the back door. "All right, Noodlehead."

I stared dumbly as Darden took his dirty shirt off and started to wash away what I expect were years of grime.

"How did you ever get so filthy?" I asked.

He cracked a bright smile amid his grubby face. "You're always on the road as a soldier. I've been traveling steady now for over a month. Can't always have a regular bath," he said while scrubbing dirt out of his ears.

"Camron came home today too. I saw him."

"Yes, I know. Maybe I'll go see him tomorrow. We're still pals. He's a good salt. What is Mom making for dinner tonight?"

"Shepherd's pie. She hasn't made it in years. With the potatoes on top like we used to have, before . . . before you went away."

"How have the old folks been? How is the shop?" He sat down next to me and wiped his head, peering at me with a new, clean face.

"They've been busy. The war's been hard on the whole town. No one can pay their debts at the store, and Dad can't get much to sell besides a few staples like flour and cornmeal and beans. We've been growing most of our own vegetables in the backyard. All the customers are local, and most folks are afraid to travel far because they'll be robbed. Traders don't stop here anymore."

"Yes, I know. Things are bad. Things should get better soon. The war is finally over."

"So you're home for good? You won't have to leave again?"

His face darkened momentarily. "I see you're still a Noodlehead with more questions to ask than I care to answer. I'm hungry. Let's go eat." Darden stood, and we walked toward the house. He stuck one foot in front of mine like he used to do when we were children together and knocked me off balance.

"Why are you walking so funny?" He laughed and pulled me upright before I fell.

I punched him in the arm.

During dinner Darden regaled us with stories of the war and his travels. He'd been to some beautiful and fantastic places, like Kayolin, where the dwarves live, and some awful ones, such as the Plains of Dust, where nothing lived. When we asked about the fighting, though, his face grew somber and his answers terse.

Immediately after dinner Darden fell asleep, and the rest of us sat around the fire. Mother had me darn Darden's stockings, but all of his clothes were a mess and some would just have to be thrown away. Finally I finished and, seeing that Darden was quietly snoring, I asked if I could go to the barn.

"Yes, of course," Mother replied, "though I don't know what you do in there every evening."

"Let her go," said Father kindly. "It's her own private world."

Yes, it was my own little world, and they left me alone in the barn at night and didn't pry into what I was doing.

I headed out the back door and climbed the ladder to the hayloft, going back into a far, dark corner and pulling out a large basket. No one ever came up there. Opening the napkin I had stashed in my skirt pocket, I brought out the fatty meat scraps that Mother had discarded. There was a rustling in the basket.

"All right, all right, hold on a minute. I'm opening it."

I unfastened the lid. A small dark nose poked out of the top of the basket, sniffing the air for food. Then a clawed foot emerged. Holding out the meat scraps, I coaxed the creature out of the basket.

Camron and Darden used to keep secrets from me, back when I was a little girl. These days I had a secret from everybody.

The usual cutesy names didn't apply to the small rambunctious creature that was my secret pet. So I simply called it "Pet."

Early one morning about two months ago, I spotted a group of vultures circling around an area outside our back fence. I spied something dark flopping around on the ground. I scared off the birds and came across Pet. It was very small at first, slimy, cold, weak, and evidently hungry, so I brought it home and cleaned it up, wiping the goop off its body. Once it was cleaned up, I realized the small creature was beautiful, black as night, but with scales that shimmered and shone in the light.

I offered it some water, and it drank greedily, then actually fell asleep in my lap. Somehow it just seemed to know that I wouldn't hurt it and that it was safe with me.

Oh, did I mention Pet had wings, small but beautifully shaped wings? It probably was a very young baby and had somehow wandered away from its nest. It had small front legs with clawed feet that it used to hold large pieces of meat while it was feeding. Its snout was long and pointed, and it sniffed the air almost constantly when awake.

That was two months ago, and my pet was growing bigger and stronger. It ate as much as I could scrounge. Once out of its basket, it stood on its hind legs and lunged at the scraps, grabbing them out of my hand almost before I could pull away. So far, I'd been lucky not to have lost a finger.

I watched it proudly as it gobbled the meat scraps. It was a muscular pet now, its wings growing larger and more beautiful and sturdy by the day. Comfortable with me, it finished eating and sprinted in a circle, stretching his legs and wings. It squawked and squealed as I watched and clapped. It couldn't fly yet, but I knew it would be only a short matter of time before it could; then it would leave me. But for the time being, it was mine, my secret Pet.

I fetched some milk from a pail. I kept the milk hidden, or the creature would drink an entire pail at one meal if I let him. I could never spare that much, or Father would notice. After it was done eating and drinking, my pet sat in my lap and let me stroke its back and touch its wings, purring almost like a cat.

"Emberlynn! Time for bed!"

"Yes, Momma!" I shouted back. I nudged the creature back into the basket and fastened the latch before I went to bed.

That night I woke to a sound coming from Darden's side of the room, on the other side of a curtain Mother had put up as a divider.

"Uh . . . ashes, ashes falling on us like snow . . . we must get to the port!" Darden's voice was like an eerie moan. "No, no, no, you can't take our boat; we'll die here without it! The city is burning; all of us will burn! We'll die here! Please, I'll pay . . ."

I jumped up and ran over to Darden, touching him lightly on the arm.

"Darden. Darden, it's Em. You're having a bad dream. Wake up!"

"Can't get air! Can't breathe! Help me!" Darden cried, his head rolling back and forth on the pillow. Then he opened his eyes, gasping for breath, his brow covered in sweat. Darden stared, searching the room with his eyes, remembering he was safe.

He let out a heavy sigh, pulling his hands to his face.

My father came to the bottom of the stairs. "Is everything all right up there?"

"Yes, Father," I said, glancing at Darden, who sank back on his pillow, his hands across his eyes. "Everything is fine."

****

The next morning, Darden went over to Cam's house, and I saw to the animals and the garden. He was gone all day, but I was busy and I didn't miss him. I'd hardly gotten used to his being around again anyway.

He returned at eventide, and we had family supper. He told interesting stories again, polishing his sword at the table. Afterward, he fell asleep as wearily as the night before. Seizing my chance, I asked to go to the barn again. Father looked at Mother, who rolled her eyes and said yes. I kicked Darden, waking him with a start.

"What?" he asked in alarm.

"Nothing," I said with a sly smile and kicked him again while shifting my eyes toward the outside.

He finally got the hint. "Uh, I think I'll get some air with Noodlehead," he said to Mother and Father, who were starting to clean up and not paying much attention to us anyway.

Outside, he regarded me skeptically, playing with his sword as he spoke, flipping it around his head, swiping it up and down, and making stabbing motions in the air.

"All right, you got me out here. What do you want?"

"Follow me."

I took him up the ladder to the hayloft and, smiling at his irritated expression, pulled the scraps out of my pocket for Pet. The basket started to rumble and rustle.

"What is this? A dumb green snake or something?" Darden asked with an impatient chuckle.

"No, much better than a snake," I said smugly. I unfastened the basket's lid, and as usual, the creature tipped the basket over as it crept out. It was slowly crawling toward my outstretched hand when it caught the smell of something strange and different, something that made the creature stop in its tracks with a surprising hiss. That smell was Darden.

"What is it, Pet? Darden? He's not—"

"Paladine's breath, Em! Do you know what that foul thing is?" Darden raised his sword. "Em, move away from it! Slowly."

"What? No! It's my pet!" I blocked my brother, with him and Pet both frozen and glaring at each other. "Stop, Darden!"

"Em, you foolish, foolish girl. Do you know how dangerous—?" Darden said, slowly trying to move around me while bringing his sword up and around. Again, I moved to block him, as Pet let out another low hiss and slithered back a few steps.

"No, Darden!"

"Em, it's a wyrmling. They kill people. It'll kill you!"

"Darden, of course it's a wyrmling, but it's just a wee one. A baby. I found him and saved him, he couldn't take care of himself, poor thing. He's my pet. I'm like his mother. So please put your sword down."

I didn't want to look stupid in front of Darden, so I only pretended to already know the creature was a wyrmling. I knew it was something out of the ordinary, but until he said the word, honestly, I didn't know exactly what it was. I thought maybe it was some sort of rare giant lizard baby.

Darden stepped around me faster than I expected and took a wild swing at the wyrmling. It raised its wings and backed up with a quick shriek that was so loud it hurt my ears.

But I shrieked even louder at Darden. "What do you think you're doing?" I threw myself in front of the wyrmling. "This is my pet! I just wanted to show you! You're trying to kill him!"

"Em, please. Get away from this foul wyrmling. I've seen creatures like this do terrible things. Have you gone crazy, keeping one as a pet? Mother and Father would be horrified—"

The terrified, black, scaly creature raced over to its basket and jumped in. Darden made a dash toward it, but I moved faster and swept his leg out from under him. He landed with a thud, and the astonishment held him for a moment. That was long enough for me to grab the basket, slide down the ladder, and push the ladder aside with him yelling from the hayloft.

Then I ran as far and as fast as I could, tears blurring my vision and streaming down my cheeks. Whoever that was, that man who wanted to kill my pet, that was not the brother I used to love. I had a head start on him but knew I had to keep running and running.

And why shouldn't I? Darden left home when he was my age. Maybe it was time for me to leave and make my way in the world too. If I didn't get away, he'd kill Pet, plain and simple.

By dark I had gotten pretty far, going down side paths and trails that Darden wouldn't know about or remember, until I was on the far southeast side of town. I kept hidden in the surrounding woods but wasn't far from one of the main roads.

But I was tired and so was my pet. I checked on my beautiful creature, opening the lid. It was ready to strike at anyone except me, and I cooed and let it smell me until it settled back down to the bottom, trusting I would protect it. What was I going to do with it? We'd both have to eat eventually.

I slid behind a tree for a brief rest, and heard a strange sound coming from near the road. I grabbed the basket and headed deeper into the wood. I had just put a safe distance between me and the road when I stepped wrong on some twigs and wet leaves and stumbled face-first to the ground. When I looked up, I saw the entrance to a cave just ahead. It was a small opening, just large enough to squeeze one or two people through.

I felt a few raindrops on my face. I was very cold and very hungry, and it was a black night. I was out later than I'd ever been out before. I looked around nervously and couldn't think of a reason not to head into the cave and sleep for a while there. I might as well explore the cave, maybe get some rest, and see if things looked any brighter in the morning. "They usually do," my father always said with a grin. I had to choke back tears as I thought of my father, whom I might never see again.

I set the basket aside and knelt down to crawl underneath the outcropping that hid the mouth of the cave. Once inside, I reached back and pulled the basket in with me.

"Are you all right, Pet?" I reached into the basket and ran my hand over his back, neck, haunches, and wings. All seemed to be intact.

"Well, I guess this is home for the night."

I wiped cobwebs away from my face with my hands and slumped down. A small amount of moonlight trickled in from the outside, along with a cold draft. I rubbed my chilled arms to warm them and pulled my dress down as far as possible to cover my bare ankles. I opened the basket and let the wyrmling out. It crawled onto my lap and buried its head in the crook of my arm.

I woke from a shallow sleep with a start when I felt something odd: warm air. And whatever the source of the air, it smelled bad.

****

"Bastard son of a whore!" I cursed. Em's swipe at my legs had caught me by surprise. I was struck speechless, and it took me a moment to get my breath back enough even to let out the curse. Where'd she learn to do that? And secondly, where had she gone? I needed to find her . . . and to kill that little dragon.

Believe me, I witnessed what those wyrmlings can do in the war. I know how destructive they can be. I had watched as hundreds of people were slain by a dragon, and the one Em was protecting could grow up to slay just as many with one killing stroke. I would never forget the burning of Balladmore port. I could still feel the acrid smoke in my lungs. I had watched from the bow of a ship offshore as the fire consumed the entire town. I had almost drowned swimming to that ship. My leather armor wouldn't come off; the buckles were stuck. But I had had to jump into the water, armor and all, then shimmy out of everything I was wearing or else sink like a stone. If I'd stayed on shore, the fire would have engulfed my body.

The streets of Balladmore had been littered with bodies. Many had died from the smoke, mercifully. The rest had burned to death in their homes. I could remember the night sky glowing brightly, almost like noonday, as the ashes of the city fell to the water all around me.

I worked my way down from the hayloft and rushed to saddle a horse. I needed to find Em as fast as possible. Never mind our parents. They would have plenty of time to yell at us both later when I brought Em home. If only I could find her before the wyrmling turned on her.

The trouble was, I had no idea where she could have gone. I guessed that she'd head south; after all, she's more familiar with the woods to the south than any other direction. We used to have grandparents who lived in the country over on that side of Alban. I kicked my heels into the horse's belly and felt the animal rear and lunge forward at a gallop.

****

It was still dark outside the cave where I crouched with Pet's basket, though I could hear birds chirping outside. It would be light soon. I looked to the dark end of the cave, where the smell was coming from, but couldn't see anything past a few feet. My pet crawled back into the basket but hissed anxiously and made scrambling noises. I stood and tapped the basket with my foot, shushing my pet. Although, if there was something in the cave, chances were it already knew we were there.

The air and smell thickened in the cave; whatever was back there was drawing closer. I started to think that maybe running away from home and into that cave hadn't been the best idea.

Squinting into the pitch of the cave, I faintly glimpsed the shine of two eyes. Though I strained my ears, I couldn't hear anything, which was strange. Then something underneath the eyes moved. Something furry seemed to be opening and closing—its mouth; no, it didn't move like a mouth; it moved like mandibles.

Furry mandibles. A spider.

It was the biggest spider I had ever seen. I fought back the urge to retch and stood back against the cave wall as quietly as possible. Maybe it wouldn't bother us. Maybe if I remained really still, it would move on or back, deeper into the cave.

Drool fell from the creature's mouth, and a plop of it landed on the dirt floor of the cave. It knows I'm here, I realized. It's eyeing its next meal. The giant spider was big enough to eat me and my pet whole in one furry bite.

My lips felt dry. A chill went through my already-cold body. My stomach grumbled, loud enough that the spider's eyes flickered.

I slowly slid down the cave wall onto my knees, watching the shining eyes watching me from the back of the cave. I stared in horror as the huge cave spider moved one hairy leg into the light. More of its hairy body followed, slowly inching closer. It was so large, I could barely make out where its body started and the darkness began. It loomed over my head, brushing the ceiling. Whenever I shifted, it shifted with me. Whenever I stopped still, it inched closer. I was being stalked.

While still on my knees, I nudged the basket toward the mouth of the cave. The spider moved too, but still slowly. Once the basket was in place, I took a deep breath. In one quick smooth movement, I lunged head-first on my belly toward the mouth of the cave and the light outside. After propelling myself outside, I reached back to grab the basket.

I felt something wrap around my wrist, something sticky but taut. In spite of myself, I screamed and let go of the basket. I was yanked back through the mouth of the cave and across the floor into darkness. I was back inside, and as I stared in fright, the exit was gradually blocked by a huge shadowy form.

****

I heard Em's shouts of fear from the road nearby. There was no mistaking her voice, or the fear. Her cry sent chills down my spine.

I rode at breakneck speed, smashing through bushes and around trees, desperately looking for a path. Again I heard her scream, and just then I came upon a rocky outcropping.

"Emberlynn! Is that you?" I shouted. I heard something muffled; then I heard something unmistakable: the hiss of the wyrmling. Following the sounds, I jumped down from the horse and looked around. Immediately I spotted the opening to the cave. I slid underneath a rock and into the cave. I couldn't wait for my eyes to adjust to the light, so I quickly lit a small torch.

When I laid eyes on the spider, I immediately pulled my sword from its scabbard. The creature had enveloped Em in a gray, gauzy web. Her mouth was covered, but she was still breathing. I knew she was breathing because I looked into her despairing eyes and saw them flicker with hope. Tears were rolling down her cheeks.

"Hey, over here!" I yelled to get the spider's attention. It quickly moved away from Em and scuttled toward me. I waved my torch at it with one hand and moved in to stab it with my sword. Nicking its furry foreleg did little to slow the creature down, however. It raised its injured leg and shot out a filmy web to ensnare my sword arm. I quickly brought the torch in closer and managed to burn the web away without scorching myself. My sword arm came free.

That was when something hissed directly behind me. I turned to see what it was just as something struck me hard. I fell, landing on my side and dropping the torch and my sword. My arms were covered, immobilized, by something sticky and quite strong.

"Paladine's stones!" I yelled. The web spread to cover my mouth. Then I noticed the wyrmling near the cave's entrance slithering away from its basket. The spider was busy dragging my web-encased body deeper into the cave, setting me near a wall. Then the spider did the same with Em. For some reason it didn't notice the small dark creature moving about stealthily in the corner near the cave mouth.

It was a struggle to raise my head and check on Em. Tears streamed down her cheeks, but I saw she had a disappointed look in her eyes. Disappointment in me, her brother, her hero.

Then I noticed her gaze shift to my left. Out of the corner of my eye, I saw the wyrmling was moving toward us. Things were going from bad to worse. What was the wyrmling going to do? Join in the fun? Call Momma to come torch us all?

Meanwhile the filthy spider had drawn close to my sister, eyeing her. When she started to struggle, the spider picked her up and spun more and more web to entangle and trap her.

My mind filled with rage, but I could do little more than thrash around inside my own webbed prison, trying to distract the monster from my sister.

Noticing my frantic thrashing, the spider moved away from my sister and turned its attention to me. Good, leave her alone.

I looked around for my sword. I had dropped it somewhere, but where? There it was, on the cave floor, halfway between Em and me. Somehow I had to reach my sword, impossible as it seemed.

Then I saw the wyrmling furtively maneuvering behind the spider.

Infernal creature! I hope the spider at least kills it and saves me the bother, I thought.

I shifted my gaze to my sister. I could see in her eyes

that hope was gone, lost. She wouldn't fight anymore.

This isn't over, Em. C'mon, you've been a stubborn pain in the arse for as long as I've known you, and now you give up?

I could move only one hand. The other was pinned against my chest. I started to grab at twigs from the ground with my free hand.

Just then the spider pulled itself up close to my face. Its fetid breath made me spasm, but I struggled against it and my thrashing around brought my fingers into contact with the sword. With all the strength I could muster, I brought up the sword and managed to cut the creature before dropping the weapon in the struggle. The creature scuttled back, making very little noise but wounded enough to worry. Its two glowing eyes studied me, seeming to be considering a change of tactics.

With a great whoosh of air from the other direction, I felt something launch itself over my head and let out a great screeching sound.

It was the wyrmling. It flew at the spider, spitting a stream of saliva into the spider's eyes. The spider recoiled, then drew itself up like a big balloon on legs before fearfully drawing back into the cave until it shrank away.

The wyrmling dashed over to Em and began gnawing on the web that covered her. I caught my breath and tried to find my sword.

Then I felt something on my wrist and realized the wyrmling was gnawing on my web like a dog after a bone. It pulled and sawed at the web with its nasty little sharp teeth.

The wyrmling made its way through one strand of web, then another, making some sort of weird spitting, gurgling noise all the while. It's going to eat my hand next! I thought.

Emberlynn pulled her upper body free from the tough webbing. She grabbed my sword and awkwardly sliced at the web around her legs and feet.

I pulled my arm free, shoved the wyrmling away, and pulled webbing off my mouth and the rest of my body.

"Em! My sword! Quick, give it to me!" I shouted.

She tossed the sword to me. I snatched it out of the air and rolled to the side to prepare for the spider's imminent return. I could hear it writhing and moaning deep down inside the cave. I crept toward the noise, choosing my moment, and stabbed the spider through the head, pinning it to the ground.

I turned and raced back to Em. She was free of the web, the color coming back to her face. Indeed, she was grinning at me, triumphantly.

"Em, let's get out of here before more spiders come."

"All right, but what about my pet, Darden? Admit it: you were wrong. He is the one who rescued us. We shouldn't leave him here."

"Noodlehead!" I said exasperatedly, but I had to grin back. I had to admit she was right. That infernal wyrmling had saved our lives. I looked over at the creature, standing next to Em's skirt and watching me intently with its infernal creature's eyes.

"All right, it saved my life, so you were right and I won't try to kill it. But it can't come home with us. Sis, you know it's going to get bigger—a lot bigger—and it'll start eating more and more. More than we can feed it. It's a wild creature, Em. This is a good place to leave it. This is where it belongs. If there are other spiders here, well, they'd better keep their distance, eh?"

Em laughed. Then her face grew dark as she looked fondly down at her pet. It looked up at her.

"All right, we'll leave him here," she said, understanding. She sniffed as she spoke, kneeling and pulling the wyrmling to her breast.

"Thank you for saving us, Pet," she whispered, hugging it.

"All right, Em, let's go home." I held out my hand to her.

"All right, home," she replied, her voice tired and hoarse. She took my hand. We made our way out of the cave, and I let Em ride the horse while I walked us out of the woods to the safety of the road.

****

I am home too. Only instead of a basket, I'm back in a cave like the one where I was born and where I belong. Once the humans were gone, I scoured the cave for food. Past the spider's corpse, I smelled its other victims. On its web lay three creatures, hearts still beating, for me to feast on. Starving, I reached for the one nearest me. With the webbing around it, I couldn't make out its exact species, but I didn't care. I unwrapped it slowly like a sweetmeat and ate it feet first. It struggled at first, then went still as I finished munching on its fingers.

The other two I saved for later, though I was still hungry.

I am growing bigger and stronger every day. I like my home and will thrive in my cave. I am old enough to care for myself. And when I have reached my full size and strength, this entire town of silly humans will be mine to rule and mine to feed on.

Chain of Fools

Cam Banks

Cam Banks leads a quiet, pastoral life in central Pennsylvania with his beautiful wife, their two sons, and an enormous cat. He regularly interrupts this peaceful existence by answering obscure Dragonlance trivia questions and writing books to explain them. A member of the fan-based Whitestone Council, Cam has been published by Sovereign Press and Dragon Magazine as a freelance author and game designer and has a novel in the works for Tracy Hickman's *Anvil of Time* series from Wizards of the Coast.

Chain of Fools

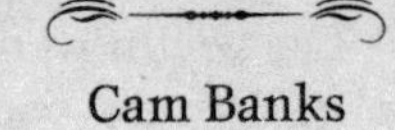

Cam Banks

Age of Despair, 357 AC

Hullek Skullsmasher was cursed.

Three weeks earlier, Hullek had been Dragon Highlord of the Green Dragonarmy of Her Dark Majesty, Takhisis. Successor to Highlord Salah-Khan, he cut a bloody swath across Goodlund and Balifor. He had ridden a mighty green dragon, holding aloft a terrible axe with which he separated the heads from the bodies of men. The blood of ogre warlords and nomad princes ran through his veins. Elves feared him; dwarves loathed him. None could stand before his power.

None, that was, but the wizard who cursed him.

Hullek sat on a rock near a long wooden bridge. A chain ran from a thick iron manacle on his right wrist to a similar manacle on the left wrist of a goblin three feet away. The goblin droned on incessantly, but Hullek wasn't listening. Hullek was trying to think.

The wizard's curse filled Hullek's head with a fog that clouded his thoughts. His had been a cunning mind, sharper than most of his particular ancestry. Hullek knew of only one half-ogre smarter than he, and that was Highlord Lucien of Takar. A role model, Hullek always thought. Lucien wouldn't have been caught off guard by a wizard.

"So I told the boss, you aren't gettin' me in that wagon, no thanks!" The goblin went on. "An' he told me, Mudskip, you worthless rat, you're gettin' in that wagon, an' I said, suit yerself, an' I walked off. That I did, an' then he yelled, like all hobs do, Mudskip, you better get back here! An' that's where I left 'im, still yellin'."

Hullek grunted. You are a worthless rat, he thought. I should toss you over the edge of the chasm, see where that puts you. Except, he thought, we're chained together. He opened his mouth to tell the goblin all of this, but his mouth said only, "Hullek."

Hullek scratched his head with his free hand. He tried again. "Hullek." No good. This blasted curse! He couldn't even berate a goblin.

"All right, you lot," called out one of his captors. "Get up. Time to go."

Their captors were mercenaries, signed on to the Whitestone Army. Hullek recognized the uniforms. He'd killed many of them while he was highmaster, even more once he made highlord. Mercenaries had little confidence and no spirit for a job that barely paid for beer and a cot in a common room. They would be an easy victory for him, if only he could think straight.

Hullek, the goblin Mudskip, and the three other prisoners along the chain stood up. Hullek looked the motley group over again as he stretched his aching legs. A goblin, two surly humans, and a gnoll. The gnoll had potential. He looked like one of the gnolls Hullek had recruited months ago in Goodlund: tall, muscular, and rangy, with a grin like an idiotic hyena. Hullek made a mental note but soon lost it to the fog in his head, as he had all the other mental notes.

The mercenaries stood to one side to let the prisoners shuffle along, out onto the wooden bridge. It swayed precariously, barely wide enough for Hullek's massive bulk. The boards beneath his boots creaked. It was a long way across, and there was a lot of wind. Hullek looked down and saw what he thought was a river at the bottom of the gorge. The fog swam before his eyes, distracting him. A plan, he thought, I need a plan.

On the far side of the bridge, other mercenaries had arrived and were waiting. Hullek and his fellow prisoners were being handed over. There was something about a contractual agreement, borders, jurisdiction, and a prison camp. The mercenaries had talked about it, and Hullek had tried to listen but, between the curse and the chattering goblin, he couldn't keep the issues straight. Hullek did know one thing: once he crossed the bridge, he wouldn't have another opportunity like this one.

"Where we goin'?" Mudskip asked, halfway across the bridge.

To perfidy and damnation, thought Hullek. "Hullek," said Hullek.

The gnoll was growling and making a lot of noise

at the far end of the chain. The two humans cursed in Nerakese. The wind had picked up and added rain. The bridge became slick and unstable. No other opportunities, thought Hullek. Forcing the idea through the fog, he came to a decision.

"Hullek!" he shouted. The other prisoners looked at him, not comprehending. The mercenaries on both ends of the bridge, many yards away and bored, just laughed. Hullek grew frustrated. Can't you see, you fools? This is our chance! He yanked the chain, and pointed down to the river. There! Now do as I say! "Hullek!" he said.

"Hang about," said Mudskip. "I think he means to jump." The other prisoners looked shocked. The gnoll licked his lips in uncertainty. The mercenaries hadn't yet noticed the prisoners had stopped moving at the very center of the bridge. "You're mad, you are," the goblin said, clutching at the rope handrail. He looked at Hullek, then looked at the others. "He's mad!"

Hullek could wait no more. Trusting the others would get the idea, he flung his weight to one side, against the handrails. The bridge swung backward with loud creaks. The mercenaries began to realize their captives had stopped and something was happening. One of the soldiers on the receiving end of the bridge stepped out onto the wooden slats, then thought better of it.

"Hullek!" yelled the former dragon highlord, glaring into the faces of the other four captives. They seemed to understand, even if they were terrified. They, too, lurched backward and forward. The rope bridge swung out again, then back, and with a series of cracks and snaps, the center gave out. Rope flayed back toward the sides of the chasm, pieces of lumber spun crazily into the gorge, and out into the void, buffeted by rain and wind, Hullek and his four associates fell end over end, linked only by a chain.

****

Hullek Skullsmasher was wet.

He was wet and cold, more to the point, and lying facedown in mud beside the river's edge. Turning his head to one side, he saw the other four escapees were still with him and still attached to each other by the chain. The highlord pulled himself into a sitting position, feeling along his chest for broken ribs or anything that may have dislodged. It's a miracle, he thought, a miracle or incredible luck. "Hullek," he said, voicing his relief.

One of the humans was the next to stir. He said something in Nerakese, which he spoke with a very thick accent. Hullek struggled to understand him. He'd picked up the language by necessity, but the wizard's curse had buried the meaning of the words deep in his skull, somewhere between the proper way to torture an elf and the recipe for gorgon garlic steak. "Hullek?" he asked, rubbing at his head. The Nerakan cursed in frustration and turned instead to shove his companion awake.

While the others returned to consciousness, Hullek studied their location: healthy green forest, burbling river, muddy bank, blackberry bushes. Beside the bushes, a path led off into the forest and, by the looks of things, it went somewhere specific. You don't just make a path to nowhere, Hullek thought.

In short order, Hullek, the two humans, Mudskip the goblin, and the gnoll were trudging along the path, stopping only long enough to fill their bellies with berries. Hullek had convinced the others with a series of meaningful intonations of "Hullek!" that he was the leader and, as such, he was to be followed. You can take the armor and the weapon and the dragon away, Hullek mused, but you can't take away the highlord. Being at one end of the chain didn't hurt either.

Mudskip rekindled his fondness for chattering, and time passed as they walked with little else but a running commentary from the goblin and the occasional grunt from the humans. The gnoll brought up the rear, looking over his hunched shoulder at the dense trees on either side of the path. He's a smart one, Hullek thought. Knows where he'd ambush us if he were the one doing the ambushing.

By the time the prisoners emerged from the forest and began walking through a waist-high tide of golden grain, Hullek had cobbled together some kind of master plan. Every few moments, however, he needed to stop and press hard at his temples to keep the plan from plunging below the level of conscious thought. It was apparent to Hullek there was a village, a town, perhaps a farmhouse nearby. The grain fields were indication of that. That meant people, and food, and possibly a blacksmith to remove the chain.

Hullek was only partly right. There was a town around the next hill, with a stream and a millpond and farmhouses. Over a footbridge, there were cobbled streets and swinging signs over tailors' shops and bakeries. Cottages with thatched roofs had well-tended gardens with little painted kender statues standing in between the hyacinths to keep the birds away. It was very pleasant. Hullek hated it already.

The goblin was the first to state the obvious. "There's no people," Mudskip said, looking around as the group stopped on the other side of the footbridge. The gnoll eyed the stream warily; the running water was an unwelcome reminder of the dangerous circumstances of their escape. The humans frowned and looked to Hullek—for inspiration or an excuse, Hullek wasn't sure which. What are they expecting me to do? he thought. If we weren't all attached by a chain, I'd send out the goblin as a scout, post the gnoll over by the town gate, and take one of the Nerakans with me to look inside the buildings.

"Hullek," said Hullek, lifting his arm to rattle the chain.

"He's got a point," said Mudskip. "Can't split up. We hafta stick together."

Up ahead, Hullek saw a fountain burbling in the center of the town square. He advanced along the street with the others trailing along behind. They had become used to how the chain worked, especially after the gnoll had stopped once or twice to sniff at something and the others had almost fallen over. Every once in a while, the gnoll would jabber or growl something in his strange tongue. As soon as the group entered the square, the gnoll did exactly that.

The village was definitely deserted. People had left in a hurry too. Hullek looked to see what the gnoll was bothered by. To one side, smoke was curling out of the windows of a bakery. The Nerakan men exclaimed loudly and pointed at it, and Mudskip helpfully yelled, "Fire!"

By the Darklady, thought Hullek. We only just got here, and there's already a fire. The building beside the bakery looked like a surveyor's guild or a mapmaker, judging by the compass sign hanging over the door. That meant it would have maps, and maps were vital information Hullek would need. "Hullek!" cried the former highlord, pointing at the bakery, then at the fountain. "Hullek!"

"The boss's right," Mudskip said, helpfully translating. "Grab that horse trough; we can fill it up with water and put out the fire." The five escaped prisoners ran in unison to the trough, filled it at the fountain, and hauled it to the bakery door, its watery contents sloshing about.

Hullek didn't see any point in being graceful. He used the front end of the trough and their combined momentum to act as a battering ram, knocking the door from its hinges. Flames licked around the brick oven inside the bakery, dancing along the tops of wooden shelves nearby. The bakery was deserted too, and Hullek was curious to know what sort of thing would cause somebody to leave in a hurry with a substantial fire unattended. Don't have time to worry about that, he thought. With a mighty heave, the chain gang upended the contents of the trough into the fires of the oven, dousing it instantly.

A second troughful of water took care of the rest of the flames, and the half-ogre nodded appreciatively.

"Hullek," he said, gesturing at the others and the scorched bakery. Fine work, he thought. This might turn out all right, after all. At that sign of approval, Mudskip placed his fists firmly at his hips, and his pointy little features looked smug. The gnoll grinned, with his tongue lolling out of his muzzle of a mouth, and even the Nerakans were smiling.

Now to business, thought Hullek.

****

Hullek Skullsmasher was perplexed.

According to the map he had found in the surveyor's guild, the town he was standing in didn't exist. Or rather, it didn't exist a century ago. He could tell they were still in Qwermish, near the border into Solamnia. The Dargaard Mountains were west of here, where the prisoner exchange was supposed to have taken place. But by Hullek's addled estimates, there wasn't any kind of settlement along the river. It was either too new or too insignificant.

It was also too empty. While he and the escapees had found plenty to eat, and were idling on wooden benches in front of the town's inn, that kind of respite didn't seem right to Hullek. He had chased people out of towns before, but that always came with the work of looting and stealing and setting fire to buildings. Easiest town I've ever taken, he thought, smiling to himself, but still somehow troubling. What was going on here?

The former dragon highlord was about to rouse the others and go searching for a blacksmith's forge when a tremendous gust of wind whipped through the town square, scattering his maps in all directions. "Hullek!" he cursed, grabbing for the parchment. The Nerakans had dozed off but woke up with a start. Mudskip dropped a mug of sour cider in alarm, and the gnoll growled thickly.

Folding the maps together in a rough semblance of order, Hullek rose from the bench, dragging the others with him. He blinked up into the weak afternoon sunlight, but there wasn't a cloud in the sky. For a terrible moment, he thought that perhaps another wizard was around. Wizards could make winds like that. But wait, the wind was familiar.

His fear felt like a knife had been thrust into his skull. Clutching at his head, he turned away from the heavens and saw that the other four were just as frightened.

Perhaps because the wizard's mind fog blurred all of his thoughts, including the terror, Hullek overcame the lancing pain enough to take hold of the chain in both of his hands. He hauled the other four prisoners by sheer strength away from the open square and through the door of the inn, falling into a shaking and terror-struck dog pile on the floor of the common room. Hullek risked a glance through the crosshatched windows of the inn and caught sight of the source of their fear.

It was a dragon.

Hullek, as Dragon Highlord of the Green Dragonarmy, was used to dragons—as much as anybody could be said to be used to dragons—and thus had built up a certain amount of resistance to their supernatural dragonfear. But nobody but a kender could be truly immune to it. Caught off guard, he was as vulnerable as anybody. The other prisoners were likely scared out of their minds; Hullek was merely petrified.

The dragon was quite large, clearly fully grown. None of the signs of youth remained, and its wings and horns and tail seemed mature and developed. Because of the sunlight outside and the poor lighting inside, Hullek couldn't make out the color. Was it a red? A blue? He knew it wasn't a green dragon—he could spot one of those by the size of it. Emperor Ariakas had made a point of isolating all of the dragonarmies from one another for the most part. That, combined with the deadening effect of the wizard's curse, made it impossible to guess.

"Hullek!" he hissed, pushing the others back farther into the common room. They went willingly, still too afraid to object. He needed a better look at the dragon, needed to know what it was doing. Maybe he could bargain with it. And was he not a dragon highlord? He didn't look much like one at the moment, admittedly, chained to a quartet of rogues and bandits who were busy soiling themselves.

A dragon's senses were excellent, far greater than any mortal's. The wyrm outside would doubtless hear them banging around inside the inn, maybe start looking into the windows or the door. Hullek needed the others to snap out of it.

Mudskip was the first to pull himself together. "W-what's that doing here?" the scrawny goblin stammered. "M-maybe that's where everybody w-went . . . the dragon et 'em!" It wasn't an entirely unreasonable supposition, Hullek thought. He'd have made it himself if he could think straight.

Hullek pointed up the stairs that led to the second floor of the inn. "Hullek!" he said. Mudskip nodded, and together they bundled the others up the stairs and into the upper hallway. At the end of the hallway was a single bay window; Hullek wanted to take a look out of that window, perhaps get a clearer picture of the trouble they were in. If the dragon were a red, it would probably be beyond rational discourse. If it were a blue, maybe they had a chance of talking peaceably. The half-ogre hugged the wall, and the chain clanked noisily against the paneling as the others followed suit. Inching along, the buildings across the square came into view, then the fountain, then the courtyard. But where was the dragon? Had it taken off?

The dragon's head burst through the window, showering the hallway in glass and lead and plaster. Hullek was dragged back rapidly as the gnoll and the humans shrieked in panic and hauled on the chain in their efforts to escape. The dragon's eyes were the size of dinner plates, wide, expressive, and very intelligent. He could feel its hot, dry breath from ten feet away. "Hullek!" he shouted, landing on his back and still moving away from the dragon, which was advancing as much as it could down the hallway to the extent its long neck would allow. Hullek had the bizarre sensation of being examined like a child examines an ant. The fog lifted in his mind just long enough for him to notice the dragon's scales were a rich, burnished brass. Brass? It was one of the good dragons!

The gnoll collided with a door at the opposite end of the hallway. The humans and the goblin collided with the gnoll. Their combined weight forced it open, and all five escapees tumbled into what was once the innkeeper's private office. Although the dragon couldn't pursue them any further, that didn't stop Hullek's companions from trying to get as far away from it as possible. Hullek was able to crane his neck around long enough to see the others were heading straight for another window on the far wall. Then the world dropped away.

****

Hullek Skullsmasher was sore all over.

In some ways he would have preferred for the big brass dragon to have given chase. It might have stopped the others from dragging him clear across the grassy back lot of the inn, through a wooden fence, and into a hay barn. When the gnoll, the Nerakans, and even Mudskip had stopped running, exhausted, Hullek was bruised and battered, wedged against a horse stall.

Hullek scratched his lumpy head as the others caught their breath nearby. A brass dragon wouldn't chase people out of a town. They were among the smallest and least-threatening of the good dragons, barely used by the Whitestone Armies in the war. Of course, he thought, nobody had known there *were* any good dragons until they came back out of exile. And only the people involved in the war itself, in Solamnia and Neraka, would have even seen any. Most, like the rubes of the town, would think all dragons were evil serpents.

The villagers had run away from a friend.

If he weren't so sure he would never make it out of

the town alive, Hullek would have found the situation amusing. Even though he appeared to have some degree of influence over the other escapees, that wouldn't last long. He tried to force another plan through his cursed brain, but kept coming up with the image of the dragon bursting through the window. I should be grateful it didn't breathe fire all over us, he thought.

Hullek leaped to his feet as if he'd been stung. That was the answer! "Hullek!" he shouted, yanking on the chain. Mudskip and the others made an effort to rise, but the humans were still shaking uncontrollably, and the gnoll was very likely about to be physically sick. "Hullek!" said Hullek again, grabbing the goblin about the shoulders and pointing out the barn door. Mudskip warily followed his gaze, squinting away the streams of tears he'd been leaking for the past ten minutes.

"Wot?" asked Mudskip, slowly. "The mill?"

Hullek was pointing directly at the stream, the millpond, and the big wooden millwheel turning lazily with the meandering current. "Hullek!" He mimed flames coming from his mouth.

"Fire," said one of the Nerakans in accented Common. Hullek stared for a heartbeat at the human, awed by his newfound mastery of communication, and nodded. He pointed at the millwheel again. He started to look around for the things he would need inside the barn.

With the help of the others, the former dragon highlord assembled a wagon full of farming implements: a pitchfork, four large barrels, rope, a horse harness, and several bales of hay. They dragged the wagon out to the barn doors, looked out, and hustled out into the open and along the back of the town, toward the mill.

Focus, thought Hullek. Focus and watch out for flying dragons. He trusted the gnoll's powerful danger sense to warn them; he trusted Mudskip to relay his orders to the humans, who would no doubt do what they were told. It seemed ridiculous to Hullek to think he had the makings of a strike unit, chained to him by iron links and manacles. But he couldn't get distracted. Focus, focus.

At the mill, Hullek and his desperate band set about filling the barrels with water and tying them to the millwheel with rope. He positioned the wagon next to the millwheel, filled with hay bales. And he handed the horse harness to one of the Nerakans and the pitchfork to the other.

It was an elegant plan, he thought. The dragon would see them, and it would charge in with every confidence. Before it could use its fiery breath, they'd douse it with the barrels like they'd doused the bakery oven. And with the horse harness and the pitchfork, they would bring it down and pierce its heart, all of that reinforced by the very chain that bound them together.

All he needed was the dragon.

Panic started to set in. Was it the dragonfear? No, it was different. It was actual panic. He looked at the others, who were wiping sweat from brows and trying to blend in with the side of the mill house. The dragon might already have taken off, tired of waiting. It was a good dragon. It might just have wanted to talk. But then again, there he was, a half-ogre with two swarthy men of the evil Taman Busuk region, a goblin, and a grinning gnoll. Good dragons spent their free time hunting down people like them.

As if aware of the irony of its timing, the brass flew directly overhead, huge sail-like wings causing wind shear that raised a fine mist from the stream. The dragonfear struck like a velvet hammer, a soft yet potent blow to the small of his back. He was expecting it, but it was enhanced by the brass's overhead motion, that iconic silhouette against the last rays of evening sun that colored everything golden-orange.

"Hullek!" shouted Hullek. Without rehearsing, and with the wizard's curse swamping his second-guesses, Hullek led his cohorts to the millwheel and flung himself across the millpond with the goblin sailing right after him. The humans, armed with harness and pitchfork, landed with a bang on the paddles of the mill wheel. The gnoll clung on to one side of the wheel as it hauled him upward off the ground. Hullek and Mudskip held on to the other side, their backs against the brick wall of the mill house. All five of them rose up with water spraying all over, drenching them completely. So far, so good.

The dragon swung about in midair, wings tight against its body, dropping like a stone for twenty feet before it threw its tail out behind it and let its wings catch the air again. It flew straight at the mill house, beating its wings to pick up speed. Hullek couldn't believe his luck. It was actually going to take them on directly. He could always count on the arrogance of dragons.

Wait for it. Wait for it. Hullek looked over at the two humans, who stood ready with their fork and harness. The gnoll nodded back at Hullek. Mudskip's teeth chattered, whether from the cold water or the dragonfear, Hullek couldn't tell. It didn't matter. They all knew their roles. The dragon seemed to know its role too; it was almost upon them, mouth opening wide to exhale or bite.

"Hullek!" yelled Hullek, hauling back on the chain and pulling it as tight as he could. On the other side, the gnoll did the same. The sudden jerking action lifted the humans up even farther, astride the mill wheel paddles, water streaming out around them. The pitchfork was out. The harness was thrust before them. The gnoll would release the barrels and . . .

The brass dragon angled sharply to the left and away from the millpond. Hullek cursed inwardly, with the usual outward comment. The humans grunted, and the mill wheel kept going. "The wheel . . ." one of them said, as if it had only just dawned on him. They flattened themselves against the paddles. "The wheel!" shrieked Mudskip. The gnoll just grinned stupidly. Hullek closed his eyes.

The wheel turned. The chain, tight across the front of the wheel, caught on something important. An axle, a strut, Hullek really didn't have the mental acuity to notice what. There was a tremendous crack, the mill wheel lurched suddenly, and the whole operation—including Hullek, Mudskip, the Nerakans, and the gnoll—plunged into the millpond.

Hullek broke the surface of the brackish water, gasping for air. Broken pieces of wood floated about him, and he pulled himself with all of his strength to the edge of the millpond. He could only trust the others to come up after him, but he was mentally kicking himself repeatedly. Wiping pondweed from his face, he saw that the dragon had landed on the side of the stream and was looking right at him.

"What in Paladine's name were you thinking?" said the dragon in a clearly feminine voice. She had her head cocked to one side, that same ant-inspecting look she'd had before.

Hullek spit out a mouthful of water. "Hullek," he said, not sure whether to be furious or embarrassed. Mudskip and the others reached the edge of the pond and collapsed in exhaustion. They were possibly the most ignoble collection of dragon fighters ever assembled.

The dragon laughed, a strangely alien sound, yet one familiar to Hullek from his exchanges with the green dragons. "Oh, my," she said. "Feebleminded? What was it, a wizard? Oh, dear."

Furious, thought Hullek. That's what it is. I'm absolutely furious. I am a dragon highlord, he wanted to shout. "Hullek!" groaned Hullek.

"Well, if it matters," the dragon went on, preening. "I was only coming back to apologize to the townspeople. I don't intend to stay. I spent hundreds of years in the Dragon Isles, and now that the war's over, I find myself missing the old haunts in the Plains of Dust."

"Hullek?" said the half-ogre, indignant. That's it? Sorry, it's time I left?

"Yes," she said, stretching her wings. "So if you could pass on my sincerest regrets to the mayor and all of the nice people here, I would be forever in your debt." She paused, looked down at the five of them, soaked through like wharf rats. With what could only be a dragon's version of a shrug, the brass lifted one mighty claw and brought it down.

****

Hullek Skullsmasher was cursed.

Three days earlier, he'd escaped from a band of mercenaries, chained to four other prisoners. He had leaped from a bridge across a gorge, survived a fall to a river, and awoken on a forested shore only a few miles from a town. The town had been empty, save for a dragon. Hullek and his fellow prisoners had faced down the dragon, and with great personal effort and struggle, they had failed.

Still, it had been nice of the dragon to break the chain before she left.

The former Dragon Highlord of the Green Dragonarmy was reclining in a chair in the inn. The people had come back, slowly and cautiously. They had found the five unchained ex-prisoners, the signs of a mighty battle, a broken mill wheel, and no sign of the dragon. The curious band of adventurers who had driven off the dragon were standing around, much the worse for wear. But there were blankets and dry clothes to be had and food and drink to be offered. The townsfolk knew heroes when they saw them!

Hullek knew he would never be rid of his curse. He would never be able to express properly how mistaken the townsfolk had been about the brass dragon or who he really was or who the riffraff he was standing around with were. He'd never ride a green dragon again or lead an army for the Dark Queen. Then again, at least in the town, he'd never go without food in his belly or a roof over his head.

Hullek looked over at the goblin seated at his table,

then the grinning gnoll at the bar, and finally the two Nerakans telling their story about the dragon to the children by the fireplace. Mudskip raised a glass to Hullek and said, "To us, what saved the town from the dragon. May we live long an' well."

"Hullek," said Hullek.

Jaws Of Defeat

Paul B. Thompson

Paul B. Thompson lives in Chapel Hill, North Carolina, with his wife, Elizabeth, and children. A freelance writer for seventeen years, his many novels include *Thorn and Needle, Firstborn,* the Ergoth Trilogy, and the ongoing Elven Exiles series. He frequently collaborates with Tonya C. Cook, and has written a new book with his daughter, Sara Thompson.

Jaws of Defeat

Paul B. Thompson

Age of Mortals, 385 AC

Every sweep of his wings sent a twinge of pain through his massive crimson shoulder. It was particularly noticeable when climbing, which put extra strain on the joint. Cold air or snowy weather made the old injury ache as well. For Raider, red dragon and beloved companion of the Dragonqueen, the twinge was more than a harbinger of advancing age. It was his badge of dishonor.

Long ago, he had failed one of his first challenges, receiving a broken shoulder in the bargain. It was his worst injury, earned in his tumultuous youth. Bones knitted and muscles healed, but the sting of his long-ago defeat never went away.

As Raider swept through the broken clouds over the Bay of Karthay, memory of his shame filled him with burning rage. Perhaps it was the sight of the Worldscap

Mountains off to the east that inflamed his heart, for there the debacle took place, one thousand one hundred fifteen years ago.

He needed to shed blood to assuage his shame. Sailing in formation across the sunlit bay was a fleet of ships. Their white lateen sails marked them as ships of the Seafarers, the dark-skinned race of humans who lived over the northern horizon from the mainland. Raider bore them no special grudge, but at the moment he wanted to vent his rage on someone.

Lowering his good right wing, he dived at the serene fleet with murder in his head and revenge in his heart.

****

How different life had been, all those centuries ago. After a few decades of life, Raider had been little more than a hatchling when he left the peaks of his birth. He was driven out, really, by his sire, the mighty Potanz. The old dragon had no desire to shelter hatchlings under his broad wings. One by one he drove them out, starting with the weakest, Keropas. His largest and strongest offspring, Raider, he saved for last. The young red dragon considered resisting, but Potanz could have torn him in half without strain. So he had left after a single bone-shaking buffeting from the old sire's tail. Raider flew out over the broad sea, south by east. He passed some islands, mostly small ones, inhabited by men. They were too little for a red dragon, and all lacked the lofty peaks favored by Raider's kind. So he flew on. From a great height, he caught a scent on the wind. It was the tang of dragon flesh—not his own red race, but a metallic beast. Raider had never met a metallic dragon, for the simple reason Potanz would not allow any to live within his domain. He recognized the scent the same way he knew the smoke of human campfires from wild flames or could tell fresh water from salt from four miles up: his senses told him so.

The smell became stronger as the red dragon picked up an unfamiliar coastline. Not an island, this place was a continent. Rocky cliffs reared up from the sea, which beat itself frothy against the high stone walls. Beyond the sea cliffs were higher mountains, great enough to be treeless at their height but not so lofty as to be permanently snow-capped. It was a promising range for a young dragon. The metallic stink persisted, but Raider was confident he could overpower any metallic wanderer he might encounter.

He climbed higher, feeling his youthful wings surge through the thin, cold air. A strong headwind hit him in the face, bowing his head back as he beat against the powerful tide. Raider waded through the fast-moving stream of air and emerged above it into a high, cold stillness.

Below, the broad landscape unrolled in all directions. He saw brown peaks and blue valleys, sinuous strips of river, and here and there the silver jewel of a lake. He saw no cities or smoke, no scars on the terrain made by habitants. If anyone lived down there, their presence on the land was light. It, Raider decided, would be a good place for a fledgling dragon to carve out his domain. He put his nose down, folded his wings, and dived.

Down he hurtled, like a scarlet thunderbolt, wind

ripping past his slit eyes. He had never dived from so great a height before, and it was exhilarating. Gradually he put his nose on a likely valley off to the east. It was a high valley, with four mountains standing one at each corner of the hidden vale. It was spring, and the valley was transitioning from winter gray to summer green.

His velocity was great, so great Raider began to feel severe buffeting on his chest. His ribs could withstand a catapult ball, but it was time to slow down. He let his fore and back legs dangle to create drag. Raider slowed, but not enough. Tentatively, he opened his tightly furled wings. Instantly the air seized them and bent them back. Raider roared with pain and quickly clapped his wings shut.

He was falling even faster now, and the ground leaped up with unnerving clarity. The valley floor was thickly covered by pine forest. A stream meandered around the stout pines. There was no lake for him to crash into. If Raider hit the trees at that speed, he'd be spitted twoscore times.

At lower altitude the stench of the other dragon seemed stronger than before. He must be close to leave such an intense trail. Hardly had the thought crossed Raider's preoccupied mind than a flash of something bright flared on his right. He glimpsed a large shape with a reddish aura passing between clouds ahead of him. The shape was at least as big as he, and it gave Raider a desperate idea. He twisted his stretched-out frame and managed to arc through the steadily warming air toward the other beast. The red dragon hit a cloudbank. So great was his speed that the cloud turned inside out and disintegrated, leaving thin streamers of cloud clinging to Raider's rough hide.

Then he was upon him. He roared a challenge, but it was too late for the other to avoid the collision. With a sound like forty thunderclaps, Raider slammed into the other dragon. For an instant, there was some frantic grappling, much hissing, and a flash of talons and teeth, then the momentum of their diverging paths pulled the dragons apart.

Raider was satisfied, even though his head rang from the collision. As he hoped, the impact slowed him enough to allow him to open his wings again. Barely under control, he glided down to a ridgeline that connected the two eastern peaks standing at the corners of the valley. Front and rear feet windmilling, he piled into the stony ground, digging his chin into the turf. It was a miserable, mucked-up landing, but considering how close he'd come to drilling himself into a deep hole in the ground, Raider was in no mood to complain about niceties of form.

He shook the dirt from his barbels and sat up. In spite of his awkward arrival, he'd come to a grand place. The air was clear, and his senses tingled with the abundant life around him. It was all of the lower orders. He detected none of those pesky humans or smug elves about.

What about the other dragon? Raider swept the sky, searching for signs. He saw nothing. Perhaps the collision had been more serious for the other. After all, Raider was a red dragon, strongest of Potanz's brood. Maybe the other dragon had been driven to the ground by the mighty impact.

He speculated on that until he heard a high, ululating call echoing down the naked peaks. It was not a red dragon's voice, he knew that much. But Raider was too unschooled to recognize the race of his unwilling savior. Whatever he was, he wasn't dead.

Flexing his foreclaws, Raider gnashed his jaws, clacking his great ivory fangs together. It sounded like stone breaking, and hearing it, any wise creature in earshot would quit the area at top speed.

The ululation ceased. Raider inflated his chest and bellowed a full-throated roar, proclaiming the valley to be his. The answer was only silence. Nothing stirred, so he descended the ridge on his hind legs, keeping his forelegs free to fight if needed. At the treeline, he noticed a line of conical boulders, streaked with a red stain. He tasted the color. It was rust, not blood. The boulders puzzled him. Their arrangement was too regular and even to be natural. There were scores of them, ranging in size from half Raider's weight to tiny ones no greater than his little talon. They extended in a straight line exactly where the stony mountainside stopped and the forest began. The largest ones were in the center, and they diminished evenly in size down the line until they vanished into the mossy turf.

A flock of birds stormed aloft, screeching. Raider focused on the spot. Tall pines were waving to and fro. No wind stirred the valley.

He leaped into the air, flapping hard. Hopping over the treetops with his tail and hind claws parting the green spearpoint tops, Raider raced to the disturbance. Before he reached it, a solid beam of dense flesh rose up from the pines and smacked him square in the face. He fell backward into the trees, landing on his rump and smashing four sturdy trees to kindling. Bounding to his feet, he roared a challenge.

"Noisy brute, aren't you?"

Rising above the trees was a long serpentine neck, topped by a narrow, angular head. The other dragon's scales were burnished red, inclining to green at the edges. His eyes were large and round, with round pupils, unlike Raider's vertical ones. His opponent was a copper dragon.

"Begone, stripling, lest I rend you limb from limb!" Raider shouted. The trees quivered at his words. He was doing his best to sound like Potanz.

"Unless you plan to ram me in midair again, I don't think I have much to worry about."

More of the copper dragon rose above the pines. He had a long neck, bulbous body, and wings of astonishing length. Twice Raider's length, and maybe more than twice his weight . . . no matter. No copper dragon was going to drive a son of Potanz from his chosen domain!

He stalked forward, knocking aside trees as he came. His first idea was to use his breath on the smug intruder, but he changed his mind almost at once. The big copper would probably shrug it aside. Very well, let it be claws, teeth, and tails!

"Come on, then, let us try conclusions," said the copper, using seven words when none were needed. "In case you're curious, my name is Cirrus."

Raider stopped in his tracks. A female name? No matter.

"I am Raider, offspring of the great and mighty

Potanz! This valley is mine! Leave or die!" he bellowed. He started forward again, but Cirrus wrapped her tail around one of his legs and tripped him. Raider sprawled among the broken trees. Outraged, he took hold of the copper dragon's tail and sank his talons into it. Cirrus hissed loudly and wrenched her tail back, causing the younger red dragon to roll over and over in the dirt. He tried to rise, but she struck him across the face with her tail, sending him crashing down again.

Mad with fury, Raider snatched up a pine tree and flung it. Cirrus batted it away. She countered with another swing of her tail, catching the red dragon in the ribs. He was braced, though, and caught her tail under his foreleg. He yanked hard, jerking Cirrus off her hind feet. Her tail was already slick with blood from his first clawing, and she managed to pull free. Wings wafting, the copper dragon rose into the air.

"You're an ugly piece of work, son of Potanz. Follow me if you dare." She took off across the valley, skimming over the treetops. Snarling, Raider gave chase. Aside from some bruising, he hadn't suffered much hurt, save to his pride. He meant to have the arrogant copper's head for daring to humiliate him.

His short, wide wings beat much harder than Cirrus's long narrow ones. Raider barreled after her, rapidly overtaking the slower-flying copper. Just as he had closed to within pouncing distance, she banked away. The eastern ridgeline was dead ahead. Raider couldn't avoid it. He piled into the stony summit, demolishing it. Speed lost, he plummeted head-down along the reverse slope, causing a major avalanche in the process. By the time he stopped hard against the slope of the next mountain, he was half buried in loose dirt and assorted boulders.

Every fiber of his being wanted to rise up and tear after the elusive copper. But anger was clouding his judgment. Cirrus was easily avoiding his clumsy attacks, then punishing him with her ripostes. That had to stop.

He clasped a handy boulder in one claw and hurled it. His aim was true, hitting Cirrus on the chest. He flung a second stone and had the satisfaction of striking one of those long, fragile-looking wings. The copper dragon spun down into the trees. For the first time, Raider laughed.

Digging himself out of the avalanche, he noticed the stones he had thrown with success were white crystalline quartz. Holding one close to his head, he felt a trickle of power in the boulder—latent but definitely there. Why should there be magical power in raw stones? Examining them more closely, he saw the boulders were veined with greenish yellow metal. So that was it! Cirrus's interest in the valley—and her willingness to fight for it—became clear. The mountain was riddled with gold. Raider knew enough about copper dragons to know they craved precious metals, hoarding them in great cave complexes that grew longer and more complicated as the centuries passed. He stalked up the ridge on all fours. "Copper! Copper, can you hear me?"

Cirrus was nowhere in sight. He sensed her nearby but couldn't pinpoint exactly where.

"Copper, I know your secret!" He tossed a boulder into the forest. "Gold, isn't it? That's why you're here?"

Still, Cirrus was silent. Raider drew back his head and set fire to the pine woods with his breath. That would smoke her out.

The flames moved quickly down the slope, fed by decades of dry underbrush. A pall of gray smoke collected over the valley. At that rate half the forest would be on fire before the sun reached its zenith.

A tremor passed through the soil under Raider's feet. At first he thought it was Cirrus; then it happened again, more strongly. Loud cracks echoed up and down the valley as tall trees teetered and fell. A hump appeared in the midst of the blazing forest, streaming gravel and blackened trees. Raider's first thought was Cirrus was burrowing under the fire, but the mound was bigger than the copper dragon, and it didn't move about like a burrowing beast would. It rose, undulated a few times, then sank down again only to rise in another part of the conflagration. The disturbance occurred several times, and the fire began to die down as the burning forest was smothered under heaps of dirt.Raider was so distracted by the strange spectacle, he failed to detect Cirrus bearing down on him from behind. She struck him square between the shoulders, knocking him off the ridge. He rolled, horns over tail, into the charred landscape. Looking back, he saw the copper dragon was well singed and had a lovely ragged tear in her right wing membrane.

Hold!

He heard and felt the word spoken aloud. It was spoken so loudly, it rattled his teeth.

"Had enough?" replied Cirrus, thinking she'd heard the voice of the red dragon.

Raider shook off hot ashes and gravel. He was battered and sore all over, but his senses were screaming a silent warning inside his head.

Cease your combat at once! You shall have no other warning!

"Who is it?" Raider asked carefully. The power behind the voice convinced him not to challenge the unseen speaker.

I am the Master of the Mountain. You are intruders here.

"Show yourself," Cirrus called out. When there was no response, she added, "I do not take orders from human wizards, no matter how big their bag of tricks!"

I am no human. I am the Master of the Mountain. Behold.

Where the forest met the ridge, there was another line of rust-streaked boulders, cone-shaped and eroded with deep vertical grooves by the action of time. As the red and copper dragons looked on, the line of boulders flexed upward, shedding a layer of topsoil a foot deep. Under the dirt was an array of dark gray shield-shaped plates, six feet wide and eight feet long. They, too, were streaked with rust, especially at the joints.

"Those are . . ."

Raider recognized them too. The plates were scales . . . dragon scales.

A young flyer such as Raider had scales six *inches* wide, and the somewhat older copper dragon's hide was similar. Raider's mature sire, Potanz, had scales commensurate with his age and size, eleven inches across. The scales of the beast calling himself the Master of the Mountain were so enormous in comparison, it was almost beyond belief. If his scales were so large, it meant the conical "boulders" they'd seen were the typical horny nodules that grew along a dragon's belly.

As if drawn up by strings, Raider and Cirrus launched themselves into the air. The ground heaved beneath them where they had stood.

"Forgive us, master. We won't trouble you further," said the copper dragon, rising higher.

Forgive? You come into my valley, scream and roar and burn my forest, and you think you can just leave?

The voice seemed to come from everywhere at once. Cirrus circled away from the red dragon, rising higher with each circuit. "It was a mistake," she said to no one in particular.

Raider had no intention of challenging so enormous a dragon. He couldn't even see the monster's body in total, much less do battle with it. But he was a red dragon, and pride ran hot in his veins. Safely aloft, he shouted, "I need no one's leave or forgiveness! Keep your valley. The world is wide."

He darted away westward. Before he'd flown a hundred yards, he felt his wings harden and grow stiff. His tail and dangling limbs likewise turned to stone, and bereft of lift, Raider dropped to the ground. Behind him, Cirrus also wavered and fell.

Raider landed hard on his side. He could breathe and he was conscious, but otherwise he was paralyzed. It wasn't hard to imagine his copper enemy was similarly smitten.

Long have I lain here, watching the dragons of later ages pass overhead. For centuries they knew this place was mine, and none dared alight here. Now, in the space of a day, two interlopers have come. Has the world forgotten me?

Who are you? Raider thought frantically. The Master of the Mountain heard his thoughts.

I was called Ro the Venerable. Kings and wizards deferred to me, once.

The name meant nothing to him, but then Raider had paid scant attention to the lessons of his elders. The monstrous Ro apparently was listening to Cirrus, for the red dragon heard his reply to the copper's unspoken question:

I could snuff you out as easily as a man does an ant, but I will not.

Raider struggled against the paralysis. His limbs were set like cast iron. Unable to muscle his way out, he tried to think of an escape. Ro was the biggest dragon—the biggest living thing—he'd ever seen or heard of. Not even the kraken of the ocean, often mistaken for an island, was as big as the entire valley. Yet the master lay buried under tons of soil, stones, and living trees. How long had it been since he'd flown? Or moved? Maybe Ro's sheer size confined him to his place.

My life ebbs. Already I have chosen this place to die, but before I become part of the mountains forever, I would see my valley delivered to a worthy successor: one of you.

The deadly rigidity faded. Raider leaped up excitedly. Could he win the valley, with all its gold, with the monster's blessing? What did he have to do?

One of you must prove you are better than the other.

"I am ready!" he bellowed, gnashing his teeth.

Do whatever must be done to vanquish your enemy, but

do not damage my valley further. That is the only requirement. The victor will remain here with all my worldly treasure. The defeated will pay another price.

Raider shot into the air, looking for Cirrus. The copper was not in sight. He flew slowly over the trees, searching for his foe. Smoke was thick from the forest fire, and Raider's head didn't feel quite right. The paralysis had been lifted, but his senses were curiously numb. Normally distinct, the scent of the metallic dragon was lost in a fog of smoke and blooming mountain flora. Raider had to rely on sight alone.

He glided through a heavy column of smoke and promptly smacked into something hard. Roaring, he grappled with the obstacle, but it wasn't Cirrus. It was a lanky pine, thrust into the splintered trunk of another tall tree to create an obstacle. As dragon and trees crashed to the ground, Raider could hear a deep thumping sound emanating from the earth. Venerable Ro was laughing at him.

Shaking off the broken trees, Raider whirled about, hissing with rage. He caught sight of Cirrus flying slowly in circles around him. Using his powerful hind legs, he catapulted himself aloft. He'd overtaken the copper dragon once in midair, and he was confident he could do so again. Sweeping in a wide left turn, he tried to come in on Cirrus's tail. She beat her long wings at what appeared to be an absurdly slow rate, yet easily pulled away from Raider. She held the turn, banking steeply over the smoke-stained forest. The red dragon tried to cut inside her turn, and found to his annoyance he could not. His stubby wings and heavy torso were made for straight-line speed, not tight maneuvers. Cirrus's lengthy wings, even with the stone tear in the membrane, gave her far better maneuverability.

Round and round they went. At last Raider cried, "Are you going to fight or fly in circles like a crazed vulture?"

In answer, she rolled right, banking out of her continuous turn, and began climbing. Raider broke after her, shouting dire threats. Every so often Cirrus bent her long neck to look back at him. "Don't give up," she called. "You'll catch me yet."

Stung by her taunts, Raider tucked in his limbs and flapped harder. Again the copper dragon showed she was a superior flyer, outpacing him as she climbed higher and higher. They passed the highest level attained by the smoke and entered a region of thin, icy clouds. Cirrus vanished into them. Raider hastily checked his upward rush. He had always come to grief when pursuing her through smoke or clouds.

He hovered, panting. He was working hard, and the altitude was not helping him. Frost formed on his nose barbels when his breath hardened in the cold. Where was she? What would she do next?

She would attack from behind, of course. Raider turned in time to see the copper dragon hurtling down at him. He belched fire at her. Cirrus shut her round eyes and plunged through the stream of flame, emerging singed but intact. Raider twisted aside to avoid her claws. In turn, he received a blast of the copper dragon's acid saliva full in the face. The red dragon's hide was proof against the nasty caustic, but it burned his eyes and nostrils. Half blind, he lashed out with his tail and felt it connect solidly with Cirrus's flank. She bleated with surprise and pain. A blow from a red dragon's tail, even a youngster such as Raider, was enough to demolish a stout stone tower.

He flew away, slinging his head from side to side to throw off the acid droplets. Ducking into a cloud, he let the cold vapor soothe his stinging face. Waxy tears formed in the corners of Raider's eyes. He shook his head, sending lumps of ambergris flying off.

Where was the impudent snake? Valley or no valley, Raider had suffered too many indignities to consider any outcome of this battle but death. He would pluck Cirrus's head from her serpent neck and fling it into the sea!

He descended watchfully and spied his enemy far below, circling the desultory forest fire. He wasn't about to do endless caracoles again. His first instinct was to drop on her from above. From that height he would have considerable speed and perfect aim, but surely she knew that. Why would a clever dragon circle in plain sight far below her adversary unless she had another devious ploy to spring on the guileless Raider?

The red dragon came down like a falling leaf, diving at a shallow angle, then pulling up, reversing direction, and diving again. In stages, he came down to Cirrus's level.

"Tired, young red? We've only begun," she called. "Come, let us settle matters. Play 'follow the leader' with me. If you catch me, I'll concede the fight."

Concede? Raider would settle for nothing less than the copper dragon's heart crushed in his claws. Nevertheless, he feigned acceptance and flew at her.

Leisurely, Cirrus turned away and dived for the western ridge.

She wove in and among the high pines with extraordinary skill, leaving the more powerful Raider to blunder through the treetops in hot pursuit. Reaching open ground between the forest and the rocky ridge, Cirrus turned north and flew parallel to the woods. She was so low, the tips of her wings dragged the ground, stirring up a cascade of small stones and grit. Raider bored on through the stinging hail. She was remarkably fleet, in spite of her bulky appearance.

They were fast approaching the northwest peak that marked the corner of Ro's valley. Slowly, almost imperceptibly, the red dragon began to close the gap. First by a few feet, then by yards. Cirrus looked back in alarm. She made evasive swings left and right, and when a stand of lordly cedars loomed ahead, she climbed just enough to clear them. Seeing Cirrus rise, Raider put on a burst of speed. It was his last surge. He hadn't eaten since leaving his sire's domain, many days ago, and the furious action of the day had worn him out.

Cirrus's tail flipped up as she topped the cedars. She was diving to the ground. Raider would do the same, and if his speed were greater, he would overtake the copper dragon directly over her exposed back.

He rose a bit to clear the cedars, then put his head down in a dive. At that moment he saw the trap. Directly ahead was a stone spire, joined at the top by a natural bridge and open in the center. Cirrus was flying slowly enough to avoid it (no doubt she had spied the formation when she was circling overhead) but

Raider could not. Headfirst, he plowed straight into the narrow opening.

He was a powerful creature, but the spire was made of black basalt, a relic of the distant days when the mountains were volcanoes. Raider's head and neck rammed through, but his right wing caught on the stone. Inside the shoulder, the bones snapped loudly. Hot pain shot through the red dragon's body. He stopped halfway through the formation, caught fast.

Cirrus alighted gently a few yards away. The edges of her wing tear were turning black, and all the barbels had been scorched off her face. She settled onto her haunches and looked on Raider with deep satisfaction.

"There you are, and there you will remain," she said, gloating.

"I will kill you!" he thundered.

She wasn't fazed. "What next, I wonder? Perhaps I'll pluck your eyes—"

"Yes, come close enough to try!"

She reconsidered breathing acid on him. "Maybe blind you'll be more docile."

"I'll be docile when I taste your blood!"

Her globular eyes glittered as she took aim, working her jaw muscles to summon another spray of vitriol. Before she could, the penetrating voice of Ro proclaimed, *Hold.* Cirrus stopped. Wedged tightly in the stone trap, Raider continued to struggle.*You have won, copper daughter. You have bested the red dragon with wit and cunning. You have proven to be far more dangerous than he.*

"My thanks, venerable one. Will you now destroy him, as you promised?"

Raider ceased squirming and felt a sensation he'd never known before: fear. The Master of the Mountain could extinguish him in an instant.

No, Ro said.

"No?" Cirrus was confused. "Shall I blind him, then, or tear off one of his limbs?"

No. His fate is no longer your concern.

The air shivered from some invisible disturbance. As Raider looked on, gray tendrils as thick as his foreleg erupted from the ground around Cirrus. They looked like granite, but they were as flexible as garden creeper. The copper dragon opened her wings and tried to free herself, but the stone tentacles rapidly reached her chest and dragged her down.

"Treachery!" she cried. "This is not what you promised!"

What did I promise?

"You said the victor would get your domain and all your treasure!"

So you shall. You shall become part of it—forever.

As Raider looked on in amazement, the copper sheen of Cirrus's scales grew lighter, changing from red to golden yellow. She gasped and flailed her free forelegs, clawing at the hardened stone gripping her hind legs, tail, and torso. An icy crackling sound filled the air as the gold color advanced up Cirrus's body. When it reached her forelegs, they froze in mid-whirl. She spewed acid on herself and the granite bonds.

Nothing will eat through my gold, golden daughter.

Ro was giving Cirrus his treasure, all right. He was pouring it into her veins, transmuting her into solid gold. She thrashed her neck and head against the metallic immobility of her own body. When the tips of the horns atop her head went yellow, she ceased moving. Stinking steam rose where puddles of acid bubbled at her golden feet. The stone tendrils relaxed and withdrew into the soil. In the place of the clever copper dragon was her life-sized image in gold, caught in final agony.

Raider was certain his turn was coming. He put his shoulder against the stone ring and tried to free himself. The broken ends of his shoulder joint grated one upon the other, sending a thrill of pain through him. But instead of gripping tentacles of stone and a creeping transmutation, the red dragon heard a loud gong-like tone. It sounded again, shaking Raider's rocky restraint. A third deep chime, and the hard stone collar around his neck cracked and fell apart. Raider tumbled to the ground, rolled, and came up in a fighting stance. He couldn't fly with a broken shoulder, but he was prepared to die fighting.

Go, scarlet son. You are done here.

"What do you mean, go?"

Leave my domain at once. If you are found within it on the next rising of the sun, I will do worse to you than I did to the copper daughter.

His right foreleg and wing hung limply at his side. It would be a long walk out of the valley.

"Why do you do this?" Raider demanded. "Why do you spare me, the defeated, and destroy the victor of our contest?"

Again the rumbling rattle of Ro's ancient laughter sounded. *My answer to selective breeding,* his voice boomed. *By destroying the fit and preserving the vanquished, I weaken the line of red dragons.*

It was too much for Raider's young mind. He cried, "For what purpose do you weaken us?"

I am old, very old. I was old when your sire was born, and older than old when his grandsire broke the shell of his birthing. I've grown so old, I cannot walk or fly, so I lie here, buried in pines and creeper, basking in warm sunshine like a common lizard. But I did not achieve my hoary age by tolerating challenges. Many are the dragons I have fought and killed. I tired of battle and sought solitude here in the mountains of this elf-stained continent. And still the dragons come, seeking new lands to conquer. But not my valley. Not my home.

The ground heaved under Raider's feet. He started walking, dropping down on his good front leg. His progress was slow and humiliating. It didn't matter where he went, the voice of Ro could be heard.

You, scarlet son, are like so many I slew in epochs past: violent, bold, stupid. So long as your kith persist, there will be balance in the world, balance between the dragons of darkness and the guardians of light. That's my gift to the world: your survival. Live long and bear many ignorant offspring, scarlet son!

Venerable Ro's mocking laughter continued a long time. Overwhelmed with shame, Raider considered halting and letting the monstrous old beast kill him. Then his pride stirred. Stupid, was he? A detriment to the cause of the Dragonqueen? Not this son of Potanz! He would go. He would live. And he would prove the ancient giant wrong. The red dragons and their brothers would rule the world one day. Then he would return and laugh at Venerable Ro.

He didn't laugh at that moment, though, nor for a long time after. Raider limped over the mountains into the next valley, a stark and stony wasteland. There he dwelt till his shoulder healed. When his limbs were sound again, he went forth to become the strongest, most cunning, and most terrible adversary known among dragons.

****

The fleet went down, ship by ship, sails blazing and hulls torn asunder. He crushed all the longboats in his claws so no one survived. When the sea was strewn with wreckage and dead sailors, he flew off, pleased with an hour's destruction. He had business beyond the mountains, business ordained by the Dragonqueen. Even so, he was careful to skirt a certain valley high in the mountains, the one with four towerlike peaks at the corners. And though he flew around the empty valley at a great height, he listened for a deep, unspoken voice reaching out from the dark pines.

UNFORGOTTEN

Jean Rabe

Jean Rabe is the author of twenty novels and more than three dozen short stories. Most of her work is in the fantasy and science fiction fields, but she has penned cat-mystery tales, military stories, and coauthored a true-crime book with F. Lee Bailey. In addition, she has edited several fantasy, science fiction, and horror anthologies. In her spare time, she pretends to garden, visits museums, tugs fiercely on old, knotted socks with her two dogs, and adds to her considerable pile of "to be read" books. Visit her online at www.jeanrabe.com.

Unforgotten

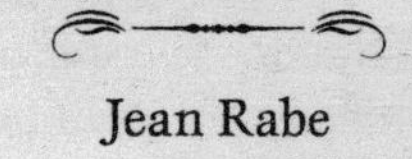

Jean Rabe

Age of Mortals, 400 AC

The map felt brittle in Rurik's stubby fingers, and it smelled terribly old, the moldy mustiness of it clinging to his nostrils and settling heavily on his tongue. To him the taste was heady and . . .

"Rich," Rurik pronounced as he smacked his lips. "We are going to be very, very rich, Nador Ironfist."

"If we're in the right spot." Nador glared across a small campfire at Rurik.

Both dwarves sat far enough from the flames that their beards were safe from errant sparks, and yet the light was bright enough to read by. They looked nothing alike, Rurik being considerably younger, with not a streak of gray in his bushy red beard and mass of long hair, and Nador having a short beard and mustache the color of cold ashes and a bald head gleaming with sweat in the firelight. They both appeared haggard, and their clothes were worn, their pants and boots caked with dirt. Their hands and fingernails were reasonably clean, though, so they would not smudge the map halves they held, and their eyes glimmered in anticipation.

"This has to be the right spot," Rurik said. He tipped his head back, appearing to study the constellations for several moments. Then he dropped his gaze and studied the other dwarf's deeply-lined face. "The rock formations match, Nador. The buzzard's neck is right over there." He nodded to a granite spindle rising to the east. "We passed Reorx's Anvil yesterday. Besides, partner, we're just about as high in the Khalkists as we can go."

"If the Khalkists are the mountains on the map." Nador's pitch-black eyes locked onto Rurik's. "How about you give me your half of the map so I can put them together and be certain." Nador held his half of the parchment in one hand and waggled the fingers of his free hand in Rurik's direction. "How about it, *partner?"*

"How about you pass over your half instead?"

"I'm the one who knows mountains, Rurik, knows all about natural features and—"

"I know about mountains too."

"Not as much as I do."

"Only because I'm not near so old as you and don't have my skull filled with pyrite and my belly filled with weak elven ale. You've got to be pushing two hundred, Nador. I'm half your age."

"And you have less than half my wits. Now let me see your half of the map." Nador looked daggers at Rurik.

Down the slope in the distance, a wolf howled mournfully. Closer by came the scraping sound of a shovel against dirt and gravel, and the high-pitched screech of some night bird hunting. A breeze picked up, ruffling the edges of the map halves and stirring the embers and the dwarves' beards. The fire popped, and another mournful howl sounded, little more than a whisper—the wolf was moving farther away from the base of the mountain.

Both dwarves were frozen, glaring at each other. "Why don't you just make things easy and give me your half, Nador? You afraid I can read the map better than you? Afraid I'll take all the credit for the find? I'm the one who's in charge here. I'm the one who knows about very old things."

"Antiquities."

"Huh?"

"My point is made, Rurik Rustbucket." Nador released an exasperated breath. "Just hand over your half. I'll give it back when I'm done examining it properly."

"Examining it properly! Why you toad-bottomed excuse for a—"

"What if you two just gave 'em both to me?" The third dwarf was thinner and shorter, not much taller than a kender. His face was smooth, evidencing his youth, and his wheat-blond beard was braided and tucked into his belt so it wouldn't get in the way. "I'm the one doin' all the diggin', and I'd like to know if I'm diggin' in the right place."

He'd been digging several yards beyond the opening of a cave, a hooded lantern on the floor casting shadows up his face and making his eyes look like hollow sockets. "I'm tired of listenin' to you bicker." He paused and let out a deep breath. He wiped the sweat off his brow with a sleeve, which simply streaked the dirt. "Maybe I'm just plain tired."

Rurik and Nador growled in unison.

"Yeah, I know. Shutupshutupshutup," the thin dwarf said.

"That's right. Shut up! I hired you to dig, not talk," Nador growled.

"*I* hired him," Rurik corrected.

"Hired? I overheard you two arguin' in that tavern about needin' help diggin', and I came up to you and told you I was lookin' for work. I kind of hired myself." The thin dwarf kept digging at a steady pace with a wide spade that had a handle so rough that splinters bit at his palms.

"You'll get paid, just like we promised," Nador said. "When we find the treasure."

"But it won't be an equal share," Rurik whispered so softly he was certain only Nador could hear. "It'll be fair payment." Winking at Nador, he held his thumb and index finger about a half inch apart to indicate the miniscule amount.

Nador nodded in agreement at that, got up from the fire, and carefully folded his half of the map and placed it in his front pocket.

Rurik went back to studying his half, inhaling deeply and letting the smell of the parchment fill his senses again. He fixated on the oldness and the mystery, shutting out the steady noise of the shovel, the screech of the night bird, and his partner's continued grumbling.

The ink was faded, but Rurik could make out mountains, the formations he'd mentioned to Nador, and a half sketch of a dragon statue at the bottom of the parchment. Nador's map showed the other half of the statue and other stuff; what else, he really didn't know.

He and Nador had met at a small marketplace in Khur, both of them veteran treasure seekers, both spotting the map at the same time, and both recognizing that it was valuable and could lead to something hugely rewarding. The shop owner also had a hint of its worth, and so demanded more coin than either dwarf had. By pooling their resources, they were able to purchase the map, but promptly got into an argument over who was in charge and tore it in half, neither trusting the other to keep the entire map.

Rurik gingerly touched the half sketch of the statue. "Forgotten," he said. "But not for much longer."

"Remind me, just what's so special about the statue we're looking for?" That came from the thin dwarf, still digging. Again he paused to wipe at the sweat, only managing to move the dirt around on his face. "I've been diggin' here and there for days. At least humor me."

Nador growled.

But Rurik cleared his throat and began, not out of sympathy to sate the hired help's curiosity, but to take the opportunity to expound upon his archeological expertise. "This statue we're looking for, it was forgotten by a god. And we aim to unforget it."

"By a god?"

Nador nudged the thin dwarf and mouthed: *Dig!*

"Paladine," Rurik supplied. He tried to make his

voice as smooth and polished as possible, like he'd remembered the academics talking in a library he'd once visited. "It was in the Age of Starbirth, after the High God awakened and the rest of the gods were called." Rurik glanced away from his map to see if the hired help seemed impressed; he couldn't tell as the thin dwarf kept digging and huffing, his back turned to them. "Paladine, the Platinum Dragon, and Takhisis, the Dragon of All Colors and of None, helped Reorx create five rulers for Krynn. They were the first dragons, crafted from metal, and they would have been good for the world. But Takhisis craved power and corrupted them, tarnished them and turned them into her own image."

Rurik returned his attention to his half map but kept on with his tale. "Paladine would not rest after that. He entreated Reorx to forge dragon statues from precious and perfect metals to balance what Takhisis had done. Reorx did just that, and Paladine breathed life into these statues, birthing the good dragons of the world." Rurik sucked in a breath, held it, and almost reverently continued. "But some say Paladine didn't breathe life into every statue, that he forgot one or two. According to this map, he forgot this one. The one we seek."

"Yeah, Rurik thinks you're gonna find a Reorx-forged statue at the bottom of this hole your diggin'," Nador said to the thin dwarf, still busy digging. "But that's not the statue you're going to find. See, I know what the map really refers to. My version's different. The correct version. The statue we're looking for? My sources tell me it's a totem, enchanted by a silver dragon sorcerer during the War of the Lance and left in these mountains for safekeeping." He paused and tugged at his beard, adding under his breath, "If these are the right mountains." Louder, he continued: "The dragon sorcerer put lots of dragon magic in the statue and then, after the war, hid it to keep it safe and eventually forgot all about it. And here it's been all these years and years and years. Forgotten to the world . . . except unforgotten to whoever found this map and deciphered the clues."

The thin dwarf stopped digging and gently rubbed his blistered palms on his trousers. "So it's a dragon statue that either was made by a god or by a silver dragon sorcerer, that might be from the Age of Starbirth or the War of the Lance, and that might be filled with dragon magic. Or maybe some other kind of magic. Or maybe something else entirely." He climbed out of the hole and leaned wearily against the side of the cave. "And here I am thinkin' you two are fools for arguin' all the time. I'm the fool for comin' with you to dig for somethin' that may or may not be anything."

Nador's eyes narrowed to needle-fine slits, and his upper lip curled in a snarl. "That dragon totem's valuable, and you'll get paid well once we find it."

Rurik had joined Nador, standing at his shoulder and carefully folding his half map. "My story's the right story, and it's an artifact you're digging for. One Paladine forgot."

"He's not digging for anything at the moment," Nador grumbled.

"I'm takin' a well-deserved break." The thin dwarf looked from Nador to Rurik then back again. He gestured to two more shovels, propped up just inside the cave entrance. The blades were shiny, having seen little use. "How about you pitchin' in and diggin' for a while?"

Nador and Rurik glowered.

"Right. I remember. You two are the brains of this operation, and I'm the muscle." He picked up his shovel and got back in the hole. "One statue, and there's three of us. How do you figure on turning it into coin and paying me my fair share?"

Nador scratched his head. He didn't like that phrase, *fair share.*

"We'll sell it," Rurik said vaguely. "To some sorcerer or a library or just sell it to somebody with a lot of coin. We'll sell it and divide the coin." But his voice lacked conviction. He unfolded his half of the map, took another look, and reverently touched the half sketch of the dragon statue. "We'll sell it for more coin than we can possibly count. More than we could spend in a lifetime."

Nador watched Rurik refold the map half and put it in a pouch at his side. "I'll be the one doing the selling," Nador said. "I'm better at dealing with people, not so gruff as you, Rurik Rustbucket. I'll be able to get a higher price for it. More for us to divide."

Rurik reached for one of the shovels, closing his fingers so tightly around the handle that his knuckles turned ghost white. *"I'm* the master negotiator," he said. *"I'm* the one who'll get the best deal." He ambled over to the hole and started digging on the side facing deeper into the cave. "I'm very good at talking to folks. I can mediate better than you, Nador Ironbrain."

Nador grabbed the other shovel and clambered into

the hole. "You cannot mediate better than me! No dwarf in all of the Khalkists can mediate better than me!"

The thin dwarf shuddered and worked quietly.

"Fine," Rurik spat. "You mediate all you want. I'm gonna get busy finding Paladine's forgotten statue."

Nador dug a spadeful of dirt and pitched it out of the hole, angling it so some would splash on Rurik. "I keep telling you, it's not Paladine's statue, it's a dragon statue filled with dragon magic made by a silver dragon sorcerer!"

The two dwarves continued to argue, digging furiously in their anger and occasionally tossing shovelfuls of dirt on each other to emphasize a point. The thin dwarf paused, listening to them and taking a rest, finding a corner where the dirt wasn't flying and he could breathe deep.

"What if this hole leads to nothin' too? Like the other holes I dug for you?" the thin dwarf asked. But Rurik and Nador didn't hear him; they were busy disputing the merits of silver dragons and dragon magic and whether the statue on the map was from the Age of Starbirth or sculpted during the War of the Lance, or whether Paladine had anything to do with it.

"What if both of you are wrong?" the thin dwarf pressed.

Rurik and Nador heard him that time.

"I ain't wrong this time," Nador insisted. He squinted through the darkness, trying to see the thin dwarf so he could glare at him. The hole was nearly twenty feet deep, and they'd left the lantern up above, so only a feeble amount of light filtered that far down. "And don't be impertinent. I hired you to dig, not to ask questions and insult me."

"Well, you're wrong about one thing, Nador," Rurik cut in with a chuckle. "*I* hired him to dig. And I'm right about the treasure coming from Paladine, about it coming from the Age of Starbirth, and about it being a dragon waiting to be brought to life. It's more valuable than anything I can think of, Nador Irongut, and when we take it to town and sell it, I'll be famous."

Nador dropped the shovel and stomped. "You'll be famous? *You'll be famous?*" He made a harrumphing noise and climbed out of the hole, dislodging some of the dirt on the side and sending a big clump falling on Rurik's head. "*I'll* be famous, Rurik Rustbucket. I'll be the one people talk about for centuries because I'm right about the statue. It was made by a silver dragon sorcerer, I tell you."

"In the Age of Starbirth," Rurik said. He put down his shovel and shook to get some of the dirt off.

"That's right," Nador returned. "In the Age of Starbirth, and—no! In the War of the Lance."

"Filled with dragon magic," Rurik added.

"No, not filled with—" Nador's face was red, and he breathed unevenly. "Yes, it's filled with dragon magic. You're trying to trick me, Rurik!"

"Like that would be difficult," the thin dwarf muttered under his breath.

"It's you who is trying to trick me, Nador." Rurik started climbing out of the hole. "It's Paladine's dragon statue. I did the research on it. I'm the one who's right. And so I'm the one to get the fame and the—"

Nador reached a hand down to help Rurik out of

the hole. "You'll get nothing if you don't stop nattering, Rurik Rustbucket. I can't believe I shared the map with you, I can't—"

"Shared? I'm the one who did the sharing," Rurik sputtered. "I'm the one who, out of the goodness of my heart that day in the marketplace, pretended I didn't have enough coin to buy the treasure map just so we could share this adventure. I'm the one who—"

Chink.

Chink. Chink.

Rurik and Nador held their breath and peered over the hole. Nador grabbed the lantern and dangled it over the edge so they could see better.

Chink. Chink. Chink.

At the bottom of the hole, the thin dwarf, back at work, had struck something metal.

"Be careful!" Rurik shouted.

"Use your hands to brush the dirt away," Nador said. To Rurik, he added, "I'm the archaeologist, after all. I know how these sensitive things should be uncovered."

"Lower the lantern so I can see better, please." The thin dwarf propped his shovel against the side of the hole and motioned to Rurik and Nador. "I don't want to break anything."

Nador fumbled with a rope and lowered the lantern, gasping when a patch of silvery blue metal glimmered up from the bottom.

"I was right!" Nador beamed. "It is the silver dragon sorcerer's statue!"

Rurik got on his knees and gripped the edge of the hole. He hoped to smell something old and instead smelled only dirt. "Use your hands to push some of the dirt away . . ." He'd meant to add the thin dwarf's name to that, but he realized he'd never asked his name. "Move it careful."

"Whatever you say, boss." The thin dwarf started scooping dirt away, slowly revealing a statue, its precise shape still vague.

"I'm the one who told him to use his hands," Nador gloated. "I'm the archaeologist."

Rurik kept his eyes on the work below. "Gentle, careful."

"You be careful with that!" Nador echoed. "Gentle! Gentle, I say!"

The thin dwarf brushed dirt away from the edges of the statue, uncovering a snout and curving horns.

"See, what'd I tell you! It's the silver dragon sorcerer's statue!" Nador exclaimed.

"I'll be famous," Rurik said. "I'll go down in history for having discovered Paladine's forgotten statue."

"Famous and rich," murmured Nador to himself.

The thin dwarf continued to work.

"Take your time," Rurik told him. He wanted to savor the moment.

The silvery blue statue was indeed that of a dragon, and it was a little more than two feet tall and half again that thick. The dragon sat on its haunches, tail wrapped around it in the pose a contented cat might adopt. Its head was straight, and it had a proud, intense look on its visage. It wasn't silver or platinum, but perhaps a meld of the two metals, and the horns were polished and gleaming like a still lake hit by a full sun. Its closed eyes were blue-steel, like an armorer would color a

Dark Knight's breastplate, and its teeth looked impossibly sharp.

"Beautiful," Rurik breathed.

"And all mine," Nador said in a hush. "Mine. Mine. Mine."

"Mine!" corrected Rurik in a low voice.

The thin dwarf worked the statue free of the earth, straining from the weight of it. He stood it up at the bottom of the hole and shined its stomach with his sleeve. Then he looked underneath where it had been to see if, perhaps, there were another one hiding there.

At the same time there was the soft *shush* of a knife coming free from a scabbard.

"Rurik Rustbucket, what in the nine layers of the Abyss do you think you're doing?"

"Taking what's mine." Rurik advanced on Nador, who was quick to pull his own knife and crouch to meet the red-bearded dwarf's leap.

"Yours?" Nador bellowed. "Over my dead body, Rurik Rustbucket!" Nador slashed out with his blade, cursing when he managed only to snag the leather of Rurik's jerkin.

Rurik retaliated, thrusting forward and finding only air when Nador dropped beneath his swing. "Mine. Mine. Mine, I say!"

"Why, you sorry excuse for a gully—" Nador's throat felt suddenly dry and his ears were filled with a great whoosh. His eyes flicked over to the hole.

Rurik risked a glance over the edge and smelled something older than the parchment.

The thin dwarf seemed to be growing, changing,

his clothes melting like butter in a hot pan. His unlined ruddy face was spreading, the mouth and nose elongating and all of it picking up a metallic hue. His blond hair dissolved in a heartbeat, and hands that had been blistered from digging became claws that stretched and stretched and sparkled dangerously in the faint lantern light.

Rurik couldn't move; he was transfixed. A part of him worried that Nador would skewer him, but the other dwarf had shuffled next to him and was looking over the edge too.

The thin dwarf continued to transform.

For a moment, he adopted a pose similar to the statue, as a tail sprouted and wrapped around his hind legs. The skin of his chest and stomach thickened, looking like a ridged carapace that appeared as sturdy as a shield. His face continued to elongate into a snout, giving him an almost horselike visage. At the same time, his teeth multiplied and formed sharp points that glistened as white as fresh snow. A tongue snaked out, red and forked, and licked lips that were thin and leathery.

The thin dwarf's eyes also enlarged, becoming black pupil-less pools that suddenly looked up and focused on the two dwarves. Bony crests formed above the eyes, and horns sprouted above them, curling up and ending in wicked points.

His skin bubbled and popped, as if he were being boiled in a pot, and scales began sprouting. They were small at first and flat against his limbs. But as he continued to change, they became larger, the size of steel pieces. It was difficult to tell the color of the scales as the light from the lantern was low and the shadows were thick. But they were metallic.

The metamorphosis continued, with the thin dwarf turning into a dragon clutching the precious statue in its front claw. Within heartbeats it was bursting out of the hole.

Rurik and Nador cringed and trembled like terrified children, shaking and babbling, lips trembling with drool and fingers unable to hold on to their knives. They couldn't speak another word, could barely breathe in the presence of the massive creature that loomed over them, staring with blackest-black eyes. They could only quiver and gasp and retch and pray.

The dragon opened its mouth, and Rurik and Nador couldn't tell whether it intended to say something or to spit some horrid gas or flame upon them. Then it slid gracefully by them, scales brushing against them and pressing them up against the sides of the cave, squeezing them as it squeezed by and eased out of the cave opening.

It turned its head, eyes regarding them and holding them in place, opening its maw wider.

The air turned fetid and musty from its breath.

As one, the dwarves jumped into the hole, pitifully clutching at each other. The light from the lantern cast shadows upon their faces, making their eyes look like hollow sockets.

Their hired help that had transformed into the dragon was at the top of the hole, peering down at them, with eyes like ebony mirrors that reflected their shivering images back at them. There was malevolence in the gaze, and for an instant Rurik thought he glimpsed a flash of pity.

Then the dragon was gone with a great whoosh and flutter and a roar that shook the mountain and collapsed the entrance to the cave.

It took several long moments for their fright to leave the two dwarves, and longer moments before they were able to climb out of the hole, holding up the lantern to confirm they were trapped.

"That was a silver dragon," Nador said in a shaky voice at last, "that flew off with our prize. Hoodwinked us into thinking it was a dwarf, having us lead it to the statue it forgot. Had to be that same silver dragon sorcerer that made that statue during the War of the Lance. Had to be!"

Rurik shook his head and made a *tsk-tsk* sound. "Wrong, wrong, wrong. Wrong again. That was Paladine," he said. "Come to get his forgotten statue."

"Gods don't forget anything, you simpering addle-minded—"

"Gods can forget whatever they want, Nador. If I was a god, I would surely forget you!"

"Admit it. I was right, Rurik. That was the silver dragon sorcerer."

"It was Paladine, I tell you! Paladine. I was right. And when folks hear all about this, I am going to be famous!"

****

High above the Khalkist peaks, the dragon could still hear the dwarves arguing, even through the rubble covering the cave mouth. It closed its eyes for just a moment, the lids looking like blued steel, and it focused on more pleasant sounds—the screech of some night bird hunting, the whispery howl of a wolf. Then it glanced at the precious statue cradled in its claw, and banked higher and higher.

I READ IT IN *THE FLYING DRAGON*

Douglas W. Clark

Douglas W. Clark has been a full-time nonfiction writer and editor most of his professional life and has written numerous short stories and four novels, including his most recent novel, *Saving Solace,* set in the Dragonlance world. He has also worked as an environmental consultant, a laboratory director, and a lecturer and teacher.

I Read It in *The Flying Dragon*

Douglas W. Clark

Age of Mortals, 419 AC

Randall Wicket glowered at the piece of paper before him, straining to block out the sounds of tavern revelry swirling around him. Not that there were any words to read on the paper, for it was blank. In fact, that was the problem. Randall—known as "Sticky" to his friends in honor of the scrapes to which he was prone—had until noon to fill up the sheet with a scintillating account of the previous night's weekly meeting of the local quilting society. The man for whom Sticky worked, Arnold Dreary, had made it clear he wanted the story in time for the next edition of the twice-weekly paper, *The Flying Dragon.* For once, Sticky hadn't bothered going to the quilting society meeting to take notes for the story. He'd been right there at The Reeking Harlot, drinking with the same friends who had bestowed his nickname on him.

****

Sticky had started his job in the naive expectation of bringing meaning and significance to people's lives after the gods vanished from Krynn, taking magic with them. Instead, three years later, he found himself writing the same endless quilting society pieces, something he swore he could do repeatedly in his sleep—except not, apparently, without first having attended the meeting.

Smells of broiling meat and baking bread from the kitchen warned Sticky lunchtime was drawing near. His deadline was almost upon him. Then, as if even the tavern's patrons were conspiring to keep him from writing, a huge man with red hair and beard and a pilgrim's staff pulled a bagpipe from under his stool and began playing. Its shrill skirling drowned out the other sounds in the tavern and drove coherent thought from Sticky's ale-muddled brain.

The only certainty remaining to him was that Dreary would have his head for his failure. Without the quilting society piece, there would be a hole in the middle of the paper's front page, a blank space without text. If only something meaningful ever happened in Nutter's Ridge, this flyspeck of a town a hard day's ride from Palanthas—or anywhere else, for that matter. Then he could write a story that mattered for a change. Something people really cared about.

Sticky tried to imagine what a sufficiently interesting story might be. It would not be about the quilting society, that was for sure, nor Goodwife Hensley's new calf. Her two cows supplied milk and butter for The

Reeking Harlot's kitchen, and she had been after Sticky again that morning to write about how one of the cows had just delivered. As if anyone cared! If it had been something a bit more unusual in the way of bovine parturition, that might be newsworthy . . . or at least entertaining.

Sticky struggled to think despite the bagpipe's noise, then, on impulse, wrote a heading across the top of his paper: "Cow Gives Birth to Snakes!"

Pleased with his imaginative start, he signaled to the elf, Harrow Bitterroot, who was forced, through some disgrace among her own kind, to work as a barmaid in that no-account settlement. Harrow sauntered over to his table with her usual look of disdain, as if she were doing Sticky a favor by taking his order rather than simply doing her job.

"Another tarbean tea, please," Sticky said, having sworn off ale after the previous evening's debauch. Harrow rolled her eyes scornfully and drifted in the general direction of the kitchen. Sticky chewed the feather end of his quill and considered what to say next about his astonishing revelation.

He needed to place the event somewhere suitably distant from Nutter's Ridge. And he needed someone he could cite whose authority would lend credence to the account. He glanced irritably at the bagpipe-playing pilgrim, wishing for a moment's peace from the cacophony, and smiled with sudden inspiration. He threaded his way through the busy tavern to the pilgrim's table.

"Excuse me," he shouted, leaning close to the pilgrim's ear to be heard over the noise. "Can you stop that for a moment?"

The man unclenched his teeth from the bagpipe's mouthpiece, and the noise trailed away in a diminishing wail as the bag deflated. "What? You have something against beautiful music?"

"Oh, no, I enjoy beautiful music just fine. I wondered if you might tell me your name."

The man scowled suspiciously. "Who wants to know?"

"Randall Wicket," Sticky replied. "I write for the local paper here in Nutter's Ridge."

The scowl deepened. "Paper?"

"Yeah, it's a newfangled thing, a kind of broadsheet that comes out twice a week with news of what's going on around town."

"It'll never catch on," the pilgrim said, dismissing the notion with a shake of his head.

"Probably not, but meanwhile it's my job to write for the thing."

"I see. And so you want to put something about me in this . . . paper of yours?"

Sticky nodded.

"Well, the name's Rance Hodbarth," the man said, his chest swelling like the bag of his recently inflated instrument.

"Rance?"

"Short for 'Rancid.'"

Sticky gave a slow nod. "Uh, I take it your parents didn't like you very much."

"Not much. Eventually, I had to kill 'em."

"Ah?"

"Wrapped my hands around their throats and squeezed—"

"I see," Sticky said hurriedly. "Well, from your staff, I gather you're a pilgrim. Seen many shrines?"

"Shrines?"

"You know, religious sites."

"Oh, no," Rance said with a booming laugh. "Why would I want to bother with any of those?"

"Because that's what pilgrims do."

"It is?"

Sticky gave another nod.

"Huh, who'd have thought it?" Rance's countenance clouded. Suddenly, he beamed. "I make it a point to travel wherever the ale is said to be good, is that close enough?"

"It'll do. So you've seen lots of places?"

"You could certainly say that. Why, just last week I was all the way over in Hardpan—"

"Thanks," Sticky interrupted again. "I appreciate your time." He hesitated before turning away and whispered, "You know, they pay itinerant musicians better down at The Swan."

"That a fact?"

Sticky gave him a final nod. As Sticky made his way back to his own table, he glimpsed Rance packing up his bagpipe and hurrying from the tavern.

Sticky's tarbean tea was waiting when he returned. He scarcely allowed himself a hurried gulp from the mug, however, before shoving it aside and picking up his quill to resume writing. "News of this wonder reached Nutter's Ridge from the town of Hardpan this week via the person of one Rance"—he paused, trying to remember the man's last name, then shrugged—"Dogbark, a devout pilgrim who has traveled extensively across the land, visiting all manner of shrines and temples. As evidence of his claim, Master Dogbark allowed this reporter to see one of the tiny reptiles, which sported a diminutive pair of bovine horns. When asked what he intended to do with the creature, Master Dogbark replied with characteristic humility that he planned to take up showing it for a fee 'in order to found an orphanage, that little tykes who've lost their parents might not have to wander the face of the world, friendless and penniless as the likes of me.'"

Sticky continued in that vein for several more pages, by which time he almost believed his own invention. Life certainly would be more exciting if stories like his were true. He drained his lukewarm tea in a single gulp and hurried from the tavern.

When he reached the office of *The Flying Dragon,* he found Arnold Dreary behind his desk, drumming his fingers on the wooden surface. Through the open door behind him came the hiss and clatter of the gnome-engineered, steam-powered press used to print the paper. Sticky had just time enough to glance into the back room, where the infernal clanking machine stood half obscured by belching steam and smoke while the wizened, nut-brown figure of Glubb danced around it, twirling knobs and adjusting levers in the technological ritual that kept the press running. But Dreary didn't give Sticky time to dwell on the scene.

"About time!" he snapped. "I was ready to give up on you, Wicket. Do you have it?"

Suddenly feeling a bit defensive, Sticky cleared his throat and handed Dreary the scribbled sheets.

Dreary grunted, hefting the stack. "Kind of long for

a quilting society story. Still, there ended up being more space for it than I figured, so that's just as well."

Sticky was heading toward the door, amazed at having gotten off so easily, when a bellow from Dreary rooted him where he stood.

"Wicket! What in the name of all the absent gods is this?"

Sticky turned to see Dreary thrusting the pages at him in evident fury.

"This isn't a quilting society story. What's the meaning of this gibberish?"

Sticky's chin jutted out defiantly. "It's not gibberish. It's . . . well, every word of it's true. Or almost so, anyway."

"It is, huh? What makes you say so?"

"Sources quoted."

"And why should I trust these sources?"

Sticky thought fast. "Can't elaborate. Reporter's credo," he said quickly. "But I assure you his truthfulness is impeccable."

Dreary stared. "You've got to be joking."

"Look, readers might be more interested in this piece than in the usual quilting society story we run every week," Sticky said, beginning to grow resentful of Dreary's distrust.

"What readers—!" Dreary broke off, straining for breath.

"Well, I just figured—"

But Dreary cut him off with an impatient wave. "Never mind the explanations. I don't have time to change any of it now, so this . . . this *thing* you've saddled me with will have to do." He hunched over his desk, already occupied with editing Sticky's text.

"Will that be all?" Sticky asked coldly, still standing in the middle of the room.

Dreary mumbled something indistinct, his attention obviously leagues away. Sticky made it to the door and fled, feeling lucky to still have his job.

****

Several hours later, Arnold Dreary still sat at his desk, drumming his fingers with impatience. It was dark out, and the paper was ready to print . . . all except for one last item.

The door swung open, and a lean man slouched in, his face obscured by a weathered cap pulled low over his eyes. "It's about time," Dreary said, holding out his hand.

The man handed Dreary a single sheet of paper, on which was scrawled a nearly illegible note. Dreary scowled at it. "A cattle auction to be held two nights from now at Blind Dog Crossing, eleven o'clock?"

The man nodded.

With a grunt, Dreary began marking up the notice for inclusion in the paper. If the time or remote location of the auction surprised him, he gave no evidence of it. The stranger slipped back through the door as quietly as he had come, checking the darkened street before stepping outside. Dreary ignored him. He examined the items slated for that issue of the paper and considered where to put the auction notice—somewhere easily overlooked.

Right after Wicket's story, he concluded. No one

with the brains of a gully dwarf would read through Wicket's mad raving to notice the auction piece there.

Humming to himself, Dreary set about his work.

****

When Sticky arrived at The Reeking Harlot the next morning, conversations stopped as people at many tables turned to watch him, then whispered eagerly among themselves when he had passed. Nods and hellos greeted him from several individuals he scarcely knew. Puzzled, he ordered breakfast from an apathetic Harrow and tried to become invisible to the furtive stares of those in the room. Around him, conversations resumed, stray bits of which reached his ears.

". . . not since the gods left Krynn . . ."

". . . first interesting thing to happen since the mages lost the use of magic . . ."

". . . almost makes you believe the glory of the old days had returned . . ."

He glanced around. In every case, the speakers held copies of that morning's edition of *The Flying Dragon.* He ducked his head to hide a surprised smile. Evidently, his piece was being noticed. Perhaps he had stumbled onto something.

It was, he told himself, the mark of a good reporter to recognize the validity of a story such as his and to insist on seeing it through to publication, even in the face of editorial objection.

After breakfast, he strolled down to Dreary's office. The editor raised his eyes from a copy of the paper when Sticky walked in, his expression downcast. "How is the edition selling?" Sticky asked, daring to sit for a change in the dilapidated chair across the desk from Dreary.

"Sold out," Dreary said miserably.

"Huh!" Sticky exclaimed, feeling a surge of pride. "The whole issue sold out? Already?"

Dreary's face sagged as if cast in wax left too close to the fire. "Every last copy."

Sticky thought about that, momentarily at a loss for words. At last he asked, "Huh! Has this ever happened before?"

Dreary awarded him a baleful stare. He looked ready to cry—from sheer happiness, Sticky assured himself. "Never."

"What do you suppose is responsible for it?" Sticky had a pretty good idea but wanted to hear Dreary say it out loud.

"Responsible? You want to know about responsibility?" Dreary roared. "It's all because of one of the two people in this room, that's who's responsible. And it sure wasn't me!"

Sticky flinched from the vehemence of the older man's anger.

"All I wanted was the usual piece about the quilting society meeting," Dreary went on, addressing a spot high on the wall. "Was that too much to ask for? Instead, I get this." His hand thwacked the front page of the paper where Sticky's story lay displayed.

"But apparently people want to read my story," Sticky said, thrusting out his jaw again. "Apparently, they think what I wrote is more interesting than the standard quilting society story."

"Who cares what people *want* to read? This story you concocted—"

"I didn't concoct it!"

"—doesn't contain the slightest shred of truth," Dreary finished as if Sticky had never interrupted.

"There are a few shreds of truth," Sticky insisted. "Here and there."

"What will I say to . . . to our advertisers?" Dreary moaned.

"I should think they'd be glad of the rising readership. It means more exposure for their ads."

Dreary glared at him as if he wanted to say something to that but held his tongue.

Undeterred, Sticky returned to The Reeking Harlot, smiling and enjoying the many greetings he received along the way. At the tavern, he began planning a piece for the next edition, an article that would feature a unique solution to the age-old problem of kender. He couldn't wait to hear people's reaction to it. In fact, once he'd thought of it, he couldn't understand why no one had come up with this particular solution before. It was a good thing they had Randall Wicket to point them in the right direction.

The only disappointing aspect of the morning was the customary indifference with which Harrow served him lunch, apparently unaware he had become something of a celebrity about town.

****

The following day Sticky whistled as he sauntered into Dreary's office, his contribution for the next edition ready early for a change. As usual, the gnome-run printing press rumbled and groaned in the back room. Sticky handed Dreary the new pages with a flourish and plopped into the chair across from him.

"What's this?" Dreary demanded, eyeing the pages with evident distaste.

"My next piece, of course."

"Healer Announces 'Kender Cure,'" Dreary read aloud. "Process Reverses Legendary Acquisitiveness." He scanned the text, an interview with an itinerant healer about a process that hypnotized kender into emptying their pockets of such items as ordinary rocks, empty seedpods, balls of lint, unidentifiable former foodstuffs, and bits of stick.

"What are you doing to me, Wicket?" he moaned when he had finished.

"Boosting circulation. And bringing the truth to a blighted public."

"I take it, then, that you're going to insist this tripe is true as well?"

"Of course. And I have something even better—totally different—in mind for the following edition."

"Totally different? Well, I should hope so."

"I was thinking of an in-depth exposé on the number of the deceased who have been secretly reanimated and put to work here in Nutter's Ridge, taking jobs away from the living. It's a serious problem, let me assure you."

Dreary spluttered, but no words emerged.

"Or maybe a spread on the ghost legion of Solamnic Knights that marches the length of the town's main road in the wee hours every night."

Dreary managed a squeak. His eyes looked ready to pop.

"Or maybe—"

"Get out," Dreary croaked. "Just get out."

Sticky did so, irritated by what he could only assume was jealousy on the part of Dreary. But he knew the crotchety old editor wasn't going to fire him . . . not for turning the somnambulant *Flying Dragon* into an overnight success. He headed with jaunty steps toward The Reeking Harlot, his chest swelling at the accolades to which he was treated along the way. The stories he wrote had to contain some measure of truth, a voice whispered in his head. Otherwise, why would so many people believe them?

****

Two days later Dreary sat at his desk, staring morosely at Sticky's kender story, which had just appeared in the latest edition. Even with Glubb, the gnome in charge of printing *The Flying Dragon,* pushing his steam-operated press dangerously close to the bursting point to produce additional copies, the entire edition had sold out within hours.

Dreary couldn't have been more distressed.

The sound of the door opening distracted him and he looked up. It was the man with the weathered cap pulled low over his face. "You!" Dreary hissed. "What are you doing here now? It isn't even dark out. You might have been recognized."

The man dismissed Dreary's objections with a flick of his hand that managed to convey annoyance. "You want to know what happened at Blind Dog Crossing last night?" he asked, then went on without waiting for a reply. "I'll tell you what: over a dozen people who shouldn't have been there showed up. And you know what they were there for? A cattle auction! Do you have any idea of the danger that placed us in?"

Dreary groaned but said nothing.

"We were hard pressed to come up with excuses for why there wasn't going to be an auction, not last night or any other night," the man continued. "Some of the people there were mighty unhappy, I've got to tell you. Threatened to horsewhip the lot of us for playing such a prank and putting them to so much trouble." He yanked the chair in front of Dreary's desk back and dropped into it, placing himself on a level with Dreary's eyes. "Now how do you suppose so many people came to the conclusion that there was to be a cattle auction there in the first place?" He pulled a copy of *The Flying Dragon* from inside his cloak and unfolded it on the desk. " 'Cow Gives Birth to Snakes,' " he quoted, not bothering to glance at the paper. "But wait, here comes the good part: Some vagrant is supposed to have shown your reporter one of the horned serpents produced by this unholy event. Now what in the name of all the vanished gods were you thinking, putting an item as sensational as this in the paper? And right on top of the notice about last night's meeting!"

"What can I say? I didn't figure on the reaction. The boy's got a knack for spinning out stories people want to read."

"You're the editor, aren't you? Fire him."

"And what reason do I give? 'Wicket, your writing is

too successful; I'm going to have to let you go.'"

"Well, come up with something," the man said, regaining his feet. "Because if you don't put a stop to this nonsense, we will."

Dreary shuddered, remembering the demise of the last person who had held Wicket's job, a lad foolish enough to threaten going public with what little he knew about the paper's true goals. "All right, I'll think of something. Just don't do anything . . . hasty."

"Three weeks," the man said, making his way toward the door. "That's when we're meeting again. You've got exactly that long to bridle your boy or else." As if to punctuate this threat, he slammed the door behind himself.

At his desk, Dreary winced from the violence of the man's departure and wondered how to convince Wicket to seek his fortune elsewhere. Anywhere would be fine, as long as it was far away from Nutter's Ridge.

****

A couple of weeks later, seated at his personal table in The Reeking Harlot (for such was his fame that a corner table was reserved there for his exclusive use), Sticky held court, acknowledging the greetings of his fellow patrons with a benevolent smile and a wave. He snapped his fingers, and a properly deferential serving girl appeared at his elbow to take his order. Having finally tired of Harrow's blasé attitude, Sticky had seen to it the elf was fired and replaced with someone more respectful.

He ordered a repast appropriate for an epicure,

then returned his attention to the task at hand. So far he'd done pieces on Thorbardin ("Giant Dwarf Lurks in Depths of Mountain Stronghold") and Qualinost ("Elf Sentenced for Laughing; Levity Declared Capital Offense"), in addition to human communities suitably distant from Nutter's Ridge ("Vigilantes from Beyond: Dead Wives Hound Killer-Husband to Death" and "Torch-Wielding Tots Terrorize Town, Demand More Cake . . . or Else!"). With each new story, his fame had grown. But today he wanted to try something closer to hand, something that would really make his readers sit up and take notice. He thought for a moment before dipping his quill in the inkpot, wiping excess drops from the nib, and poising his hand above the blank piece of paper before him. He waited . . .

And waited . . .

And . . .

He was still sitting there some time later, staring moodily at the empty page, when a dark-haired, freckle-faced boy a couple of years younger than Sticky came over and stood by his elbow. "What?" Sticky barked at last. "I'm not giving out any more autographs today."

"Master Dreary wants to know when he can expect to get the latest story," the boy said hesitantly.

"He'll get it when it's done," Sticky growled, still studying the page, which persisted in remaining blank.

The boy shuffled but didn't leave.

"What!" Sticky repeated, more vehemently, wondering how he was ever to get his story written with the incessant interruptions.

"Master Dreary said you might say something like that. He said to tell you if the story isn't there by midafternoon, he'll have to put the issue together without your contribution."

"Huh! And just how many readers does he think that'll bring him?" Then, when the boy still didn't move, he added, "All right, you've delivered your message, now get out of here. Go on, scoot!"

The boy mumbled something as he turned to go.

"What's that?" Sticky demanded, suddenly alert. "What did you say?"

"I said I have to go cut clothes out across the alley for my beast of a master, the tailor—"

"Did you say something about a beast of Cutthroat Alley?" Sticky interrupted.

"No, sir." The boy looked at him as if he were mad. "Why would I say something as peculiar as that?"

But Sticky wasn't listening. He spun away and grabbed the abandoned quill. "Attack of the Beast from Cutthroat Alley," he wrote in bold strokes across the top of the page.

"Knowledgeable locals in Nutter's Ridge refer to it as 'Cutthroat Alley,' but even they think it refers to the shrewd business practices customary in that part of town. Few among even the usually-well-informed know about the beast that is the true cause of the name. But with the latest round of attacks, some of them occurring in broad daylight, that situation is about to change."

If Sticky felt any qualms about inventing a fictitious beast terrorizing a street right there in Nutter's Ridge, it wasn't sufficient to stay his hand. Weeks ago, he had convinced himself that his stories were reported for the common good. Perhaps he merely acted as the mortal vessel for some higher cause. Not for the gods, of course, for they had vanished from Krynn, but some unquestionable good. If so, who was he to argue? He dashed off several more paragraphs, including a couple of gruesome eyewitness accounts of victims whose throats had been slashed "as if by giant claws or talons," then hurried to the office of *The Flying Dragon*.

Dreary, who had looked more and more disconsolate with every story Sticky turned in, scarcely glanced at the latest piece. "'Cutthroat Alley,' eh?" he said.

Sticky nodded, his feet casually propped on the other man's desk.

"A mysterious beast, huh?"

Absently, Sticky examined his fingernails. "Yeah."

Dreary shook his head, the motion made ponderous by the certainty of defeat. "Wicket, what did I tell you about turning out any more of these blatant fantasies of yours?"

Sticky shrugged. "You know better than to think I'd make something like that up. Besides, if you don't like it, don't run it. Though how you'll explain the absence of my stories to expectant readers, well . . ." He let the words trail off into pregnant silence.

Dreary peered at Sticky, and for a moment the young reporter had the uncomfortable feeling his editor was looking at him from a long way away. "Right," Dreary said at last, turning back to the story. "Well, I had best get this ready for tomorrow's edition."

Inexplicably, Sticky shivered. "I'll leave you to it, then," he said, suddenly eager to leave. But once outside, his customary bravado returned. He sauntered back toward The Reeking Harlot, where his admiring public would be waiting to hear whatever tidbits Sticky chose to let drop about his piece in the next day's paper.

He was unaware of the man in the weathered cap who stepped into Dreary's office from the back room as soon as Sticky left. "Well?" was all the newcomer said.

Dreary let out a huge sigh. "Get a couple of the men together."

The man in the cap nodded and slipped out the front door after first checking the street. Dreary stared glumly at Sticky's latest story a while before he eventually became aware of eyes studying him from the doorway to the back room. He turned to confront the sad countenance of the gnome, Glubb, who had paused in his task of tending the printing press to peer in at him. "What do you want?" Dreary demanded.

Glubb shook his head, setting his long, soot-streaked white beard to wagging. Behind him, something sputtered and popped.

"Then get back in there and see to that blasted machine," Dreary snapped. "I want this edition out on time tomorrow."

Glubb abruptly withdrew his grizzled head, leaving Dreary alone with his thoughts.

****

Scarcely had the paper come out the next day before Sticky was summoned to Dreary's office. "There's been another sighting," the older man said before Sticky had the opportunity to prop his feet up on the editor's desk.

"Sighting?"

"The Beast of Cutthroat Alley."

"What? I mean . . . well, there has?" Sticky peered about him, concerned lest someone might overhear. He leaned in closer and whispered, "Look, are you sure . . . ?"

Dreary waited in vain for Sticky to finish.

"Ahem, as I was saying, the beast has been seen by several reliable witnesses."

Sticky, who knew just how easily such "reliable witnesses" could be come by, studied the older man with a judicious frown. "You're putting me on, right? I mean, this is some trick. You never have liked the idea of me doing these stories."

Dreary grunted noncommittally and added, "I want you down there tonight to write a firsthand account of the creature."

"You want me *where?*"

Dreary pushed a scrap of paper torn from the morning's edition across the desk at Sticky. "Here's the address. The town guard is keeping word of the deaths quiet because they don't want to alarm the citizenry. But I figure people have a right to know, don't you?"

Sticky picked up the piece of paper delicately, still expecting to be made the butt of some joke.

"Go down there tonight and check it out. Write up an exposé for the next issue."

"Me? But—"

"This is your story, Wicket. No one else could do it justice."

Sticky opened his mouth to speak, but found he had no more objections. Dreary was finally coming around. He was recognizing the unique contribution Sticky made to the paper. He was giving Sticky the chance to follow his story through several editions. He closed his mouth, his chest swelling. It had taken long enough, but at least Dreary was behind him finally.

As Sticky left the office, he wondered whether Dreary might consider renaming the paper to incorporate Sticky's name, perhaps calling it something such as *Randall Wicket Presents 'The Flying Dragon.'* He entertained himself with that possibility all the way back to the tavern, where he decided he had time for a couple of ales before heading out on his errand, an assignment that looked to make an exciting story for his fellow patrons afterward. Sticky grinned. That night's excursion would be good for a free ale or two from eager listeners at the tavern.

Thus it was that he emerged again from the tavern a few hours later in much better spirits. Whistling jauntily, he made his way on unsteady feet to the alley indicated in Dreary's instructions. His way was somewhat lengthened by the quantity of ale he had imbibed.

Outside, the silence came at first as a pleasant relief after the revelry and tumult of the tavern. Then it began to weigh on him. Darkness, too, reigned at that hour, wrapping Sticky as if in a shroud. But the gloom that lay upon the town by night was as nothing compared to the darkness that enveloped the alley. At its mouth, Sticky stood for a moment then snorted and strode forward with his newfound swagger into the inky depths. He was the fearless reporter who had first broken the story. Why should he hesitate?

At first, his footsteps were the only sounds he heard. Then a low moan emanated from the far end of the alley. Sticky froze in midstride. Something clumped toward him like a peg-legged giant. Gradually, it loomed up out of the darkness, huge and horrible. Sticky put his hands on his hips and cocked his head as he studied the apparition. A dark cloak hung from its shoulders, shrouding its form. Each blunt-boned footfall reverberated in the alleyway with a sound like that of approaching doom. A few paces away, it paused and opened its gaping maw. "Randall Wicket," it intoned in a voice both raspy and deep. With a lurching gait, it advanced another step.

Sticky, not fully convinced, almost snorted and stood his ground, but thought better of it. Cautiously, he backed up, keeping his gaze on the improbable creature before him.

So it was that he didn't see the pairs of arms waiting to grab him from behind, didn't see starlight glinting on the naked blade held by one of those hands. But he felt the searing coldness of the well-honed blade as it drew a crimson line across his throat. He tried to cry out, but the sound emerged as a gurgle, bubbling on his own blood. The night grew suddenly darker still. He sagged as his legs failed to hold him.

All consciousness had faded before he hit the ground.

****

"Tell me," Arnold Dreary said to the dark-haired, freckle-faced tailor's boy seated in front of his desk a few days later. "Do you have aspirations of becoming a celebrated reporter?"

The boy swallowed hard, his Adam's apple bobbing, visibly awed by the editor's presence. "N-n-no."

Dreary leaned back. "Good. That's excellent. Now the first thing I want you to do is attend a meeting of the local quilting society and write up a report of the occasion. Can you do that without elaborating on the bare facts of the event?"

The boy nodded, then mumbled something too indistinct to hear.

"What's that? You'll have to speak up."

The boy mustered his nerve. "What happened to Master Wicket? Why did he leave this job?"

Dreary glanced at the corner of the room, where a drab and shabby blanket, with a hole cut out of its middle as if to admit a wearer's head, hung about a pair of stilts. "Oh, he departed rather suddenly. I wouldn't worry about him. I'm sure the bod—that is, the *boy,* I'm sure the boy will turn up eventually."

Then Dreary stood, signaling an end to the discussion. "Welcome to the staff of *The Flying Dragon.* Keep your sights low and your ambition in check, and I'm sure you'll work out fine."

Aurora's Heart

Rachel Gobar

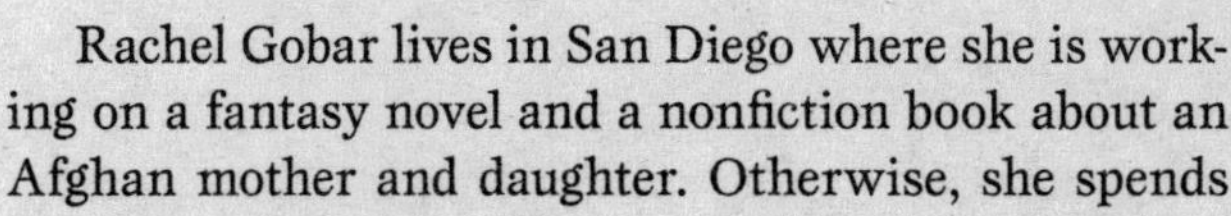

Rachel Gobar lives in San Diego where she is working on a fantasy novel and a nonfiction book about an Afghan mother and daughter. Otherwise, she spends her time teaching meditation and practicing various forms of martial arts. This is her first published short story for Dragonlance.

Aurora's Heart

Rachel Gobar

Age of Mortals, 422 AC

The sun hung low to the west, dripping soft light across the wheat fields of Jolithia as Aurora walked across the land. Her tall, slim shadow faded behind her with the late-day sun. She did not wonder why the wheat had not been sheared. She was headed toward her home, which was still another month's journey south in Lemish.

She walked along the side roads, cutting through pastures. Her objective was to avoid the main roads. She was just as afraid of the vigilante turnip-eaters as she was of the soldiers and mercenaries raping Jolithian towns and lands.

They said the Dark Queen's war had ended, but Aurora knew better. She saw the pillaged towns that were still being fought over. The soldiers and mercenaries who battled over dwindling spoils used the same brutalizing tactics to control the civilians as they had wielded in war. The sad truth was that sometimes savage methods worked.

Aurora was tired of fighting. The main roads guaranteed a fight, so she stayed clear of them.

Although she wore the uniform of a soldier, that was not the main thing that proved her occupation. It was too easy to get a uniform from the dead. Anyone could pose as a soldier. But her fine weapons, the only things of real value, gave her away.

After seven years of service in the Solamnic Army, she had seen to enough killing and torture. Some would say she excelled in the art of war. But her abilities as a soldier were not what drove her to volunteer, nor to quit earlier than her release date.

It was her father, whose voice tortured and pushed her. Aurora had thought she could escape him in the war. If anything, the war only strengthened his hold. She heard his voice before and after every battle. He was her real commander, ruling her far more strictly than any general. His voice came strongest when she was in mortal danger. Even at that moment, the memory of his voice was fresh and made her stomach clench.

"Get up." His guttural voice would demand. "Fight!"

She was never good enough or strong enough, for her father. Aurora was not as resourceful as her sister had been and would never be the warrior her father imagined his son could have been. For a long time, Aurora tried to fulfill those dreams and prove her father wrong. She understood as she walked toward home that he had only been trying to tell her the truth.

Aurora slowly took her canteen from her shoulder and untied the leather pouch. Her movements were controlled as she drank greedily and remembered.

The faces of her dead brother and sister came alive. After years of burying them in her heart and in her mind, as far and deep as she could, she saw them again.

There was nothing in her gait betraying the turmoil inside her. Her face appeared serene. Even the purple darkness of the scar that covered her left ear to her cheekbone didn't disturb the calm and soldierly poise with which she carried herself.

The old purple wound did not diminish the smooth texture of her features. In fact, it enhanced the fragility of her countenance. She was five foot seven but small-boned and appeared nothing like a warrior. Often Aurora was thought to be far younger than she was.

She exploited her appearance as an advantage and was frequently used in reconnaissance and information extraction. Aurora had learned to use her weaknesses to her benefit or hide them.

Aurora had one other asset not immediately apparent. She moved and fought with speed and flexibility. However she realized time would diminish her strengths.

Her gray eyes were focused ahead as she walked. She listened to the gentle sounds of the wheat bending and breaking under her footsteps, the sparrows calling to one another, and the supple movements of the country mice, which had free rein there.

She immersed herself in her surroundings in order to bring herself back from the past into the present.

Aurora paused a moment, took a deep breath, and continued walking as the orange glow of the setting sun bathed the sky and meadow.

Suddenly a loud, sharp scream echoed across the pale yellow field. The birds and mice stilled as Aurora squatted to the ground.

Again, the howling voice cried out. Aurora was certain it was a child's voice she heard. The fierce screams continued as Aurora peered through the rising wheat fields toward a stream of smoke. A small farmhouse of wood and stone stood north of her.

It might have been just a child injured or being punished, but Aurora suspected worse. She had seen women, men, and children tortured in war and recognized the high-pitched wail for what it was. There was anger and defiance that carried through the voice.

They hadn't yet broken him. The thought slid into her mind as cold sweat skimmed down her back.

Fear followed with the rapid beat of her heart because she knew he would eventually break down and surrender. Everyone had a breaking point.

Children were innocent and expendable and incredibly useful to the Dark Queen's army. They observed things hidden to scouts and assassins because they were easily overlooked.

There had been rumors that one small group of the Dark Knights were using children as spies. Until Aurora had been given her last assignment, she didn't think it was anything more than a kender's tale.

Aurora had been asked to infiltrate the Dark Army. She was trained and prepared and given all the right documents to fit in among the Dark Knights.

The Solamnic Knights had clear lines distinguishing right and wrong. Aurora had held to those principles until she joined the Dark Army and had to blend in. She had expected to be appalled by everything the Dark Queen's Army stood for. While serving within the Dark Army, Aurora found the knights were often no different than the Solamnics. In the Dark Army she made friends. In many ways she became one of them.

But obtaining secret documents that proved the Dark Army exploited children as informants and spies brought her back to the revolting reality. Aurora was freshly disgusted not only by the Dark Knights, but by her own lapse; she admitted to herself that she had come to admire some among the Dark Knights whom she had come to know.

Aurora crouched, listening hard for any footsteps or other sounds that might indicate people were close by and cautiously scanned the vicinity.

Someone was torturing the child.

Who?

It was possible the family was torturing their child. She had seen worse and learned by her father's hand that children were no more than property.

Once she was sure there wasn't anyone else around, Aurora guardedly continued to walk toward her home. As she did so, her father's voice screamed into her mind.

"Get up girl! Do you want your sister to have died for nothing?" His voice echoed inside her head as it always did when she tried to retreat from a battle. "Fight!"

"Damned if I will!" She answered to the ghost in her head.

Instinctively, she thought about fighting and calculated the risks. If the torturers were bandits, maybe she could do something. If they were the parents, she couldn't really help the child. A kid wouldn't be better off with her. She wasn't going to be anyone's mother. Even if Aurora managed to rescue the child, she would have to leave him to his own devices, and there was a good chance he would die anyway. The cold logic of the warrior she had become agreed with her assessment. There was very little reason to intervene.

The pain that came with her decision was unexpected. It surprised her as much as the regret that followed. Usually all she felt was the emptiness.

However, she persisted walking through the fields away from the farmhouse, trying not to listen to the memory of her father's voice, calling her a coward. The sun slid into the western edge while Aurora inhaled the past.

Nearly every time, what she remembered first was the smell of rotting meat and vomit. In the summer it didn't take long for the dead to smell.

One day her father had gone to the next village to sell cheese and some chickens they raised on the farm. He wasn't coming back for another two days. It was dawn when the bandits came. They had been watching and waiting for her father to leave.

The three men raped and killed her mother, sister, and brother. They left Aurora alive, cutting off her ear when her sister bit off the ear of the bastard raping her.

They threatened that if her sister did not do what they said, then they would continue to cut off Aurora's other body parts. Her sister did not struggle or cry out again. The silence of her voice was as painful to remember as the sacrifice. The bandits finally left in the middle of the night on the second day.

While Aurora tried to push away the faces of her family, she could not disown them. Aurora had not killed her siblings and mother, but she had killed others like them. She had become akin to the monsters who butchered her family and raped her sister. And she had seen too many other victims caught in a war not of their own choosing.

Aurora continued to walk through the fields, toward the trees ahead. As a trained warrior, she noted the darkening sky and the rush of cool wind. Automatically, she searched for the best place to take shelter and rest, even while another part of her relived memories.

For some soldiers, the killing was what haunted them, what eventually made them careless. Aurora had seen it happen often enough among soldiers and watched for the signs. But for her, it wasn't the killing that began to slow her instincts and reactions.

It was the doubt that plagued her after her time serving as a spy in the Dark Queen's Army. Before that, she had managed to keep the past at bay. Aurora, who took risks, who did not question orders, found herself unable to do either.

She had infiltrated the Dark Queen's Army in order to find out how far the Dark Knights had penetrated into the Solamnic forces. That was all: no more and nothing less.

It wasn't just spying within the Dark Queen's Army that had made her question her actions. It was the war itself. She had killed civilians; there was no denying it. It had happened accidentally and mistakenly, but there was no such thing as a clean war. She had inflicted torture on the enemy, and had done it well enough to be commended for it. She knew torture, understood it as well as an old friend.

When she had the required information about the Dark Knights, Aurora returned to the Solamnics with her report. She couldn't get her release papers until after the debriefing. Everything had to be done according to code and rule. Solamnics prided themselves on how organized and civilized they were.

She spent the first three months after returning from her assignment writing letters to the proper officials. It took another two months until her case was heard and she was actually granted leave. They docked her five months of back pay before allowing her to go.

In the five months she had waited to be released from her commission, she relived every moment of what she had seen, experienced, and done. The Solamnic interrogator was as thorough and harsh as any she had witnessed in the Dark Queen's Army.

Aurora explained all the details of her duties and activities in the Dark Army. As she did so, she wondered if her interrogator suspected that she had also liked and admired some of the Dark Knights. Quite a few of the Dark Knights she worked with had the same strength of conviction as she once had when she joined the Solamnics.

Her testimony to the handler and interrogator gave her no reprieve from her memories and nightmares. They could not grant her any real clemency. However, they insisted that what she had done and the information she had intercepted would save many lives. If anything, those salves disgusted her even more, making Aurora realize that the Solamnics were no different from the Dark Knights; both sides justified anything in war.

In all the years Aurora served, she never drank until those last five months. She always had hated ale, though it was available and cheap. Waiting for her leave, she took to drinking. Drink offered the illusion of oblivion.

She focused on going home. Aurora did not allow herself to think beyond that. She was tired of fighting and was ready to die. Aurora needed to confess all that she had done in the war. If her father were still alive, she preferred to die by his hands.

She was surprised at the wet, cool drops sliding down her face. She didn't wipe away the tears. The last time she cried was when her father kicked her down while teaching her to fight. She could hear him again, taunting her, telling her to get up and fight.

She heard the tortured scream again, faintly in the distance.

No. She would not run away from it, even as every part of her mind screamed at her to continue south. There was another part, deep within, which held out for redemption.

"You're an idiot," she whispered, even as she turned back toward the farmhouse. Walking fast, she knew the new moons would hide her. The instincts she had developed and the knowledge she had gained in war automatically helped her devise a strategy.

The only light was the stars of the night, etched across the valley, as the evening fog lifted from the ground. She weaved through the field toward the house, pausing to listen.

The mist draped across her. The wet cold sank its invisible teeth into her bones and joints. She would be slower in the mist and cold.

A quarter of the way there, she saw the front door open, spilling light into the night. To her surprise, a soldier walked out wearing an old uniform marking him as one of the Dark Queen's. The weapons he carried confirmed his occupation.

She hesitated. For some reason she had expected a civilian. It was uncommon for soldiers to be so far from town. If they were there, there ought to be more of them.

Why are they here?

Aurora melded into the caked, dark brown soil beneath her as she listened. She had no intentions of walking into a fray without knowing what she was going to face. Her father would have criticized her cowardly hesitation. But it was patience that had saved her when better soldiers than she died.

She watched the Knight of Takhisis patrol the grounds. He was at least ten years her senior and diligent in his vigilance. He was stocky in build and appeared to favor his right side for some reason, perhaps an old wound, but it was hard to be certain in the darkness.

She heard a burst of laughter from inside the house. But Aurora remained still and hidden until she was confident the Dark Knight returned indoors.

Once she was closer to the farmhouse, she bent

down, heading cautiously toward the side of the house where there was no light. The shutters had been boarded.

However, she clearly heard the sound of flesh striking flesh: unmistakable fast cracking sounds of a hand slapping skin and bone. There was no response from the child she assumed was being hit.

A slit in the boards gave her the opportunity to see inside. The single source of light was a lantern by the open door. She noted the thin shadow of the child held by red knuckles. The chains falling from his bound wrists and ankles rattled against the floor.

Aurora could see only the profile of the boy. His face was cut open. Drops of blood fell against his arms and feet, down to the ground. He didn't turn his face from the soldier.

The boy dangled from the soldier's hand. Aurora could not see his face well enough to see his expression. The boy didn't utter a sound as the soldier poked his knife into his face. In that defiant silence, Aurora recalled her sister.

"You think you're tough," the soldier said, dropping the boy heavily to the floor. "I will eat your liver and maybe you'll be alive long enough to watch me enjoy it."

The Dark Knight picked up his lantern, turned, and spit into the huddled mass, which had not moved. "You're nothing. No one will come to your rescue. And I will make sure your death is slow."

As the knight turned his back, the light found its way to the boy's dark hair. He lifted his head just enough to look straight at the slit in the boarded wall . . . at Aurora.

In the dim light, Aurora did not see his lips move. Nonetheless, a whisper of wind carried his voice from across the room.

"Help me."

He shouldn't have been able to see her at all. She shouldn't have been able to hear his soft voice as though he were whispering close to her ear. No one but she could hear him.

In the soft cadence of his voice, Aurora noted pride more than pain.

Aurora's heart thundered as she was swept by memories, all the overlapping voices of those she hadn't saved.

Aurora crawled toward the front of the house, under the open window, and listened.

"Torm, I said leave the child alone," came a voice with a hint of steel in the soft command.

"Nah. And I don't think we should reduce his medication either."

Footsteps grating against wood moved from the back room to the main one.

"Shut up, old man."

Aurora heard the scraping of a chair as the man who just spoke continued to walk closer to the open window.

"Stupid old man. You wouldn't even be here if it wasn't for Jor."

"Leave Sabe be," the authoritative voice from earlier responded more firmly.

"All I'm saying is we can't be sure what will happen if he doesn't get the full dose of the medication. They'll be coming to move him in four nights."

"I know. And I will handle it. We'll start the full dosage in two nights. Meanwhile, we might learn something if we take a break and let him think hard about cooperating."

Aurora couldn't risk looking inside.

"Torm, take the watch tonight for Sabe, and I don't want to hear the boy or see in the morning that he's suffered." Jor paused. "And walk the grounds thoroughly."

"I've . . ."

"Just do as I say, Torm."

"I'm taking a smoke," Torm said as he opened the front door.

Aurora quickly ran to the back of the house and from there into the fields. She waited to make sure they hadn't heard her. Making her move away from the farmhouse, she went half a mile out before feeling safe enough to stop and plan what she should do.

****

On the second day, late in the afternoon, she waited for the old man, Sabe, to make his rounds. She had guessed he would be on daylight duty instead of Jor.

She already knew Sabe's bladder, which, during the night and throughout the morning, was reliable in getting him outside. He had injured his left knee and sometimes would stop, leaning on his right side before moving on. The sunlight, she knew from experience, eased the pain. He liked being outside in the sun.

Sabe was cautious, but he was still foolish enough to drop his guard while urinating. There was nothing stupider than relaxing when you were defenseless.

Aurora used her knives, throwing one toward his throat and the other into his solar plexus. She didn't have unusual skills when it came to swords, although she carried one. But given a weapon to throw or shoot, she was fast and fairly accurate on the averages.

The soldier went down. Aurora pulled out her knives and wiped them on her pants. She hurried to the farmhouse, hoping the other two were resting after their large midday meal. She had watched them eat heartily, feeling hunger herself. As a soldier, hunger was a constant companion.

Jor, with his soft, steely voice, trusted the old man's assiduousness. But Jor would also become suspicious if Sabe didn't come back soon.

Aurora sidled quickly around toward the back of the house, carefully looking over her shoulder. She didn't expect to be caught from the front and shoved against the farmhouse wall. Unbreakable calloused hands grabbed her around her neck.

Aurora moved for her knife at the same time her assailant kicked her hard between her legs. Still, she didn't let go of the knife, but her swing was slow. He caught her arm and punched with the other.

She fell hard, slumping against the wall. She fought for consciousness as her father shouted. The last thing she felt was a sharp, swift kick to her gut.

****

"Gods, but you're loud. Kill me, but stop shouting." Aurora knew it was a stupid thing to say, but she needed Torm to hit her. Anything was better than hearing her father's voice in her head taunting her stupidity, her capture.

Her intestines felt as if a serrated knife had slashed through them. They had tied her ankles, knees, and bound her hands behind her as she lay with her back pressed on the dirty timber floor. Her arms were entirely numb from the pressure of her body on top of them. But she continued to flex her fingers despite the sharp, shooting pain that ensued.

"Where are they?" Jor asked as Aurora felt the blood slide down from her lips where Torm had slapped her repeatedly.

"A day's journey north," she said for the fifth time. There was no platoon coming, but she envisioned one. And she hoped for one. In believing it to be possible and true, she was better able to convince her captors.

At first she denied she was part of any group. She told them she had retired from active duty and was returning home. They had scrutinized her release papers, which they thought forged. A lie infused with the truth was always more convincing.

They didn't believe her. Thank Paladine.

Her weapons weren't standard issue. They were specially made for the elite group of soldiers in the Solamnic Army that she had been a part of, which most of the other soldiers referred to as the "General's Whores."

She didn't think Jor or Torm knew about her secret unit. They just thought she was a regular soldier sent to spy on them.

Because of that, they bound and questioned her. They worried she was part of some larger plan, some approaching force. It was the only reason she was still alive.

After all, who would be stupid enough to come to the rescue of a mere boy just because he was being tortured? Certainly not a homeward-bound soldier, retired after a long and bloody campaign. It was obvious they had been warned there was a chance of someone coming to rescue the boy.

What made the boy so special?

Aurora couldn't guess. She knew only that they hated and feared him. They called him their golden egg. Maybe they wanted to ransom him. She doubted it was that simple.

"How many?" Jor persisted.

"You'll be dead before you know the answer to that." Part of Aurora raged against the fear beating inside her. The rage was the only way to keep control and not give in to despair. She was not afraid of dying. She was afraid of what they would do to her before killing her. And she was afraid of failing.

"You will not give into fear, girl, even if I have to beat you to make you understand that."

She was grateful for her father's voice at that moment. It saved her, as it had on other occasions in the past. It helped her focus on a way out of her problem.

If she could just get to the little darts of steel in the small pockets of her pants, she would have a chance. They had searched her quickly, taking her conspicuous weapons but missing those.

"Your face is pretty. The only pretty thing you've got. I can turn your face into what's left of your ear," Torm volunteered as he toyed with his knife.

She knew her missing ear, the subject of scorn and ridicule even among her Solamnic comrades, only made the delicate features of her face stand out. She learned long ago that people were deceived by that scar and apparent fragility.

Aurora ignored Torm's threats. There was only one person to worry about, and that was Jor.

"Why would anyone be sent to rescue a mere child?" she asked scornfully, throwing the question back at her persecutors.

"Because he is your secret weapon," Torm answered.

"Shut up," Jor quickly interjected with his hard-edged voice. His voice was as sharp as Aurora's knives. "I want you to go and find Sabe's body and report back to me. Bring back his weapons if you find him. Don't take long to do it."

"Yes, sir," Torm said sullenly, as he walked out the door.

Aurora smelled the dirt and blood on the soles of Jor's boots. As Torm left, she also breathed deeply the honeysuckles that grew wild on the land. The cloying sweetness and the dizziness worsened as Jor's boot pressed against her throat. She wanted to retch. But she fought the sensation because she knew he would let her choke on her vomit.

"We can pay you more for the child than what you're being offered," Aurora rasped, trying a different tactic.

She continued flexing her fingers for the darts of steel in the small, hidden pockets of her pants. But her damn nails were too short to slice the stupid stitches she had sewn too well. She had similar sets of arrowheads on the sides of her pants, as well as by her knees.

Jor pressed harder, pointing to the door with his right hand. "That fool may be doing this for riches. But I assure you, you will never be able to buy me out, even if I was doing this only for the money. Money means nothing to me, less than nothing."

After what seemed like an eternity, Aurora had managed to get at the rapier-sharp arrowheads. She was grateful she hadn't cut her finger completely off while cutting the rope that bound her hands; she felt the blood flowing along her backside. Aurora was even more grateful that they had tied her hands behind her as she lay on them. Jor didn't notice what she was doing.

He released some of the pressure from Aurora's throat.

"I'll make this offer once. I will kill you quickly rather than hand you over to Torm if you tell me what exactly you are up to. What are your exact orders? Tell me, and I'll be merciful with your death. Regardless, you will die when Torm returns."

The arrowheads were tiny, but they would get the job done. She grabbed two more as she turned her head completely away from the boot, getting enough air and momentum. In the same instant, Aurora twisted her body, forcing her torso up while pushing the first arrowhead into the soldier's groin.

She didn't anticipate the knife that quickly plunged into her left shoulder. But she managed to throw one of the arrowheads into his throat and another into his eye as he went down. She quickly pulled one of the arrowheads from the dead soldier and cut the other strips of rope around her knees and ankles. She knew the knife behind her shoulder was more dangerous to remove suddenly than to leave.

The knife had pierced deep, going into her lung. It wasn't a mortal wound if she could find one of the healers of Schallsea. Too bad that wasn't going to happen.

Torm came into the house just as she got the light-handled knife from the table where they had cast off her things. She managed with more luck than precision to hurl it at Torm and lodge it in his throat.

It was well worth it, Aurora thought, as she did each time the enchanted knife hit its mark. She always winced to recall the exorbitant fee the old witch had asked for in the backlands of Solamnia when she had her knife blessed and her wounds treated.

She quickly went and retrieved her knife, wiping it on her shirtsleeve. The ghost of her missing left ear twitched as she gritted her teeth and walked to the room where they kept the boy.

She noted the boy's apprehension as she approached. He was barely conscious from the wounds they had inflicted. Gods. If she had the strength, she would go back and kill the Dark Knights all over again. It was a naive thought, but it made her feel better.

The room was dark; the only light came in from the open door. The boy raised his chin, tightened his jaw, and looked at her with defiance. He blinked his eyes, trying to adjust to the light.

They were a clear beryl blue. They were the color of the summer skies of Lemish. As she drew closer, Aurora saw her mistake. Those eyes belonged to the arctic, not the summer. Summer had ended for the boy long ago.

"It's all right," she tried to say, but her voice came out choked. She tried again. "It's all right, boy."

He didn't look older than thirteen. He seemed roughly the age Aurora's sister was when she was brutally raped and killed.

She swallowed what spit she had, hoping to ease her dry throat. "I'm going to free you."

Through the torn gash of his mouth, a soft melodic, nearly hypnotizing voice emerged. "You can't. I've already tried."

Part of her immediately believed him. His tone and words were oddly compelling.

"I must free you, boy," she answered, defiantly, though his words frightened her. "I haven't come this far to die for nothing."

Yet try as she might, Aurora couldn't open the manacles around his ankles and wrists. Finally, she used her enchanted knife, wedging it in where the metal was not quite welded. They seemed poorly made cuffs of iron. She didn't realize right away why his bonds were so powerful, that they had been fortified by spells.

Soon she could taste the blood in her mouth. Her lungs filled with blood. She could barely focus on sawing the manacles.

She forced what strength she had left into her arms and hands to free the boy. She was unaware that as her knife finally broke one manacle, the metal bled mercury. Nor did she notice the burn marks where the mercury touched her skin. Aurora was barely conscious as she worked on the other manacles. She didn't hear their dull metal sound as they fell to the floor. She didn't notice her knife was no longer the color of steel, but the color of obsidian.

****

The dark-haired boy looked at the woman who saved his life as he felt himself becoming stronger without the cuffs that had magicked him. He would have killed her if it were not for his dragon's blood. He hated she had seen him weak and captured and too impotent to stop the torture. Most of all, the boy hated being forced to ask for help.

He would save her and no more than that. He changed to his dragon form because he could not carry her in his human form far enough to heal her. His charcoal hair hardened as his face elongated. His clothes disappeared. He left them in the void as his power connected. Great golden wings stretched with tips of black and silver.

He flew the woman to the mountains and there drew his own blood and fed her as his father had done for him. As he felt her life ebbing, he shouted: "Fight!"

Aurora's father wanted her to fight with her body. The boy-dragon commanded her to fight with her spirit. Aurora did not have the breath to tell the boy it was all she knew how to do. She didn't feel the burning breath of the dragon, nor the blood he fed into her. Aurora did not even know if he were real. But she adhered to the power of his voice and his words, and for the first time, battled for herself and not her father.

****

The boy-dragon could do no more to help the female warrior. He left her both food and water in the cave. There was a way down through a passage made long ago by another race, which she could use.

He walked toward the edge of the cliff and paused. With a scowl on his face, he turned and walked back to Aurora. Using the full power of his restored voice once again, he roared: "Blood of my blood, live!"

As he moved to the edge of the cliff, his features softened. The scars on his face hurt, and not even his dragon powers could completely heal them. Whatever magic they had bound him with in the farmhouse could not be completely undone. However, his wide, carefree smile did not show his pain. It showed his excitement—the excitement of a boy.

He jumped. He fell thirty feet before his wings opened. Aurora opened her eyes, but not in time to see him fly into a gray sky that cloaked his path.

The Dragon's Claw

Jake Bell

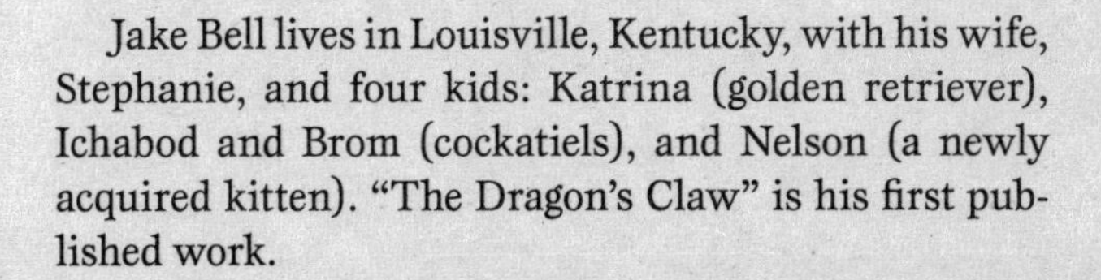

Jake Bell lives in Louisville, Kentucky, with his wife, Stephanie, and four kids: Katrina (golden retriever), Ichabod and Brom (cockatiels), and Nelson (a newly acquired kitten). "The Dragon's Claw" is his first published work.

The Dragon's Claw

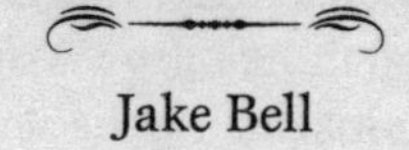

Jake Bell

Age of Mortals, 422 AC

"I wish Kabos was dead and it was his grave I was looting," muttered Damian as he shoveled dirt from a gravesite. "If he was gone, I would be doing more important things than poking about graves looking for baubles for the Blood Letting."

Damian jammed his shovel into the soft earth beside the hole he had just finished digging and climbed out. He stood among the tombstones that protruded from the dense mist that hugged the ground. As he raked his hands through his sweaty, dark locks, Damian turned and looked toward the monastery ruins where his brethren dwelt. Fires flickered in the courtyard as the sun's final rays died. A cold breeze whisked against his back, causing him to clutch his black robes closer to his body for warmth.

Damian . . .

"Who called me?"

Damian jerked about to his right and faced the skeletal remains of a dragon. He stared into the dragon's empty eye sockets, listening for the whisper he was certain he had just heard. He walked up to the skull and stood at the foot of its mouth. The lower jaw of the dragon was buried beneath the ground. The teeth in its upper jaw jutted menacingly, like stalactites over the mouth of a cave. Earth had grown over the lower part of the dragon's remains during the centuries since it fell from the sky; pieces of its wing bones lay strewn about the ground on either side of its massive ribcage.

When he was little, Damian had played inside the dragon's ribs, pretending he was a bird trapped inside a giant cage. Many of his brethren argued that his actions were blasphemy, for the dragon's remains were sacred. It was believed that one night the dragon would take flight, symbolizing the return of their lost god, Chemosh. Kabos, leader of the brotherhood and mentor to Damian, dismissed such chatter as regurgitation of some ancient tale.

Damian . . .

"Who calls me?"

Damian turned toward the monastery again. To his horror, he saw smoke and flames rising into the sky. Frantic, tortured screams bellowed from the smoldering ruins. His brethren ran forth, black robes in flames. They fell to the ground wailing, while others dumped buckets of water on them. Damian felt icy tingles in his hands and looked down to see that they had suddenly turned gnarled and gray, his skin taut with age. Blood dripped from yellow, cracked fingernails.

Damian gasped and blinked, and his hands were normal once more. He looked up to see the monastery was not on fire. His brethren were milling about, doing their nightly chores. He wiped chill sweat from his face and fingered his bone necklace, wondering if his vision had been a premonition. Kabos would dismiss his vision as daydreaming, for premonitions came from the gods, and how could a young man be touched by a god in a godless world?

Damian . . .

Damian located the whispering voice. It came from the gravesite he had just dug out. He crept up to the edge of the hole and peered inside. Wind nudged against his back, causing the hair on his neck to stand.

The lid to the coffin inside the grave was still closed.

Damian had always sought the solitude of the graveyard, felt *drawn* to it. Not only was the graveyard a place where he could escape many of the mundane tasks assigned to him by Kabos, it was also a place where he could escape the pressures of the brotherhood. Much was expected of Damian from his brethren, though Kabos acted more like a disappointed father who had little time for him instead of a mentor who trusted his star pupil. The Great Mother was his friend and advocate, that was true, but she was so weak and frail that she could do little to aid him. Damian spent more time in the graveyard than any of the other brethren, which was one reason Kabos sent him there to loot the graves. He had never, in all his years there, heard a voice whisper his name.

Damian jumped into the grave and grabbed a hammer from the sack that lay beside the coffin. The wood creaked as he pried the nails from its lid. Damian opened the lid with one hand and covered his mouth and nose with the other, the stench of decay emanating from the open coffin.

Lying in the coffin was a corpse, arms folded across its torso. The gray skin on its face was taut, its eye sockets a blank stare. A few strands of dark hair behind each of its misshapen ears rested on its shoulders. The tattered, black robe that hung loose against its bones was eerily similar to those robes worn by Damian and his brethren.

"How can that be?" muttered Damian. "Our own are buried at the monastery."

A bone bracelet in the shape of a dragon's claw lay loose on one of the corpse's wasted wrists. The emerald embedded in the bracelet gleamed in the moonlight.

Damian was pleased, for he rarely found anything of value in the graveyard. He reached for the bracelet.

The bony hand of the corpse jerked up, grabbed his wrist, and squeezed.

"What foul sorcery is this!" cried Damian, trying to free himself but failing. He struck the corpse's head with his free hand, but it would not relinquish its icy grip.

The corpse sat up. A clump of maggots fell from its left eye socket. Earth tumbled from its mouth as it spoke.

Why do you fear me, Damian? Our Lord, Chemosh, has found us after all these years!

The corpse's eye sockets glowed like dying embers.

Its grip on Damian's wrist seemed no longer threatening. Warmth flowed through Damian, calming him.

"I don't understand," he gasped. "What do you mean—he 'found' us. The gods abandoned us, as they did our ancestors during the First Cataclysm."

The corpse's jawbones scraped as it talked to him. *The gods have not forsaken us, for Takhisis stole Krynn so she might rule it alone. The gods have found Krynn and are returning to their followers. Paladine has fallen and Takhisis has paid for her sins. . . .*

The corpse pointed to the empty sky, and Damian saw that it was devoid of the Dark Queen's constellation. A hissing laugh emanated from the corpse's open mouth.

Chemosh is searching for devout followers to lead his armies across Krynn so that he may rule in the Dark Queen's stead. He has chosen you to be one of his leaders.

"Why is Chemosh interested in me?" Damian asked, though he was pleased and flattered. "I have only lived twenty-four summers. I am barely of age."

He has lost faith in Kabos, the corpse said. *It is time for someone new to lead, someone who has Chemosh's interests in mind. You must bring this news to your brethren.*

"What can I do to convince them that Chemosh has, indeed, returned?" asked Damian. "If I return to the monastery and make such claims, Kabos will have me thrown into the dungeon."

Make a sacrifice to Chemosh. Prove to him that you serve him.

"I do not mean to question the motives of Chemosh, but what do you mean by *sacrifice?* What must I do to gain the trust of my brethren? Nothing short of murder will prevent Kabos from ruling the brotherhood."

Though very little skin was left on the corpse's receded lips, it managed a toothless grin. It released its grip on Damian's wrist.

Have faith, Damian, and Chemosh will come to you in your most desperate hour. As a token of his faith in you, he offers a gift.

The corpse reached out to Damian, the bone bracelet dangling from its wrist.

Wear this bracelet, and you will glimpse the power that Chemosh offers, power that you may wield some day. As for convincing your brethren, I will go with you as proof.

Damian's mouth was dry as he reached for the bracelet. The emerald in its center glowed brightly. He thought about the corpse's offer, then thought about the mundane life he lived at the monastery. He had nowhere else to go in the world, no family to nurture him. Kabos had plucked him from a litter of ragamuffins in an orphanage. Until the moment the corpse spoke to him, all he had had was the brethren. Damian imagined Kabos counting the gold coins he would receive in town for the bracelet. Damian was the one who had found it, after all.

Damian slid the bracelet from the corpse's wrist and onto his own.

The corpse let forth its hissing laughter. The emerald burned with intense light as the bracelet bit into Damian's wrist. Blood ran down his arm. The dragon-clawed bracelet dug into his skin and clasped the bone underneath. Damian screamed in agony as the burning emerald seared the skin around his wrist. The flesh withered and fell off his hand, leaving only the bones.

A brilliant flash of green light shot forth from the gravesite. Damian clutched his skeletal hand. The emerald was embedded in his wrist above the surface of the skin; he could feel the bone, dragon-clawed bracelet latched onto his wrist bone. Slowly the pain subsided. He stared in horror at his hand that was nothing but bone. No flesh, no muscle, no blood.

The corpse was silent, as if waiting for directions.

Awed, Damian fell to his knees and bowed his head. Then, pulling his robe over his skeletal hand, he climbed out of the grave. "Let us return to the monastery so that we may illuminate our brethren of Chemosh's return."

The corpse climbed from the grave, grinning, as the emerald burned warmly beneath Damian's sleeve.

****

The dark moon, Nuitari, poised itself above the monastic ruins, its ebony glow darker than the night sky. Mist seeped through the decayed walls surrounding the monastery. The monastery needed no guardians, for it was rumored to be a cursed place where dark rituals were performed.

Kabos stood before a blazing fire. Its glow cast his shadow across the courtyard. He folded his hands, prayerlike, beneath his chin and his graying goatee. Black-robed monks rustled around him, trying to accomplish their duties before supper. Kabos walked over to the wall and caressed its eroding stone. He looked into the misty darkness, toward the distant graveyard.

"My beloved Damian . . . so devout," said Kabos.

"What treasures will you bring me this night, I wonder?"

Kabos felt a tug on the sleeve of his robe. He turned to snarl at the monk at his side.

"Didn't I tell you not to disturb me until preparations for the Blood Letting are complete? The ceremony is tomorrow night, and there is still much to be done."

"Please forgive me, Kabos," said the monk, "but I thought you should know that Master Damian has returned from the graveyard. He is on his way to the Great Mother."

"The Great Mother?" Kabos cried. "Damian was instructed to come to *me!*"

Kabos stormed toward the inner cloister of the monastery, pushing past monks heading to the refectory hall for supper. The boy was a favorite of the Great Mother. It was even rumored that Damian was the bastard child of the Great Mother, who had sent him away to an orphanage, then had second thoughts. She had lately started to hold private counsel with Damian instead of Kabos. That frightened Kabos, for she would not tell him why. He sent the young man on many excursions, most of them trivial, hoping to learn more of her motives. Kabos would do whatever it took to ensure his place in the monastery hierarchy.

He walked down the empty gallery that led to the heart of the monastery. As he drew closer to the Great Mother's chamber, the sounds of activity faded behind him. Only his echoing footfalls were present along the shadowy walkway. Kabos reached the Great Mother's chamber. Normally, two monks stood guard at the door, but they were gone.

Kabos cursed their incompetence and stormed toward the door.

He turned the doorknob and let the door slowly creak open. A putrid stench slithered from the chamber, causing Kabos to cough. He entered the building, closing the door behind himself. Dying torches gave the room a dim glow. In the center of the room, in a massive thronelike bed covered with an open canopy, lay the Great Mother, propped up like a bloated queen. Her layered, fatty skin was withered and pallid, her hair thin strands of gray. She watched Kabos with her bloodshot eyes as he came forth and knelt before her. She released her grip on the yellow skull pendant attached to her silk gown and extended her hand toward Kabos. He took her coarse hand and kissed it.

"You may rise, Kabos," she said, her breath labored.

It was rumored that the Great Mother had been a cleric of Chemosh before the Age of Mortals, her beauty dark and seductive. It was also said she had made a dark pact with the god to live forever. As a reward for her undying loyalty, Chemosh chose her to establish the Brotherhood of Death, a group of followers of the lost god who were to lay dormant until he returned to Krynn, at which time she would be given immense power.

Kabos had joined the brotherhood not out of faith, but out of greed. Having grown up in a godless world, Kabos doubted that Chemosh ever existed. He figured the tales were a way for the Great Mother to cling to her dwindling power. Kabos would have taken full control of the brotherhood were it not for some or her more loyal followers—such as Damian.

The young man came forth from the shadows behind

Kabos and the Great Mother. "I return with wonderful news," he said.

Hiding his anger, Kabos turned to smile at the young man.

"Chemosh has returned to Krynn," said Damian.

The Great Mother's bed buckled as she shifted her massive body.

Kabos raised an eyebrow.

"Damian," he said, mildly rebuking. "You know the Blood Letting is tomorrow. We do not have time for your stories. What artifacts have you brought for the ceremony?"

The Great Mother coughed and said, "Let the boy speak."

"I have proof Chemosh has returned!" said Damian. He turned to the shadows behind him and ordered, "Come forth."

The corpse loped from the shadows and stood next to Damian like a skeletal twin. Kabos walked forward and looked into the corpse's empty eye sockets. Kabos looked suspiciously at Damian.

"A trick," he said dismissively. "What do you use to animate it? Ropes?"

"This is Chemosh's doing," Damian said solemnly. He turned to the corpse. "Tell Kabos everything you said to me in the graveyard."

The corpse stood silent.

"Say something!" said Damian, shaking the corpse.

"I have far more important things to do than stand here waiting for a bag of bones to talk!" said Kabos.

"It told me that Chemosh had returned to Krynn," Damian cried.

"Silence," moaned the Great Mother. After a coughing fit, she murmured, "Damian, come closer."

Damian walked over and bowed before the Great Mother. She extended her hand, and he kissed it. Her bloated tongue poked from her mouth. Her breath was rancid and wheezing.

"Come closer," she repeated, licking her pocked lips.

Damian stood and bent over the Great Mother. She fondled his dark locks and pulled him close to her bosom. She looked beyond Damian, her lips curling into a thin smile.

"*I* believe what you say," she whispered in his ear. "Come back after supper so that we may discuss all you have learned. We do not need Kabos. He does not understand such things."

"Thank you, Great Mother."

"Damian, you must be famished," she said aloud. "Go eat, for you have worked hard this night. Kabos and I have much to discuss. Return to me soon, Damian."

Damian left the building.

Kabos stood frowning. "Surely you don't believe such nonsense, Great Mother," he said.

"I believe it enough to make Damian the Master of the Brethren of Death in your stead, Kabos," said the Great Mother, coughing.

"You love Chemosh so much, perhaps it's time you joined him!" Kabos muttered, and, drawing his knife, he walked toward the bed. "And Damian, as well."

The corpse stood in the shadows, grinning.

****

Damian . . .

Damian stood before the door of the Great Mother's chamber, but the skeletal dragon blocked his path and he was unable to enter. He told himself the dragon wasn't there, it was an illusion, but he couldn't overcome his terror and covered his face with his one good hand, hoping it would disappear. He had felt an urge more powerful than hunger eating away at him all through supper. Some of the monks had asked if he was feeling ill. Damian *had* felt faint, and he found himself outside the Great Mother's door, trembling as the whispering voice called his name.

Damian . . .

Damian slid his fingers down his face. The dragon was gone. The door that had been closed stood open.

Damian entered. There was very little light inside, for the torches were nearly extinguished. The room was cold and quiet save for a faint dripping sound. The canopy over the Great Mother's bed was closed. Damian pulled up the sleeve of his dark robes, and the emerald's faint glow guided him forward. Lying on the floor before him was the corpse he had brought from the graveyard. It was inanimate, its body contorted.

Damian stepped over the corpse and walked up to the bed. At first he could not place what was missing; then he realized that the familiar sound of the Great Mother's labored breathing was gone. Something wet washed against his bare feet. Damian did not look down; his hand trembled as he pulled back the canopy. The Great Mother lay motionless in her bed, her eyes rolled into the back of her head. Blood dripped from the gash in her throat. Her mouth was open in a silent scream—or a last curse. Damian covered his mouth with the back of his hand.

The Great Mother's left hand was clamped shut. Damian pried her fingers open; the yellow skull pendant rested in her palm. The skull faced the open door behind him, its toothy grin radiant in the emerald's glow. A bloody knife lay on the bed. His mind reeling in horror, Damian reached out and picked up the blade . . .

"What have we here?" shouted Kabos from the doorway. "Murder! That is what! Seize him!"

He stalked into the chamber. Four monks followed him. Two of them grabbed Damian's arms. The other two stood on either side of Kabos, who brandished a wooden club.

"Look at this, Master," said one of the monks, and he knocked the knife from Damian's hand.

"I am very disappointed in you, son," said Kabos, sighing deeply.

"How could you think I would do this?" Damian cried. "You know how I revered her!"

"Yet you were holding the knife stained with her blood," replied Kabos.

"She was alive when I left you with her!" Damian said accusingly.

"One thing is certain. We must solve this mystery quickly. The outcry over her death will cause havoc among the brethren."

Kabos rested his hand under Damian's chin so the two could make eye contact. "You are going to need allies to vouch for your innocence," said Kabos. He grinned. "You are lucky that I—your mentor—am now the leader of the brotherhood. If you obey my instructions, there might be a way to save you."

Damian jerked out of Kabos's grasp.

"What must I do?" he said through clenched teeth.

Kabos smiled and continued. "For one thing, do not go about the monastery proclaiming that Chemosh has returned. You must understand that such talk gives our brethren false hope. You wouldn't want to do that, would you?"

Kabos pointed his club at the corpse. "What I really want to know is where *this* came from. And by what trickery did you animate it?"

"Chemosh gave me the power to animate this corpse," said Damian. "I have been trying to tell you that the gods have returned to Krynn!"

"I grow weary of this babbling about the gods," said Kabos. "The Great Mother is dead and so, too, are the old ways. Damian, the truth is that the gods have never existed. The Great Mother used those ancient tales to control us. I am in control now, and the brethren shall follow *me*, not hang their hopes on false pretenses of gods that have never been seen! Besides, if Chemosh really does exist, why would he choose you to do his bidding? You are nothing but a weak-willed boy, incapable of leading."

Damian ground his teeth and tightened every muscle in his body. The monks holding his arms braced themselves, surprised at the boy's strength. The bracelet burned beneath his skin.

"He chose me because *I* have faith. Pull back my sleeve, and I will give you proof that Chemosh exists," said Damian.

Kabos hesitated, for he had not expected such a brave response. He pointed his club at Damian and directed one of the monks to pull back the boy's sleeve. The emerald embedded in Damian's wrist burned a brilliant green, revealing his fleshless hand.

Kabos gasped and recoiled. The monks who had been holding onto Damian let loose their grip and shrank away from him.

"This is my gift from Chemosh," said Damian. "Come closer, so you might feel *his* power."

Damian reached out and grabbed hold of the monk's hand. "In the name of Chemosh!" he cried.

There was a brilliant flash of green light. The monk gave an agonizing cry. The smell of burning flesh permeated the air. The monk fell to the floor, writhing in pain; his hand was charred black.

"Do you believe me now?" Damian demanded.

"I know not what evil magic you have uncovered in that cursed graveyard, but it dies with you!" Kabos snarled. "In honor of the Great Mother, we will have a final Blood Letting ceremony. Since you have such faith in Chemosh, *you* will be the last sacrifice to this false god."

Kabos lashed out with his club. Damian felt the emerald grow warm as pain-filled darkness embraced him.

****

Damian . . .

Damian awakened in darkness. His hands were bound and a sack covered his head. He sat propped against cold stone. He could hear the nervous whispers of the monks outside the jail that was a converted crypt located deep within the graveyard. The cell was dusty with age. A key turned in the rusty iron door, and it squeaked open. A monk removed the sack on Damian's head. Two other monks grabbed him and pushed him into the cool night. They nervously prodded Damian through the cemetery, careful to steer clear of the skeletal dragon. Mist floated between its massive bones.

Once through the cemetery, the monks shoved Damian into a cart. He sat between two monks with his head bowed, the crunch of the wheels grinding against the gravel path that led to the monastery the only sound. After a few moments, the cart stopped and Damian was taken from it. He was prodded through the crumbled monastery walls and into the courtyard.

A blazing fire burned in the center of the courtyard. Many of the brotherhood stood around the fire, chanting. Damian was led to the center of the circle. The Great Mother lay wedged in an open casket beside the blazing fire. A gigantic wooden bowl had been placed in front of the fire. Inside the bowl was a chair. A circular wooden clasp with small holes around its perimeter was attached to the chair's back. A table with long, needle-thin blades resting on it stood beside the chair. The monks forced Damian into the chair and bound his hands and feet. One of the monks stepped over the rim of the bowl and stood by the table, while the other closed the wooden clasp around Damian's throat, then stood by the Great Mother's casket. The monks surrounding Damian chanted louder, their faces hidden in the shadows of their hoods.

Mist crept into the courtyard and hovered at the ankles of the monks. The emerald in Damian's wrist was cold. No light glowed. His knees rubbed against the rim of the bowl.

"I have faith in you, Chemosh," he whispered. "I am ready to accept my destiny."

The circle opened, and Kabos came forth. He wore a horned bone mask with menacing fangs. A vest of bones was draped over his dark robes. He walked over to Damian and stood behind the chair, his breathing heavy under the weight of the mask. Kabos raised his hand, and the chanting stopped.

"A tragedy has befallen us, my brethren," he said. "Tonight's sacrifice not only represents justice for the murder of our Mother, but also it symbolizes change. For you see, my faithful, dark times can offer new beginnings."

The crowd murmured, unsure what to make of Kabos's statement. He walked over to the table and picked up one of the blades. He slid it into one of the holes on the clasp around Damian's neck, making sure that the point of the blade poked the skin but did not draw blood. He repeated the procedure with the other blades, so it appeared that Damian wore a spiked collar.

"The Great Mother was strong in her convictions, and that is to be admired. However, times have changed. No longer can we lie dormant, waiting for some god to arrive. We must take initiative, go forth into the world, and stake *our* claim!"

The murmur of the crowd lengthened. The emerald in Damian's wrist suddenly pulsed with life, and his body felt warm once more.

"Kabos lies!" Damian called out. *"He* murdered the Great Mother, not I. He murdered her because he lacks faith. Chemosh has returned to Krynn, and I can prove it to you."

"Do not listen to the murderer." Kabos sneered. "He has been cursed for the murder of the Great Mother. See for yourselves!"

Kabos yanked back Damian's sleeve and revealed the glowing emerald. He ripped the binding around Damian's wrist and raised his arm into the air. The emerald's glow revealed Damian's skeletal hand. Those in the crowd gasped.

"Fear not, my brethren," Damian shouted. "Chemosh has given this bracelet to me as a gift. I will use it to bring the Great Mother back from the dead so that she may tell you the truth. If I cannot accomplish this feat, then I will be the one to push these blades into my throat."

Damian pointed at the casket. "In the name of Chemosh, I bid you rise!"

The emerald flashed with blazing light. The casket cracked. Nails popped loose as the great Mother sat up. She stared into the crowd with glazed, lifeless eyes. She slowly turned her head toward Kabos and pointed a cold finger at him.

"Chemosh has embraced me, as he will you . . ." She gurgled, air escaping from the open wound in her neck. "Look to the sky . . . There you will see that Chemosh has returned."

The corpse of the Great Mother pointed to the sky. Damian quivered as the magic from the bracelet coursed through his body. The ground quaked and the massive, skeletal dragon rose up from the graveyard, taking horrible flight. The undead dragon swooped low over the monastery. Fire shot forth from its skeletal maw, setting the monastery aflame. The stench of scorched flesh wafted in the air as panicked monks ran amok. Some fell to the ground burning, while others ran for water to douse their fallen brethren. The dragon continued to circle the monastery, blasting fleeing monks with its molten breath.

There were cries of, "The prophecy is true," and, "Chemosh has returned."

Damian freed himself from the chair. He stood up and faced Kabos, the screams of his brethren dinning in his ears.

Kabos ripped the skull mask from his head. He was pale and trembling. "This cannot be!"

Damian extended his skeletal hand toward Kabos.

"Pledge your faith in Chemosh while there is still time," said Damian.

Kabos grabbed one of the blades and lunged at Damian. He caught it with the skeletal hand, and the blade shattered. Kabos turned and fled toward the graveyard.

He was met by the dead, those whose rest he had disturbed, those whose graves he had long plundered. Kabos's screams faded as the dead converged upon him, clutching at his robes and pulling him to the ground.

The dragon swooped down from the sky and landed beside Damian. The emerald on his arm blazed. The dead monks rose to their feet and shambled toward Damian. Among them were a few loyal monks, untouched by the hand of Chemosh. All hailed Damian as master.

Kabos emerged from the darkness, groaning. His

eyes were a milky white, his robes torn. The flesh on half of his face was ripped clean, revealing his bloody skull. The muscles covering his jawbone flexed as he tried to speak. He raised his bloody hand, three fingers missing, and pointed at Damian; now Kabos was a mindless follower of Chemosh.

The dragon lowered its neck so its skull rested on the ground in front of Damian. Blue flaming dots of light glowed in each of the dragon's eye sockets. Its jawbone creaked as it opened its huge mouth.

Damian, hissed a voice from inside the dragon. *You have done well. I knew my faith in you would be rewarded, but there is still work to be done. I need you to convert more followers in my name.*

"As you wish, Chemosh," said Damian. "I am ready to go forth into the world and stake *your* claim."

In due time, said the voice. *First, I must give you a reward for your loyalty: an eternity of power. All you have to do is come closer.*

The dragon's mouth opened wider. Damian walked toward the dragon's mouth, his faith in Chemosh unwavering. As he entered the dragon's mouth, the emerald's glow extinguished. Icy tingles started in his hands and trickled throughout his body. Damian felt faint; blood ran down his nose and dripped from his chin.

All of the warmth that Damian had felt slowly drained from his body.

****

Damian awakened in utter darkness, his memories scattering like cobwebs blown away in a breeze. His arms were folded tight against his chest; the air surrounding him was cold and dense. Voices spoke above him, drowning his rasping breath.

"Barnabas, are you sure this is the correct site?" asked a voice.

"Yes," replied another voice. "Have faith in Chemosh, for he would not lead us astray."

Dirt fell into Damian's face as the stone slab above him was pushed aside. Years of dust floated into the air, causing the grave robbers to cough. Damian sat up, his tattered, black robes hanging loose against his skeleton, and looked in the direction of the voices. Three men in dark robes stood before him. They appeared faint to Damian, as if they were standing in the dim light of a fading torch. The eldest of the three men walked up to Damian.

"Barnabas, don't get too close," warned one of the men.

"Our faith in Chemosh has guided us this far," said Barnabas. He turned to Damian and said, "Can you understand me?"

Damian nodded.

"Chemosh has chosen me to lead his followers. He said that you can give me a gift that will aid me against Mishakal's clerics."

Damian raised his arm, bones creaking from his long sleep. He reached his skeletal hand toward Barnabas. A bone and dragon-claw bracelet hung loose on his wrist. The emerald in its center glowed dimly.

Chemosh says you have much promise, rasped Damian. *Take this bracelet as a token of his faith in you.*

Barnabas slid the bracelet from Damian's skeletal

wrist. He peered at the emerald, enthralled by its beauty. The other two men crowded around him to see it.

As Damian's hissing laughter echoed throughout the crypt, Barnabas slid the dragon-claw bracelet onto his wrist. A burst of green light bathed the crypt in a brilliant glow.

Bloodrage

Kevin T. Stein

"To succeed in life, you need two things: ignorance and confidence."—Mark Twain. Kevin Stein has been a writer, a teacher, a chauffeur, a club DJ, a dishwasher, an aide-de-camp, a traveler, and a student. He's lived in the United States, England, and Japan. Through it all, he has learned one great thing: he's confident of his ignorance.

Bloodrage

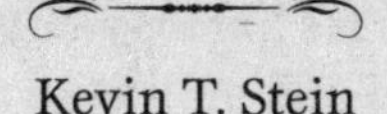

Kevin T. Stein

Age of Mortals, 422 A.C.

Fury pressed her muzzle against the scout's good side. He had fallen asleep on the bare ground. Now the sun was gone and the wolf wanted to move. She heard the call of the Hunt.

The scout didn't move. Fury pressed with her muzzle again, got no reaction. She chewed the air a moment, yelped, dug her nose under the scout's good arm, breathed warmth onto his body. She jumped back and yelped again, barked her words to him. Fury ran back and forth in front of him. She reared on her hind legs and dropped back. She wanted the scout to move.

Fury sat, panting. Her own wounds burned and bit. She licked her left side, soothed her pain. She switched sides and gnawed at her right foreleg where a gash up to her belly left something clear and foul on her tongue.

Her teeth crushed a few vermin living off the fodder.

Fury's neck strained toward the sky. Her eyes found the twin green stars among the many others. She moaned her words to Canus. She begged for another day to hunt with her master. She howled.

The scout moved his good arm and Fury jumped on him, knocking the little breath from his body. Fury licked and bit and yelped. The scout defended himself with his good arm, the other pinned under and folded against the ground. He finally got a grasp on Fury's left ear, squeezing hard and pulling backward. He steered the huge wolf away.

Fury stepped back, shook away the leaves and twigs clinging to the fur on her right side. The scout rolled flat on his back, bent his knees, pushed and twisted onto his good side. He sat up and ran a hand across his face. "Canus sends dreams, hey, wülfbunde? Of the Long Hunt. Maybe next time I not wake?"

The scout raised his good arm and Fury entered his embrace. With honed nails, long and sharp, the scout picked away some of the blood lining Fury's oldest wound, an uneven line two fingers wide running from neck to left flank. The exposed flesh was roughly cauterized and no fur grew near the injury.

"Maybe, soon, we both sleep, hey?"

Fury made a noise of refusal.

"We are old, wülfbunde. None older, you think?"

The scout leaned against the wolf. Finally stood. One shoulder sagged, one arm hung too long. His flesh resisted its own muscles as the scout forced his aging body to stretch. He bared his fangs and breathed in shallow breaths.

Fury pushed her front paws into the ground, stretched her back legs, then her front. She licked her chops and looked at the scout.

"Food." The scout sniffed the air, eyes searching the ground. He stopped, staring at the base of a tree. Fury jumped the distance, pawed the ground.

With a cross-draw of his stiff hand, the scout pulled a curved dagger from his belt. The dagger's hilt was wrapped with so much wire it filled the scout's grip. He put his fingers through the holes in the knuckle-guard. He squeezed his hand against the hilt, applying uneven pressure from the trauma suffered to his fingers. The wire bent, pressed into pads of flesh yellow-calloused to stone. His knuckles and joints quickly swelled, trapping the hand.

Dirt arced out behind Fury. She stopped digging, shuffling back. The scout leant against the wolf with his good arm, his dagger digging deeper into Fury's hole.

"There." The scout held up his weapon. Across the dagger's blade a line of thick black mushrooms slicked the edge with their oil. Fury licked her chops again, barked briefly. With a finger of his good hand, the scout slid the mushrooms off the blade onto the ground at Fury's paws. The wolf cocked her head.

"Not hungry." The wolf shuffled away from the food. The scout said, "Eat."

Fury cocked her head the other way.

"Eat."

Over the wolf's tongue and through the Bond, the scout savored the mushrooms as the wolf ate. His own stomach didn't complain, though he had not taken food in days.

With his good hand, he reached into his tunic and pulled out a folded packet made of leaves. Using only forefinger and thumb, he unfolded the packet. Powdered herbs and leaves, mixed and red. He raised his stiff arm to his mouth and bit a gash among the many scars. Raised the packet to his tongue, took a bit, pressed tongue to the new gash. The powder and his sluggish blood mixed.

Fury immediately stopped eating and stared at the scout. She felt some of her master's pain subside, some of the old stiffness leave with the rush of the powder. Fury trotted forward, sitting. The scout flexed his stiff hand. Swelling in the finger-joints diminished. He placed the leaf packet on Fury's muzzle.

"Hold."

Fury didn't move.

The scout pulled the dagger from his stiff hand, twisting to get his middle finger through the knuckle-guard. He shook his hand, flexed the fingers, returned the dagger to his belt. With his good hand, he smoothed skin near the gash he'd made in his bad arm. The gash had already healed. The scout turned, walked a few paces.

Fury yowled in her throat.

The scout didn't turn. "Forgot something?"

Fury yelped.

The scout turned to face the wolf. "Speak, wülfbunde."

Fury spoke. The scout widened his eyes. "Powder!" He returned to Fury, pointed at the packet perched on Fury's nose. "This?"

Fury moaned without moving.

"Move this?"

Fury growled.

"Hie, wülfbunde, as you will." The scout took the packet from the wolf's muzzle, refolded it with one hand, replaced it in his tunic. Fury barked, baring fangs. The scout growled as a wolf, baring fangs. The two stood, Fury draping her forelegs over the scout's shoulders. Barking and snarling, wolf's fangs on the scout's throat, scout's fangs on the wolf's.

Fury's weight forced the scout back, his stiff leg failed. The wolf landed on top of the scout. Fury plunged her muzzle into the scout's tunic. The scout tried to push her nose away, but the wolf would not be denied.

"The boot," the scout said, lifting his good leg up, over the wolf's neck. Toppling, pinning. Fury was trapped, didn't try to move. The scout reached into a wallet stitched to the boot, removed a twist of yellow lakrak. Fed a piece to Fury, the rest to himself.

"Almost gone. Like healing powder."

Fury ignored the scout. The scout tasted the lakrak in his wülfbunde's mouth, then his own. Their hearts raced. Muscles burned.

"I would not join the Long Hunt," the scout said. He ran his hand over some of the wolf's remaining fur. "Forever I would fight by your side."

Fury laid her head heavily on the scout's chest. Her breathing was shallow from the effects of the yellow lakrak. The scout looked into his wülfbunde's brown eyes, saw himself looking back from the wülfbunde's own. Though night, they saw everything clearly, they saw the truth. They were old.

"We move, hey, wülfbunde?" The scout released his wolf, slowly stood.

Fury ran toward the nearby forest, back to the scout. She could not run straight, broken spine forcing her back legs out of line. Fury clamped fangs on the scout's hand, pulled him toward the trees. Both smelled evil twisting, turning, changing.

The scout stumbled, good leg, stiff leg. Fury pulled. The scout found his stride. He and the wolf ran, finally in pace.

****

Trees roughly hewn. The scout saw the cuts were from a weapon, an axe. He sniffed the air.

"Not magic, hey?" The scout and the wolf turned to the night. The air carried the scent of the forest, many things living, some dying, others dead. Fury knew them all. What she didn't, the scout knew. Except this. "Not Chaos magic. What is it?"

Fury growled, paced. Panted, looked up to the scout. "What and who, hey?" The scout ran his good hand over a tree stump. He saw something on his fingers, something probably green, darkness preventing color-sight. He held his hand to Fury's nose. She sniffed, licked. The scout tasted nature, healing herbs and oils and care. He looked at his stiff arm, where he had closed the gash with the powder from the leaf-packet. Fury licked her chops.

The scout wiped the herb-oil on his leggings. "Healer of forests tried to save these trees. Healers of forests do not cut wood."

Fury sat very still, eyes boring into the night. "Trees were . . ." the scout started, stopped. He forgot the word. "Killed? Murdered. Healer tried to help."

Animals came, hunting them. Terrible, changed, driven to destroy. But not Chaos-driven. Another evil, ancient, forgotten.

Scout and wolf turned toward the call of the Hunt. The wolf bounded into the night. The scout leapt over a stump, forgot his stiff side. Landed, drew his daggers, bared fangs and snarled. Canus and the Bond were with them.

They ran long. Night animals watched them, moved aside, up trees, burrowing. The Hunt brought them to a stream's end. Wolf and scout caught the scent of sickness in the water. Both changed direction, upstream.

Trees gave way to more harm. Fallen timber left scattered, all cut by the same weapon. In the air, the scout tasted the herb-oil rubbed onto the exposed stumps. On the ground, the wolf saw life making new homes in the fallen wood.

Snarls in the night, teeth bared, claws slashing.

Curve forward, the scout's right dagger arced up in a cut. An animal dropped dead, left behind by the scout's pace. Fury skirted around another animal, broke its neck with a kick. The scout cut twice, killing three.

Ahead, animals shuddered and gagged near the stream. Some had died, bled out into the stream. Without color-sight, blood was black, floated on the near-motionless water. The blood reeked of the same sickness as the stream. Other animals bounded, crawled, walked toward them. Without color-sight, their eyes were black. Driven by the sickness, they sought to kill.

"Let's faster, hey?"

The scout and Fury pushed harder. The stream widened where they ran. The night-sound of the forest churned to hatred. Man and wolf heard the masses move in behind them, more converging at their front.

The scout howled as he ran, Fury joining. The rage in their voices brushed animals aside, many dying in fear where they stood. The scout's arms began slow, regular motions. Whatever the animals had become, he did not recognize them, did not register them. They attacked. He slayed them, protecting himself and his wülfbunde.

The biting taste of the yellow lakrak turned to aftertaste, slowly faded to fatigue. Scout and wolf had run long, run leagues. The stream widened more, still shallow, an arm-span across. Misshapen animal corpses lined the edges, rested in the water. Fury saw some animals had killed each other. The scout heard insects in the air feeding off the dead, black flecks swarming.

Trees felled by the axe formed a barrier across the stream. Animals behind continued chasing. The scout leapt up, onto the logs, daggers throwing chips as he dug with them, climbing without slowing.

Fury followed, shot up. Front claws caught bark. Her back legs scrabbled hard against the logs. A beast, filled with the sickness, caught her. Teeth or fangs flayed Fury's left flank.

Fury's body was the Bond, the Hunt, and she took the rage of Canus into her heart. She felt the infection start. Her howl of suffering smashed a line of trees to splinters, lasted so long no trees were left standing within fifty paces, within a half arc from where she stood. The animals not already dead from terror were disintegrated, the trees felled near the stream were gone. The stream water was vaporized. What flowed under the barricade followed the path of its bed, slowly returned.

The scout rounded, changed direction without losing speed. He took the entire barrier in a single bound, daggers raised overhead as he sailed over the obstruction. His body was the Bond, the Hunt, and he took the rage of Canus into his heart. The heart of every animal near Fury exploded from terror.

The scout landed near his wülfbunde, the impact shattered the ground, threw animals into the air, felled young trees. The scout felt whatever was in the stream, the animals, now ran in the blood of his wülfbunde.

Fury collapsed onto her back legs, the scout caught her. He wept, and his tears wet the wolf's remaining fur. They shuddered. The scout cut a line into Fury's leg where the infection began, saw whatever was in the animal's bite moved too swiftly, was not venom to be sucked and spat out.

The rage of Canus left their bodies, left them weak and empty. Even so soon, the scout smelled inevitable death in Fury's scent. He rocked the suffering wolf in his arms, kissing the animal, burying his face in her neck.

The night turned suddenly cold, mists forming. The scout sweated from the rising heat of his wülfbunde, tried to hold back the shivering, her whimpering of burning pain.

The scout heard a voice nearby, speaking Common.

He did not register the words. He moved to protect Fury, to attack.

The speaker gestured. Scout and wolf collapsed in deep and unnatural sleep.

****

A small rectangular hut. Torn clothes, dulled weapons set on a table. The sealed leaf packet was open, only a few grains of powder remaining. The final half-finger twist of yellow lakrak next to the powder.

"Wülfbunde!" The scout rolled from the sleeping mat, pushing up with his good side. He hobbled outside into green daylight. "Wülfbunde!"

Fury lay on a sleeping mat in the clearing surrounding the hut. The wolf's torn flank showed no injury. No blood flowed from wounds old or new. The scout still smelled the poison in his wolf's blood. Through the Bond, he felt an invader taking the life of his companion. This invader was not born of Chaos and he had no power to confront it.

The scout knelt, threw himself over the wolf. He smoothed fur, listened to Fury's heartbeat. The wolf's heart was a constant, unsteady drum. Her breathing was shallow, unconnected to the heartbeat. Under closed lids, the wolf's brown eyes darted toward nothing. The scout buried his face in the wolf's neck, rocked, muttered something.

Coolness and mist returned, fogging the clearing. The scout's face came up from his wülfbunde's body. He leaped, stood over the wolf, baring fangs and long sharp nails.

Yellow eyes stared through the mist. A hand was held up in peace.

The scout snarled. "Hold!"

What was in the mists moved closer.

The scout lunged into the mists. He was slowed, stopped, felt magic force him slowly back. He strained against the power, was pushed back. Gently. He found himself near Fury, was pushed back further. He swam against the power, was pushed to the ground. He clawed at the dirt and howled.

Next to the panting wolf, a robed figure knelt. The scout dug his good hand into the earth, attempted to climb against the magic separating him from his wülfbunde.

The figure pinned the scout with its gaze. Held up a hand again in peace. The yellow eyes turned back to the injured wolf.

The figure said, "She told me her name was Fury."

"Fury, aye."

The power holding the scout diminished. The scout raised himself to a sitting position.

"You are bündesphar."

"Faithful, aye."

"I found you at the stream. At the fallen trees. You scattered the animals."

The scout tested the strength of the magic holding him. He couldn't raise himself. He batted the air. "Mists. Can't see you."

"You have my scent."

"You smell of dragon."

The figure pushed itself from the mists, stood over scout and wolf. The height of a tall man. Wings folded against its back. The yellow eyes stared from a face with a large forehead. Short horns curled back over its head.

"Dragon," the scout repeated.

The figure shook its head, gesturing with a long-fingered hand. "Born of dragons, like our cousins called *draconians.* I, we, were born from the eggs of chromatics."

"Legends, I've heard," the scout said. "You are called nobles."

"We have heard of you, as legends," the draconian replied. "The bündesphar trace their history to the ages before the Cataclysm. You smell of long age and the Hunt."

"In the Age of Might, the Dark Queen brought us the word of Canus."

"You are still faithful to the fallen goddess?"

The scout brushed Fury's standing fur. The wolf shivered under his touch, growled, whimpered in pain. The same sounds broke from the scout's bleeding lips. He brushed the back of his good hand against his mouth, spit. "Too old to spend our steel, too old to want the coin of the White Lady."

The noble draconian gestured. The scout was free of the magical restraints.

"Like many of my kind born from the greens, I am protector of a forest, faithful to Zivilyn. My name is Quid."

The draconian gestured over the wolf. The scout saw only curling mist and the hint of long fingers. The scout heard Fury's breathing slow, her heartbeat steady.

"I am grateful for your entry into my forest," said Quid. "The accursed animals you saw are growing in number, and I have not the means to fight them all. I healed Fury's wounds. I cannot save her."

The scout saw the long-fingered hand smooth the wolf's fur. Fury's eyes were closed. She moaned. The scout felt her pain, the thing in her blood burning her from the inside. The scout bit his lip and pierced his own palms with his nails. His spine contracted, arm and legs curled as he felt his muscles catch fire. With fresh strength. And her pain.

The draconian said, "You will have to grant her mercy."

"Poisons have antidotes."

"Poison? This is Morgion's curse." Quid stood. The scout could not see through the mist, sight color-robbed to grays and shadows. The draconian gestured, something like wings flared out, pushing fog. Points of light appeared overhead, formed shapes from the Godhome. The draconian pointed at one of the shapes. The scout saw the long finger ended in a talon. "Morgion sends his curse from the Abyss into *my* forest."

"Morgion is not prey."

Quid moved back, fading again in the scout's vision. The scout felt the power around his body loosen again. He stood, pushed up with his good side. For a moment, he felt the strength in Fury, the invader in her blood granting him the strength to stand. The scout moved back to Fury's side. The heat from her body made him sweat. He felt his muscles tense and release, saw Fury's muscles ripple tip to tail. Her lips pulled back, revealed fangs, relaxed. Fur stood on end.

"You feel it," said the draconian. "What the animals feel. The bloodrage."

"Bloodrage?"

"It's what the axe-wielder feels. The one who fells my trees and built the barrier against which you and Fury were caught."

The scout asked, "Who is this axe-wielder?"

"He is a friend, or was," Quid said. "Like you, he came here, in need of aid. I gave it to him, and he has been—was—my ally. I made the axe he wields."

"To help the forest?"

Quid said, "Yes. Sometimes, the forest needs to be cut back to help it thrive. Now the forest needs your aid."

The scout stroked Fury's fur. Static crackled under his hand. Some of the hairs pierced his flesh, drew pinheads of blood. "She burns."

"I tried to ease her suffering, but you must understand. She is cursed by the bloodrage. She will become as the animals that made her this way. Morgion's curse may be stronger than your bond."

The scout's stiff hand grabbed Quid by the throat. "None is stronger than the Bond!"

Quid did not blink. The scales around his neck buckled under the scout's grip. The scout and draconian's eyes met. The scout slowly released his grip. "I feel her madness."

"You feel her bloodrage. I keep her in sleep, to spare her the terrible pain of waking."

The scout sat hard on the ground. For the first time, he pushed at the Bond, pushed away. The strength he felt, in his spine, in his impatient muscles, departed.

The pain of his stiff side returned. He leaned to the left to alleviate his hurts. His muscles immediately stiffened, almost crippling him.

Quid said, "The packet of powder in your uniform. It is some kind of healing herb?"

The scout nodded. "Many herbs."

"I do not know the secret of its making, but I have my own remedies. Stay here, with Fury. I will bring some to you."

Quid turned toward the hut but the scout grabbed the draconian's long robe with his good hand. "What is to be done?"

"Before I speak of that, there is something you must know, something of which you must be made aware."

The scout released the draconian's robe.

Quid said, "What you hunt cannot be defeated."

"Explain."

"I'm not sure I can." The draconian gestured. "It is something brought by, or more accurately, lost from, the Abyss."

The scout shrugged his good shoulder. "What is to be done for my wülfbunde?"

"I have asked Zivilyn for guidance. He has none to provide. Fury must be put to rest. "

"I would speak with my wülfbunde."

"She will succumb to the bloodrage in due course. I am loathe to wake her and would keep her from suffering."

"If Fury is to die, I will not bear the Grieving. By dagger and fang, I die with her."

Quid nodded his understanding. "What name shall I report to others of your corps?"

The scout shook his head. "My tour is long. Maybe the longest. I cannot remember my name."

Quid gazed at the scout long, then bowed his head. He left, returned with bottles and herbs. Mixed some into others, produced a green foaming substance from a tube. He held it under the wolf's nose.

The scout jerked his head aside, away from the powerful stench. Fury's eyes opened. The whites had turned red and bloody tears wept from the corners. The draconian stood, overturned the tube. The foam vanished before it hit the ground.

Every hair on Fury's body stood straight. Her ears pricked, tail lashed. She shook. Foam flecked her muzzle. She half-howled, half-whimpered as she walked in slow motion around the noble draconian's clearing, unsure in her pain if her paws really touched the cool earth.

The rising heat from Fury's body pushed away the draconian's perpetual mists. She glanced at the scout with nearly every step, biting the air, spitting foam. The scout felt the fire, the ferocity pumping his partner's heart to near-bursting. And she was afraid, as afraid as when first brought to the corps. She had the promise and protection of Canus then. Now she felt the invader, her destruction, eating her body from the inside.

With an arm, Quid kept the scout from the wolf. The scout pushed against the draconian, but the keeper of the forest was too strong. Quid said, "You must give her peace. You must release her."

At the draconian's words, Fury spasmed, twisting. She barked blood and foam at the draconian, ready to attack. The scout said, "She disagrees."

The scout pushed the draconian's arm aside, knelt in front of Fury. To him, she seemed to have grown. The wolf's bloodied eyes glared rage at the draconian. The scout raised his hands to brush back her standing fur. Quid said, "Morgion's curse is not restrictive. If she bites, you will join in her infection."

So near his companion, bathed in the heat of the poison, the scout again pushed at the Bond, prevented himself feeling the wolf's agony and new strength. His stiff side called for him to let go, give in, rejoice in the Bond. His stiff hand pressed against Fury's back. Felt the heat of her flesh, its vibration, the beat of the wolf's heart through her veins. Her body was straight, muscles contracted rock-hard, broken spine repaired against the brute strength of the curse. He heard Fury's words, confused, enraged, distant.

And then Fury turned toward the forest, howled, was joined by the scout. He said, "Our prey is near!" The scout rose, stiff side dragging him left, forward as he stood. "Aid me, hey?"

Quid gestured his magic. The scout straightened, swollen joints and stiff muscles cooling. Quid said, "I will accompany you."

"We hunt alone."

"My forest. My law."

Fury howled again, charged the surrounding foliage. She shredded it with fang and claw, could not penetrate the barrier. The scout said, "Let us out of this place! Canus commands we hunt!"

Quid parted the mists and the forest cover with another gesture. A near-straight path led into the woods.

Blood-foam dripped from Fury's mouth. Her four legs kicked dirt from the ground in showers. The scout gave chase.

Quid stepped into his mists, left the clearing without sound.

****

Scout and wolf raced together. On the run, on the Hunt, their feet did not often touch the ground. The path opened by Quid closed behind them, opened in front of them, allowed them to pass.

The path created by the noble draconian ended, released them back onto Krynn, into a clearing defiled by the axe. Scout and wolf halted their run, skidded on the exposed forest floor. Fury lurched forward, the invader in her blood hot fuel, the Bond and the scout barely keeping her in check.

The scout saw none of the stumps had been attended to by Quid, no green liquid covered the exposed wood. The mighty trees were stacked carefully into a barrier, much larger than the first they encountered. The barrier was hundreds of paces from where they stood. The sun lanced into the mists surrounding the draconian.

Fury lowered her muzzle to the ground, still dripping blood-foam. The fur near her eyes was matted with bloody tears. She and the scout heard the call of the Hunt, the order of Canus, but the draconian's words were right. There was nothing to be defeated. They were thwarted. The wolf's body shook with rage.

The barrier stood behind a portal. Sunk into the ground, the portal was made of metal, made of flesh, made of everything and nothing. It could let pass two horses, nose to tail. Neither scout nor wolf saw a clear image of what made the portal or its hatch. They both knew its origin.

"That is a portal leading directly to the Abyss," Quid said, so silent neither had heard him arrive. "I don't know how it got here."

Fury howled to the sky. The wood barrier vibrated, showered dust. The scout rubbed a hand against the wolf's exposed hide. Whispered something soothing the noble draconian could not hear.

The scout said, "Born of Chaos."

"And what is caught under its weight?"

Quid pointed a talon at the black mass trapped between the portal's hatch and the earth of Krynn. The mass had no definite outline and filled most of the portal. Its core was human-shaped, its head had horns and a fanged maw. Some of its many arms ended in hands, others clusters of fingers, another a bone-maul. Its bulk was pinned face-down by the hatch. The thing was covered in a writhing mucus, opaque, filled with tangles of many-legged creatures.

The draconian pointed to the mass's half-severed neck.

The scout said, "An axe."

Quid said, "The axe-wielder fought the creature as it crawled out of that portal, striking it dead, or mostly so."

"Made it too weak to hold the portal," the scout said.

"Crushing it, thus. But again, what is it?"

Fury chewed the air, throwing foam. Her remaining

fur stood up as she shifted, hunched her back, straightened, unsure and angry. She tossed her head, growled.

The scout said, "Demon." He wrapped his arms around his wülfbunde, pressed her body to his own. Her heat formed steam from the cool air. She wanted to destroy the portal, to fulfill the mission before she died of the poison in her body. She shared this with the scout, who wanted the same, could think of no way to do it. Like her, he bared his fangs at the portal, made by the great enemy, Father Chaos.

"Then it must be a demon sent by Morgion," Quid said and pointed again. One of the demon's arms lay in a stream. Its mucus covering thinned, drained into the water. "It releases its curse into my water."

"And your axe wielder?"

Quid indicated tree stumps. "What he once protected, he now seeks to destroy."

"He bloodrages?"

With an expressionless nod, Quid said, "He must have been infected during his battle. No one could fight such a thing as that and not fall to the curse."

The scout sat against a stump, pulled Fury against him. The wolf's sweat and blood-foam soaked into his uniform. Her fur stabbed pricks of quick pain into his flesh. Instead of howling with rage, Fury shivered in torment, whined. The scout felt what she felt, her heart raced, the poison in her blood clutched her every organ, boiled her brain. She desired the only possible release, combat, killing, to cool her fever. The scout was again forced to turn away from the Bond. He left them both isolated and in greater suffering than any blood-born curse.

"We cannot destroy a portal. We scout, not engineer."

Quid said, "If it can't be destroyed, it must be closed."

The scout looked at Quid, then to the portal, then to the sky. With his stiff arm, he pressed Fury to his body. With the hand of his good arm, he used long fingernails to dig a sigil into the dirt. Two curves, a crossed box. He held his free hand to his fangs and slashed his skin apart, let the blood fall on the sigil.

At the scent of blood, Fury writhed in his grip. The scout looked to Quid for aid. The noble draconian knelt before the wolf, took the animal in a gentle grasp. Fury snarled at Quid, who gestured, whispered, quieted the wolf enough for him to lend strength to the scout's grip.

The scout pressed his hand onto the sigil, looked to the sky, howled. Fury sat on her haunches and joined, shifted in Quid's grip. More blood-tears. She looked to the sky, to the scout, to the sky. The two howled until out of breath.

The scout pulled his hand out of the dirt, blood ran from his wound. He searched his tunic for the leaf-packet.

"May I heal that?" Quid asked.

The scout held up the wounded hand. Quid pulled a flask from a pouch, unstoppered it, poured a drop of pearlescent liquid onto the wound. The flesh healed instantly. The draconian replaced the flask, gestured toward the ruined sigil. "Have you gained some insight?"

The scout shrugged. Fury had fallen asleep sitting up in Quid's arms. The scout took the wolf from the draconian, holding her closely. He said, "Destroy the demon's body. Push it in the portal."

"I have tried both. Either action brought the axe-wielder, and as I've said, I cannot defeat him."

The scout said, "Canus has ordered. We defeat the axe-wielder. You remove the demon."

"The axe-wielder is in my forest now, killing trees."

"We will scout."

Quid shook his head. "I can summon him if I wish. I know what he now hates most."

The noble draconian stood, removed another flask from his pouch, a piece of cloth. He unstoppered the flask. The scout remembered the smell of oils and care. Quid took the cloth, put it over the flask's mouth, tipped both over. Green liquid stained the cloth. Quid held the cloth over the stump where they rested.

"We should return for your weapons," Quid said.

The scout gestured away the draconian's words. Quid restoppered the flask, put it back into his pouch, along with the cloth. Quid said, "I have something, that can protect you for a while against the poison in the water and any infected blood you might spill." He produced a metal compact. "May I?"

The draconian gestured for the scout to stand. The scout made sure Fury rested, then stood. Quid unscrewed the compact's lid, handed it to the scout. The draconian said, "Take a small amount, not so much, that's good."

The scout held his salve-covered fingers to his nose, smelled different oils and some back-scent of magic. Quid made motions with his hands for the scout to rub the salve over any exposed skin, reminded the scout to put salve on his eyelids, the backs of his ears, his scalp. Quid took a wide leaf from his pouch, said, "Coat this, chew it well, then swallow."

The scout asked, "Cover with this and eat?"

Quid nodded. "Unless you can keep your lips shut while fighting. Eating a little will protect your mouth and throat."

The scout did as instructed, glanced at Fury, who remained in sleep. The scout said, "Now?"

Quid took the compact from the scout, put it in the pouch, removed the green-stained cloth. "By your command."

The scout nodded. The draconian applied the oil to the tree stump.

The sound of approaching hoof-beats and a howl of anger shook the barrier, created a shower of dust and twigs. Quid continued to apply oil to the exposed wood of the stump. Fury's head sleepily turned toward the barrier, her eyes slowly opened.

Rising over the top of the barrier, the scout first saw the axe. Its blade was larger than his torso, the haft taller than the draconian. He smelled the axe's magic before he smelled the invasive scent of hundreds of animals on the barrier's far side, before he caught the scent of the axe-wielder. It was a scent he had not held in a long time, almost as much a legend as the draconian.

Half-man, half-horse, black-maned, eyes blood red, the centaur crested the barrier. Jumped out over the portal, past the demon, into the infected stream. Water sprayed up and far. Quid gestured, turned his back. Water struck a barrier around him, sliding down a glassy surface. A few drops hit the scout, the water beading on his protected skin.

Quid turned back as the centaur charged, hooves throwing water and streambed in all directions. The scout expected the axe to have dark magic but the axe was a weapon second, a forest tool first. Quid gestured with both hands. Thorned barriers and dense hedges grew instantly from the soil. The centaur raised the axe, shearing the obstacles aside. The draconian said, "I gave him that axe to help the forest."

The centaur continued to cut through the draconian's barriers, bellowing, blood-foam pouring from his human mouth. The scent of animals and infection reached the scout. A legion of cursed creatures washed over the barrier's top, scrabbled, jumped, fell to the ground. They charged up around the centaur.

Quid said, "Do what you must." The draconian gestured. Hundreds of sharp leafy spines thrust up from the ground, pierced the bodies of the animals. The stiff and mortally wounded creatures hung on the spines, spitting foam, weeping tears of blood before shivering, dying. A fraction of the total were stopped. "Go now!"

With his good hand, the scout grabbed Fury by the scruff. The wolf immediately awoke, barked, nipped at the scout's hand. The scout barked and growled, cast his gaze at the centaur. As one, the two charged across the field.

The centaur destroyed the last of Quid's barriers, bellowed at the attacking bündesphar. A number of animals washed around the centaur, were killed by another carpet of spines raised by the noble draconian.

At the point of attack, the wolf bolted under the

centaur's legs, scout above. Fury stood to full height beneath the enemy, knocking the centaur off balance. The wolf raised her head and slashed her teeth across the centaur's exposed belly, drawing a wide line of blood, soaking Fury's fur. The invader living in her guts raged for more.

The scout wrapped his arms around the centaur's torso, avoiding the haft of the axe as it was brought around to knock him aside, his good arm went across the centaur's throat, pulled. Foam and blood exploded from the centaur's mouth, his cry harshly cut off. The scout felt the unnatural heat in the centaur's body.

The scout bared fangs to rend the centaur's throat, stopped before he penetrated flesh. The centaur maneuvered the axe-haft to knock the scout away, failed, reared on his hind legs and shuffled back. Fury followed the motion, turned, stood with her forelegs against the centaur's belly to push the centaur over, onto his back.

The scout clamped his legs onto the centaur's sides as the centaur reared. His stiff leg failed, he held on with his good arm around the centaur's throat, tightened his strangle-hold. The scout used his other hand to punch nails-first into the centaur's neck, seeking critical veins and arteries.

Fury clamped jaws onto muscle near the centaur's sternum, drawing another spray of blood into her face, over her fangs. She bit and bit, stitched a line of ruined flesh wherever her teeth pierced the thick horse-hide.

The centaur skipped back a pace, fell forward. Fury was thrown on her back, under the centaur by his superior weight. Her neck cracked across an old injury. Her tongue lolled, blood streamed from her mouth.

Jarred, the scout slipped, grabbed the centaur's black mane. The centaur maneuvered the axe-haft up, around, struck the scout on the side of the head. The scout let go, staggered, did not fall.

The axe-head literally sang as the centaur brought the weapon around one-handed. A sudden wind gusted as a tree exploded out from the ground at an angle, into the centaur. Knocked him far aside and off-balance. Quid gestured, tanglevines raced across the ground, reached the bündesphar, dragging them away from the centaur.

Quid summoned a path that led to his clearing, commanded the tanglevines to follow. Leaving the centaur to rage.

****

The black wolf poked his muzzle into the old scout's stiff side. The wolf chewed the air, yowled, shuffled back.

"He will awake, hey, Shadow," Arana said to her wülfbund. "He dreams of the Long Hunt." The black wolf turned yellow eyes toward the woman. "No, none know his name."

The old scout stirred, opened his eyes. The ground was red from his bleeding. He struggled to sit, turned away from the others and vomited. His stiff side collapsed beneath him, bending him. He saw Arana, his leader, commander. He looked away and called out, "Hie, Fury."

"She rests outside," Quid said, entering the hut. "She was grievously injured." The scout attempted motion, the noble draconian held him back, held him down. "You were also gravely injured. You almost did not survive the journey back."

Quid knelt in front of the scout, with a battery of flasks held in a leather case. He performed the delicate work of opening the flasks with his left hand, where the talons were cut short. He poured droplets onto the scout's head, soaking the bandage.

The scout raised his good arm, blocked the draconian. "Fury."

The draconian forced the scout's hand aside. "She recovered on her own. The curse of Morgion has made her strong. Very strong. You might not recognize her."

The scout dropped his hand. "How long?"

"Days," Arana said. She stroked the fur between her wülfbunde's ears. "The evil god's curse has fallen full upon her."

"I hear her."

"You must turn aside from the Bond," Arana said. "Fully."

"First I would die."

Arana said, "For that, we are here to offer assistance." She turned to the noble draconian, nodded. Quid took the rolled leaf pack from the woman, took out a twist of yellow lakrak. The draconian saw Arana jerk her head at the lakrak's smell. She said "Only our strongest may take the yellow."

The scout chewed, coughed yellow saliva. He clutched his throat, stood. Spit out the root-twist and tottered on his stiff side. Quid thrust up, under the scout, helped him stand.

The scout said, "Fury."

The four walked into the clearing's sunlight and mist. The scout's body tensed, shook in the noble draconian's grip. A long growl grew in the scout's throat, his shoulders hunched.

Arana said, "Do not let the Bond posses you."

The scout turned to the other bündesphar, bared fangs. Shadow pressed against Arana, bared fangs. The woman placed a hand on her wülfbunde, silencing him. The wolf fixed the scout with a glare.

The scout turned away, to the clearing. He heard the bloodrage howl through Fury, heard the victory of the diseased god's curse. The Bond enfolded him, made him strong. His muscles tightened, tension pulling old breaks into place. He drew away from the draconian, boldly walked to Fury's side, dropped to his knees. Enfolded the wolf in an embrace. The scout could no longer wrap his arms around his companion, she had grown so large. The heat from her body made the air damp, heavy.

The scout laid his head on Fury's shoulder. He heard her battle. Her lungs fought for air, her heart beat against the tide of racing blood. Old scars were gone, separated muscles knit. His own flesh nearly burned. Her fur stood needle-straight.

The wolf slept through the magic, the scout smelled it. He followed in her dreams. She wanted only release, death, combat and killing to relieve the pain. Suffering was continual, isolating. In her dreams, the scout walked her path. Blood under his paws, blood on his fur, his fangs. The agony of the curse was diminished only by blood.

Arana pulled the scout away from Fury, out of the

clearing, into the hut. The scout remained in the wolf's semi-dream, did not awake until out of sight. His stiff side failed, he collapsed.

Arana knelt before the scout, said, "Give your wülfbunde peace. Release her."

The scout thrashed his head against the floor in denial. "I die with her."

Arana said, "Perform the rite. Join the Long Hunt."

Quid gestured healing magic over the scout and asked Arana, "Why have you come?"

"To continue, to close and seal the portal."

Quid said, "You will not succeed."

Arana said, "It has been ordered."

The draconian said, "I have failed. My power, combined with the strength of this scout and his companion have failed. How will you succeed?"

"It has been ordered."

"Based on previous results, your answer borders on foolish arrogance," Quid said. "You will fail and you will die. Or worse." He nodded toward the clearing. "I am protector of this forest, and I have the power to deny you."

The scout rolled onto his good side, gestured. Arana's wolf padded into the scout's embrace. Shadow's fur was perfect black. The scout leant his head against the wolf's body, listened. Listened.

The scout said, "Attack together. All."

Quid said, "I will not waken Fury. Her suffering is god-born. She will be mad in her agony."

Arana said, "Your wülfbunde's pain must end."

The scout shook his head, patting Shadow on the flank. The wolf dug his muzzle under the scout's chin, bit lightly at the scout's exposed throat. Returned to Arana. "Die in battle. For Canus. For the corps."

In the clearing, Fury howled in her sleep. Her breathing was loud, her legs thrashed, she coughed, bit the air.

The scout's legs thrashed in time. He said, "Her madness is on me."

Arana turned to the draconian. His yellow eyes met hers. He said "There are precautions to take. I have discovered a means to keep the animals away. Then I will prepare you all as I can."

****

The noble draconian summoned tanglevines to carry Fury out of the clearing. The five traveled Quid's path back to the portal. Found the centaur waiting for them.

Quid gestured toward the tanglevines. Fury started coughing, a stream of black foam. Shook her head, throwing spray. The tanglevines receded, leaving her standing. Her legs were unsteady, shaking.

The centaur charged. The axe sang a sweet song of forest healing. His other hand tore hair from his body, beat himself in the head, the face, pounding his chest. His pupils were without color, nothing left but twin orbs filled with blood.

Fury shook violently. She kicked the air, bit her legs and chest, puncturing holes in her hide. But she couldn't shake the fire. The invader in her blood demanded sacrifice. She charged the centaur.

The scout followed his wülfbunde. Felt the madness

in her muscles, felt it in his own. He did not turn from the Bond. He ran straight, fast.

Fury found her voice in the Godhome, borrowed once in a life from the jaws of Canus. Visible power erupted from her howl.

The centaur blocked with the axe. Stopped dead, was pushed back. The axe-blade was huge, covered his human torso and face. His horse's body was blasted. Legs shattered, he fell to his belly. Fury's howl continued as she moved. The axe-blade vibrated, cracked.

The enchanted blade splintered. Quid's cry of despair erupted from the axe-blade as it fell to shards. A piece of the draconian's spirit rose from the tool, vanished. Fury's howl ended.

Arana and Shadow had not moved. There had not been time. But Arana was quick enough to catch the grief-stunned draconian as he fell.

The scout and Fury ravaged the centaur, utterly destroying him. Fury barked at the corpse. The invader demanded she kill. Without a look toward the scout, the wolf was off, running around the timber barrier standing behind the portal.

The scout could not feel her through the Bond. She was gone and his body spasmed, every past injury cried its name. He toppled forward.

Arana left the unconscious draconian, tended to the scout. Shadow bit the scout's body, got no reaction. Arana checked the scout's throat for the signs of life, found them finally.

The scout said weakly, "Time for the Long Hunt."

Shadow stopped biting, propped her forelegs on the scout's body, lowered herself to a comfortable position.

She shifted, smoothed the scout's tunic under her chin. Arana sat beside the black wolf, laying a hand on her wülfbunde's shoulder. She looked at the mass of corruption trapped between the portal and Krynn. It still leaked disease into the stream.

She said, "The draconian will destroy the body. We will close the portal. We wait until you finish the rite."

"I would not join the Long Hunt," the scout said. He ran his hand over Shadow's fur. Coughs and spasms wracked him, convulsed him in half. Shadow was forced to move aside. Blood spilled from the scout's mouth, stained his fangs red. He said, "Leave."

Arana shared in the Bond with Shadow. The two walked back to Quid. Arana muscled her shoulder under the draconian's. The mists surrounding him were thinner, but not gone. With effort, Arana dragged Quid from the clearing, took a line directly away from the stream and tree stumps.

****

Around the scout, time passed. Darkness fell. He had no color-sight. He smelled dirt in his nose, nothing else.

An animal sniffed near him. He felt the heat from its body, knew it had the diseased god's curse. Fur needled his skin. "Wülfbunde?"

The scout turned his face. Fury stood over him, body slick with the blood of the other like-cursed animals. He knew she had killed them all. She was his wülfbunde.

He grabbed the muscles near her neck, pulled himself up to sit. His stiff arm was useless. When he touched his wolf through the Bond, he shared in her madness. He was at his end.

The scout clawed with his good hand, pressed his face, fangs, against Fury's throat. He could still open his jaws. He fixed fangs against his wolf's veins.

Fury turned her head into the scout's throat. She opened her jaws, fixed her fangs against the scout's throat.

Through the Bond, the scout said, "Forever I would fight by your side."

The scout's fangs punctured Fury's hide, the blood, the intruder in the blood, rushing to fill his mouth. He heard the scream of the curse. He saw the portal still open, the diseased demon trapped beneath it. The portal was made of everything and nothing, a thread from the mantle of Father Chaos. The portal led to the Abyss, and the armies there. The armies of Chaos left behind after the many long wars.

The scout drank his wülfbunde's diseased blood. He drank his fill.

****

Days later, Quid returned to the portal, carrying his pack of vials. Morgion's demon was still there, crushed under the portal's weight. The mists surrounding the draconian did not flow farther than a few feet from his body. He was stooped, wings tattered.

Quid unpacked vials, mixed contents into other vessels. He quickly created two solutions. The first he poured into the stream. The water slowed, hardened, turned to stone. He sighed, shook his head. He had plans to reflow the stream around this cursed area.

The noble draconian hefted the second solution. The liquid was heavy and brown, its vessel dark brown clay. He was too weak to throw the vessel a comfortable distance. When the axe died, a piece of his vitality had died with it.

Quid hefted the vessel again, gauged distance. Cocked his arm.

"Hold!"

Quid relaxed his arm, looked around. Two figures appeared around the wooden barrier behind the portal. Man and wolf. Scout and wülfbunde.

Quid said, shocked, "What have you done?"

Fury was huge with power and strength. The scout walked tall, able-bodied. His eyes were red. He wiped blood-foam from his mouth. The draconian felt the heat blasting from their bodies.

"The portal must be sealed from within."

"How do you know?"

The scout placed a hand on Fury's head. "Been to the other side. Know its working."

The scout and wolf moved to the lip of the open portal. The scout said, "Destroy the demon, the portal closes. We seal it on the other side."

"This is madness. You know the workings of Morgion's curse. And it is said none die of age in the Abyss."

The scout nodded, leant, kissed Fury between the ears. "In the Age of Might, the Dark Queen brought us the word of Canus. Canus was the faithful. Canus was the guard. Canus was the hunter. Canus brought us the Bond, between wolf and man, wülfbunde and master, both to the corps. Nothing can break this Bond. Nothing can come between this Bond. No force can sway this Bond."

Quid said, "But your suffering will be unending."

"No force can sway the Bond," the scout said. "And we will be together forever."

To the forest, Quid said, "The Abyss shall know fear."

The scout said, "Tell Arana and Shadow we are gone and what we have done."

Quid said, "She was going to sacrifice herself and seal the portal from the other side, wasn't she?"

The scout nodded. "Aye, true. The only way. There is one other thing you can tell her."

"That is?"

"My name."

Quid asked, "What is your name?"

And before he seals the portal, the scout answers.

The Vow

Richard A. Knaak

New York Times best-selling fantasy author Richard A. Knaak is a long-time contributor to Dragonlance, having published his first short story in *The Magic of Krynn.* Since then, he has appeared in more than a dozen other anthologies for the series, plus written eight novels, including the *Legend of Huma* and the Minotaur Wars saga. He is also the author of some two dozen other novels, including his own popular *Dragonrealm* series, stories for the *World of Warcraft* and *Diablo,* and, most recently, the *Aquilonia* trilogy for the *Age of Conan* series. In addition, the author has also delved into manga, scripting the *Sunwell* trilogy, the first *Warcraft* manga. Currently, he is at work on his latest excursion into Krynn—the *Ogre Titans* saga. The first novel, *The Black Talon,* is due out late in 2007. Knaak is also in the midst of the *Sin War,* the trilogy that explores the background of the *Diablo* conflict, and other various projects. You can join his e-mailing list by going to www.sff.net/people/knaak.

The Vow

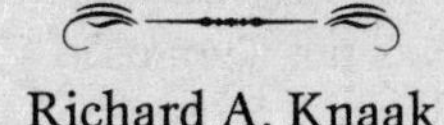

Richard A. Knaak

Age of Mortals, 423 AC

The haggard minotaur stumbled along the bleak, rocky landscape. Dust, sweat, and blood marred the once-shiny breastplate of the legionary. A sword whose upper tip had been snapped off dangled at his side, now and then clanking against the dull metal tips of the soldier's kilt. His dark brown fur was thickly matted, and hungry insects buzzed around his long, scarred muzzle, darting in for another nibble at his flesh.

Under a thick brow, the minotaur stared wearily at the path ahead. High ridges rose to the north, and empty, flat lands stretched far to the south. Somewhere days to the southwest, the barren realm—called Kern by its vile inhabitants—gave way to lush, rolling hills and thick forest. There one would find the imperial colony of Ambeon, which was the foothold of minotaur ambitions on the continent of Ansalon.

There Chonos not only could find relief, but also fulfill his vow to Ulthar.

The legionary shifted a huge battle-axe, which pressed against his left shoulder. Its magnificent twin-edged head shone in the relentless sun. Its long handle was carefully wrapped in aged leather, and just below its head were etched runes marking the five generations of family who had proudly wielded it . . . .

A family that was not Chonos's.

The weapon adjusted, he reached for the water sack tucked under his sword belt. Raising the shriveled pouch, Chonos allowed only five drops to trickle down his throat. Then he quickly cut off the flow, aware that the rest of the water would have to last him until Kern was far behind.

And he was also well aware that it probably would not.

Chonos snorted in sudden self-derision. He was a legionary. Ulthar would not have entertained doubts. Ulthar would have gone on with utter determination.

Chonos gripped the axe tighter. Ulthar was dead, slaughtered with the other members of the scouting party.

It had started out as a simple reconnaissance mission to investigate the odd, unsettling silence hanging over the realm of the empire's one-time ally and traditional enemy. Under the rule of the ambitious Grand Lord Golgren, such silence could mean a threat was gathering, even the secret formation of an organized horde such as had never been seen before. Ogres tended to be individualistic fighters whose traditional tactics came down to charging wildly into a fray and trying to crush in the heads of as many foes as possible. The shaggy, tusked giants—at least another two feet taller than Chonos's own formidable kind—were not to be taken lightly in terms of brute strength, but their cunning was rarely a match for veteran legionaries.

Yet that had begun to change under the grand lord. The ogres had become something different, something far more dangerous than in any generation past. Indeed, they were *organized.*

The minotaur's legs suddenly quivered. He staggered a few more steps; then both lower limbs gave way. Still clutching the axe as if it were life itself, Chonos fell flat on the hard ground.

He lay there, seriously considering whether to simply let nature finish him before the ogre patrol could find him again. Yet it was his duty to return to his commanders, and more important, he could *not* fail his sacred promise to Ulthar. No matter how much the heavy weight of the unwieldy axe sapped his precious strength, Chonos would do his utmost to see the vow fulfilled.

If only he could stand.

It took several long moments before the legionary finally managed to push himself up onto his elbows. The first thing he did was inspect the axe for damage. To his relief, only dust marred its sleek appearance.

"S-still will do it," he muttered to Ulthar's shade. "Still will do it, brother . . ."

At that moment a shadow swept over him, one so immense it gave him several heartbeats' respite from the sun . . . but at the same time set every nerve taut with foreboding.

As Chonos forced his gaze skyward, he beheld the dragon.

There was no mistaking the glittering brass scales. Chonos instinctively stilled; a dragon was danger enough, but a metallic dragon, so often allied with Solamnic Knights and elves, would readily identify the legionary as an enemy.

As the dragon swept through its arc, Chonos also noticed something atop the leviathan: a *rider.* It was slim of build, more so than most humans. An elf, perhaps?

The dragon shrank swiftly as it soared south. The legionary wondered if it carried some rebel scout seeking weakness in the frontier forts. That would not be at all surprising since, for most of history, Ambeon had been the fabled elven realm of Silvanost. The haughty elves still chafed at being driven from their ancient homeland. Every now and then, some group would attempt an incursion, only to be easily repelled. The minotaurs would not relinquish their claim . . . a fact that made Chonos proud even despite his own dire situation.

Seeing the rider suddenly made him yearn to sit astride the dragon himself, however impossible such a notion. How fast the miles would have flown by! He could be back in Ambeon before nightfall, his thirst already slaked, his belly full of fresh, roasted goat . . . .

With a grunt, Chonos pushed himself up on his feet. There was no dragon waiting to whisk him away to safety. One waiting to *eat* him was more likely. Leaning on the axe, he eyed the dwindling form with rising hatred. The ease with which the dragon soared over the harsh landscape seemed to mock Chonos.

From the western sky, a second, larger form dropped without warning behind the brass leviathan . . . another dragon, whom even the legionary could tell through stinging eyes was the color of blood red.

The fearsome juggernaut dived toward the unsuspecting brass. Chonos imagined the talons of the red giant easily tearing through the wing membranes of the brass. The minotaur stood and watched, awed by the rare display of power and violence he was about to witness.

However, what seemed an inevitable slaughter of the brass abruptly became a startling, madcap flapping of wings and aerial acrobatics that left the red dragon hovering madly in place, its would-be victim atop *it*. The brass moved like lightning, darting around. Clearly, the ambush had been anticipated by the smaller giant.

Chonos stumbled toward the struggle in order to view it better. He need not have bothered, though, for, caught up in their maneuvers, the dragons inadvertently battled back in the minotaur's direction. Their roars echoed throughout the wasteland, and their immense bodies caused wild shadows to dance upon the ground.

The red dragon twisted around in midair, claws and huge teeth seeking its elusive prey. However, once again, the brass was not where it had been, having already dived below, then up again behind its adversary. It almost appeared as if the metallic beast were playing with its chromatic adversary.

Outraged at the other's antics, the red immediately spun about. Its savage maw stretched wide. The brass made no new attempt to move. Its hesitation would cost the smaller dragon its life.

Just as the chromatic dragon turned to the brass, the latter opened wide its own mouth . . . and unleashed a blast of bright flame directly into the eyes and jaws of its opponent.

Aware that many dragons could breathe flame, but never having witnessed its use—much less against another dragon—the fury with which the stream enveloped the red's head stunned the minotaur. The larger dragon let out a roar of utter anguish. Its wings beat backward in a frenzy as it pulled itself away from the awful fire. Wisps of smoke could be seen near its orbs.

However, in its agony, the larger beast lashed out with its claws, ripping across the triumphant brass's torso and right wing. The metallic dragon let out a cry of its own as both the force and pain of the strikes momentarily sent it tumbling.

Still roaring, the red dragon spun wildly about then darted back in the direction from which it had originally come. One forepaw clutched at its blinded eyes.

The brass spiraled downward for several breathtaking seconds before managing to right itself. The wounded beast then hovered precariously over the area, as if taking stock. Fortunately for it, there was no longer any sign of the red dragon.

The entire dramatic duel had taken place over the space of perhaps three minutes.

The smaller dragon suddenly peered over its shoulder, as if finding something of great interest in the surrounding landscape. Chonos went still, certain that it had noticed him. However, after a tense moment, the dragon descended among the high rocks, vanishing from the minotaur's sight.

Its disappearance brought Chonos back to his own plight. Had the ogres also noticed the titanic struggle? They were reckless enough to perhaps investigate its aftermath, which meant they might even pick up the legionary's trail again.

Glancing behind him, the weary minotaur noticed for the first time he had left a haphazard series of footprints behind him. How long he had been doing so, Chonos had no idea. Worse, the landscape ahead was dusty enough that the problem would continue. The legionary would have to spend much of his time and strength eradicating his steps, a difficult task.

Unless . . .

Hefting the axe over his shoulder, Chonos stared at the high rocks. Heading upward would mean much climbing, but at the same time, his trail would become nearly impossible to follow. It also occurred to Chonos he might find water among the rocks, not an impossibility. Often such regions held hidden springs or streams fed by frost runoff from the freezing nights.

Unable to think of any better course of action, the legionary decided to take a chance. Gripping the axe tightly, Chonos headed toward the rocks. Besides the sharp, uneven terrain, he ought to be worrying about the dragon. Likely it would already be long gone, but surely, if it were not, a single minotaur would not escape its glance.

Surely . . .

****

Among the high rocks, the wind proved as relentless as the sun. The wind did not even cool Chonos, for it was so very dry and carried with it small, sharp particles that blew into his eyes and mouth.

As time passed, his wounds throbbed more and more. Climbing through the rough terrain while still protecting the axe forced additional strain on the minotaur. Twice he nearly blacked out.

Now and then, shadows gave him some respite. Unfortunately, he came across no hint of water. In fact, the region was more bare of life than its sun-drenched areas. Yet the harsh route *did* erase his trail, just as Chonos had hoped. He at last exhaled in some slight relief at that realization.

As if in response, another exhalation echoed from ahead.

Chonos reached for the broken sword. Hefting both it and the axe, he slowly advanced toward the ominous sound.

There, settled in the midst of a wide gap among the rocks, was the brass dragon.

Caught between exhaustion and fascination, Chonos merely stood there, raptly eyeing the wounded behemoth. Up close, the damage done by the red proved far more extensive than the minotaur had imagined. From its one wing hung ribbons of membrane. The brass's scaled torso was covered in red streaks that opened each time the leviathan breathed.

Chonos suddenly realized the danger facing him. He stepped back, already certain the dragon had noticed his presence, then saw that its attention was drawn to something on its other side . . . .

A body.

It took the minotaur a moment to realize that it must be the dragon-rider. A brief glance was enough to reveal the shattered condition of the corpse; he—Chonos could only assume that the human had been a "he"—had fallen to his death during the battle.

Staring at the corpse, the dragon—also a male—growled something in what the minotaur supposed was the fabled tongue of his kind and, in the Elvish language, added two last words. That done, the brass dragon pulled back his head and unleashed a stream of fire that engulfed the dead body.

The action startled Chonos. A loud gasp escaped him.

The massive head swung sharply toward him, the eyes—so reptilian and yet *not*—narrowing.

"Minotaur . . ." the scaled fury rumbled. "Minotaur . . ."

With some effort, the brass rose up into the air. Chonos made no attempt to flee, aware that it was already too late and that he had doomed himself by his stupidity.

The dragon studied the legionary carefully and, with a snort of dismissal, unexpectedly settled down before him.

"Hmmph! Not much of a minotaur! Pretty scraggly specimen! Run off, little bull! I've no interest in playing with you!"

Chonos drew himself up as best as his condition allowed. Even as low as he had sunk, he did not expect to be talked to in such a manner, not even by a dragon.

"I am a legionary of the imperium!" he rasped.

"Sworn an oath to the Emperor Faros! I am no vermin!"

The huge head darted close. Sulfuric breath cascaded over the minotaur, nearly smothering him.

"Oh, yes, that is the right word—you *are,*" retorted the brass. "Now go! Leave me be! I have a friend to mourn!"

With that, the brass whirled about and returned to the makeshift pyre. Still overcome by the creature's scorching breath, Chonos could initially only stand there, weaving back and forth. Only after several attempts did he find it possible to breathe, much less focus.

Chonos finally started to leave, but heard the dragon utter something in Common tongue.

"We vowed we would be there for one another, Skorios, but I failed you! I should've known old Furon wouldn't take to being humiliated easily!" The metallic giant let out a puff of smoke from his nostrils. "Well, let us see how much trouble he can cause with his eyes toasted, eh?"

The brass let out a halfhearted chuckle, but still stared at the dwindling fire that had consumed his rider.

Chonos blinked. A part of him knew his mind teetered on delirium, but a single word that the dragon had uttered reverberated within him so strongly that at last the minotaur stumbled not away from the great beast, but *toward* him.

He had nearly stepped within reach of the tattered wing before the brass dragon noticed, his eyes widening.

"What do *you* still do here, bull? Go find a rock upon which to lay your frying bones! Death at the whim of this befouled landscape is still a better thing than stirring my anger, especially now!"

Chonos was undeterred by the threat. His thoughts continued to fixate on the word the brass had used in connection with his rider.

"I, too, have made a vow," the minotaur declared, trying to keep his voice from cracking. "And you are my one hope of fulfilling it! I'm well aware that my kind are no friend to you, but—"

"That is an understatement, bull! Do you see those ashes that were once a brave elf? Your kind forced him into a binding relationship with me that once we both despised, yet became a kinship like none I've ever known with even my own! We were like two sides of the same coin." The brass flapped his wings in agitation. "May Furon be damned to the Abyss for this!"

Head pounding, Chonos barely understood anything the dragon said to him. "And I understand such loss!" the legionary dared to return. "This day, five good comrades perished, including he with whom I swore a blood-oath when we were children!"

The brass pulled back his head in astonishment at the vehemence in the puny creature's words.

"I ask only that I be carried to the edge of Ambeon!" continued Chonos. "From there, I can reach a fort on my own!"

"But I have no cause to save your miserable hide! Hmmph! Such a poor example of a warrior! While your fellows lie dead, you whine to me like an infant to carry you to safety! Pfah!" The last declaration was accompanied by a puff of hot smoke that enveloped the minotaur's head.

Anger overwhelmed reason. Brandishing his broken sword, Chonos lunged forward, shouting, "I am no coward! I swore a vow to Ulthar that I would reach his son and give him his father's axe!" He held the weapon high. "I will not—I must not fail!"

The brass cocked his head, gazing at Chonos as if the legionary had transformed into a stinking gully dwarf. He let out a puff of breath that knocked Chonos onto his back. The legionary fumbled his grip on his sword but held on tightly to the other weapon. "*That* is your precious memento? That *axe?*"

"It was—it was his last words . . ." They were his last *fevered* words, in point of fact. Chonos could still see the savage, tusked faces of the eager ogres, so squashed, so flat in comparison to his own muzzled one. The scouting party had been attacked without warning. The legionary could only assume his party had been spotted long before, despite their continuous efforts to stay wary.

"They're up on the rocks as well!" Ulthar had shouted. "Turn back! Head along that rise!"

Against such numbers, even the hardiest of the scouts had known better than to make a stand. Ogres were not renowned for their strategic genius, true, yet that band had not only had the foresight to set an ambush for the scouts, but also had figured out in advance just where the legionaries would choose to retreat. What the six had taken as their avenue of escape had proven instead to be a second, more lethal trap.

They had lost Dorn early, young Dorn on his first scouting mission. His steed had stumbled, throwing the legionary. The ogres swept over Dorn moments later. A dozen spears had made a pincushion of the sprawling minotaur, and one ogre warrior had taken his time beating in the corpse's skull.

Minotaur horses were not bred just for size, but also swiftness. But the scouts' ignorance of the terrain kept the ogres right behind them. Thus, it was far too late when Chonos and the others realized their fatal error.

"Rocks above! Rocks above!" Chonos didn't know who had let out the belated warning, perhaps it was he himself. The next instant, an avalanche had swept over the scouts. Timorius and Jakor had fallen then, they and their horses crushed under rubble. Chonos's own animal had been bowled over and only by swift reflex had he managed to avoid sharing its fate.

A strong hand had seized the dazed legionary by the arm. Ulthar's hand, naturally, Chonos's blood brother was there for him, just as he always had been. Ulthar, too, had been knocked off his horse, but another of their party, black-furred Golt, had not only managed to stay in the saddle, but also brought Ulthar's horse back to them.

However, before they could mount, the first of the ogres fell on them. Ulthar had shoved aside Chonos in order to take his famous axe and bury it deep in the hirsute giant's chest. At the same time, another ogre had rushed at Chonos from the side. The shaggy-haired warrior had wielded a club nearly as long as the minotaur's torso and as thick as his head. Chonos had managed to pull free his sword and catch the fiend in the abdomen, but momentum sent the ogre falling into him. Chonos struggled as the huge body threatened to crush the legionary.

And it had been Ulthar again who had rescued him, barreling into the dying ogre and shoving him over to the side. He had then pushed Chonos to the horse.

Just as Ulthar had started to follow, a kilted ogre carrying a chipped hand axe had leaped over the remains of the previous attacker. Before Chonos could act, the ogre caught Ulthar in the back between the shoulder blades, the force of the blow easily cutting through his armor.

Ulthar had stumbled into Chonos, who deflected a second strike by the ogre with his sword. The axe had shattered the smaller weapon, and the action enabled him to drag his comrade over the saddle. Ulthar somehow managed to keep a grip on his axe.

What had happened in the heartbeats that followed were still mostly a blur to the surviving legionary. Golt had perished, dragged off his own mount by two warriors. Chonos recalled Ulthar's horse rearing. There had been an ogre's meaty hands reaching to tear Ulthar from Chonos's grasp. Chonos had swung at the hands . . . and the horse had raced off with its double burden.

"An axe!" the leviathan repeated, snapping the minotaur back to the present reality. "Ha! The sun's taken any good wit you had, bull, and some of mine, too, for having spent even seconds with you!" He thrust out his wing as if to swat the minotaur with it. "Begone with you and your puny axe!"

"I made a vow!" Chonos shouted at the brass,

amazed not only that he tempted the dragon's wrath, but that he even had the strength to speak anymore. "Both of us escaped the ogres . . . but our horse was wounded, though we didn't know it until some distance later . . . when the horse, dying, threw us . . ."

Violent images once more flashed through his distraught mind: the animal's stumbling; its pained cry, presaging that of Ulthar's; the harsh, hard ground rising up to crash against Chonos's head; the long, agonizing bout of vertigo, throughout which he could hear the continuous moans of his dying friend . . . .

The slow refocusing of his gaze, revealing to him at last Ulthar's twisted body bent over a jagged outcropping.

The brass dragon did not try to strike him again when Chonos dared step nearer. Instead, almost as if weary of everything, the metallic giant sighed and said, "You two were thrown from a horse. And so?"

"And so, I crawled to Ulthar! His back, I could see, was shattered! Yet somehow he was still conscious, if barely. When Ulthar spoke, though, it . . . it was not to me, but to another . . . to his son, Kylus."

Chonos told the brass then how Ulthar had looked up at him, tried to bare his teeth in the minotaur equivalent of a smile, and finally said, "Kylus . . . g-good lad! A new legionary! Y-You get posted to Ambeon and I . . . and I'll see to it that my axe is yours, j-just as I inherited it from . . . from my father . . ."

Chonos had said nothing, letting Ulthar continue his delusion. For a few more moments, the dying minotaur went on with his praises for his son and the proud tradition of the family.

Then a sharp pain had coursed through Ulthar.

Blood seeped from his mouth. His eyes wavered and refocused.

"Ch-Chonos . . . is that you?" After a nod from his friend, Ulthar had tried to turn his head. "My axe . . . Kylus . . . Chonos, he must have my axe! I swore to him it'd be his . . . where is it?"

The surviving legionary had quickly brought the weapon up so Ulthar could see it, letting the end of the staff rest in the other's hand.

Suddenly, Ulthar had gone into convulsions. Chonos had attempted to hold him down as best as he could while still keeping a grip on the weapon, no simple task. "I've got to give it to him!" the dying minotaur had gasped. "I swore —"

"I knew that Ulthar did not remember where we were," Chonos told the brass. "Or what had exactly happened, but I nonetheless made the vow. That brought him peace . . . just before he died."

"Pfah! What a fool you and your vows are," snarled the dragon with disdain. "The axe might be useful in a fight, bull, but carrying a thing of such size surely slows you down and drains your precious strength! You would've moved swifter without such an unwieldy burden! It's just a piece of wood and metal, with some bits of leather!"

"It is the legacy . . . of a friend." Before the leviathan could respond, Chonos continued, "It is also a point of honor!"

In response, the brass dragon gazed down at the flames, which had all but died out. "Skorios knew well of honor, bull! There were aspects of it he was able to teach even me, who had lived thrice longer than he! You call it a point of honor, a vow, that which you seek to do! Ha! There was some honor in your comrade's saving of your life and even in your attempt to carry him to safety, but *this* . . . this is just pure foolishness!"

"To the edge of Ambeon! That is all I ask!"

"The edge of *Silvanost,* don't you mean?" retorted the metallic behemoth. "Raped and stripped Silvanost? My fire's at last dead, bull, and with it goes whatever interest I had in our conversation! Kern is welcome to you! A brave elf has perished, and there are those who I must tell of his fate!"

The brass dragon spread wide his wings and took to the air. It was clearly a strain for the dragon, the flying. Chonos realized he probably would have been too much extra weight, even if the brass *had* agreed to take him. But what of his vow?

"The axe, then!" he shouted up. "Just take the axe!"

He at least caught the dragon's attention. Hovering a few dozen yards above Chonos, the brass snarled, *"What?"*

"The axe! Kylus, son of Ulthar, is stationed at the fort near what was once the elven settlement of Kohoria! There is a ridge—"

The dragon snorted dismissively. "I know all of Silvanost better than any invader! I don't need your directions, or your axe. Are you telling me that you would wish me to take only the weapon, bull? That you would choose to stay behind to die?"

Chonos's expression was set. "Yes."

The airborne behemoth twisted his long neck around to gaze at the burned remains of his elf rider. "Skorios!

Do you hear him? He would give the axe to me and die here weaponless!"

"You—you do not understand!" Chonos felt his head growing light. "I swore . . . swore . . . to him—"

"Your friend was addled in the head . . . and so, it appears, are you." The brass raised his snout, suddenly sniffing the air. "I do you a single favor, though, bull. There is an odor more offensive than yours wafting in from the direction from which you came!"

A chill coursed down Chonos's spine and through his soul.

"That blade of yours would only be good for picking my teeth!" the metallic giant went on. "My favor is to let you keep the axe, so that when the accursed odor catches up to you, you will have some slight chance of saving your hide!"

Chonos could almost imagine that he heard the horns already, the horns and the thudding hoofbeats . . .

He suddenly hurled the axe at the brass. The bulky weapon flew far too low and landed short. The brass gave it a cursory glance, then, with a shake of his head, took to the sky.

"No! Sargonnas take you!" Eyes desperately fixed upon the dwindling form, the legionary rushed forward. He reached for the dragon, only to have his hooves become entangled. Once again, the ground came rushing up at his face. When he fell, he nearly cracked his jaw.

The minotaur rolled over . . . and saw that it was the axe that had tripped him. He looked over his shoulder at the heavens, but the brass dragon was no longer in sight.

"Ulthar . . ." Chonos muttered.

A sound caught his attention. His ears stiffened. It was *definitely* a horn.

He searched for the broken sword and immediately saw that the blade was of little value whatsoever. Truth to tell, he barely had the strength to raise the smaller weapon, much less the huge axe. The dragon had only spoken a truth Chonos had known all along. Carrying Ulthar's cherished legacy on his long trek had eaten away at too much of his strength.

Yet still Chonos did not regret what he had done. He would have never gone back on his word.

And so, even as the horn blared a second time—from much nearer—the legionary gathered his strength and took up Ulthar's axe. He surveyed the harsh landscape, trying as best as he could to determine his options. Flight was no longer a possibility; by the time he scaled any of the walls, they would have spotted him. Perhaps if Chonos left the axe behind, he might manage to elude them for a time, but that would only be a delay of the inevitable.

The legionary chose at last a tall outcropping large enough for him to perch upon and just level enough for the minotaur to swing the axe. Ulthar's weapon in hand, Chonos scrambled his way up, sat down with the axe across his lap and tried to catch his breath.

The ogres swarmed into the area just a few moments later. They howled with pent-up bloodlust as they rushed at the lone figure. Chonos counted at least thirty. Some were on horseback, most were on foot.

Forcing himself to his feet, the minotaur waited to greet the first, gripping the axe with two hands.

Three ogres leaped from their mounts and started

to climb up toward him. Two carried clubs, another a spear. Chonos stared into the bloodshot eyes of the foremost. The ogre gnashed his chipped, yellowed teeth. His tusks were so large that they rose up to his eyes. His hair was a dirty bird's nest. He had shoulders almost twice as large as the legionary's.

When the bestial warrior was close enough, Chonos drove the pointed top of the axe through his throat.

As the first ogre fell, the other two reached the top. Chonos swung the axe at the one on his left, catching the fearsome figure in the arm. The force of the blow sent his foe reeling backward and off the outcropping.

Without hesitation, the gasping minotaur turned to the third. The ogre lunged at him with a spear, almost catching Chonos in the chest. Out of the corner of his eye, Chonos saw a fourth foe reaching the top. He kicked out as best he could, sending the newcomer into the air. At the same time, the legionary deflected another thrust from the spear.

The ogre barreled into Chonos, sending them both crashing against the rocks behind. Another warrior climbed atop the outcropping. Brandishing his club, he moved in.

Strength flagging, Chonos was nonetheless able to shove his first attacker back. He jammed one axe blade into the ogre's unprotected chest. The tusked giant let out a gasp and crumpled forward.

Cursing, Chonos shoved the corpse back, managing to send it reeling into another ogre just climbing over the edge. The latter let out a howl of frustration as he vanished from sight.

A tremendous pain in his shoulder jarred the legionary, and he heard the crack of bone. With a groan, Chonos staggered to the side as the ogre with the club moved in for a second swing. Two more of the hirsute beasts appeared behind him.

Chonos let out a roar and swung with all his might. The axe cut a swath across the club-wielding ogre's belly. As his foe fell to one knee, the legionary shoved the point at the top through his chest.

But there were three more ogres surrounding him. He no longer had room to wield Ulthar's weapon. Pain-wracked, Chonos charged the first ogre. Both went flying off the rock.

Chonos braced himself for crashing into the ground, but even though the ogre took the brunt of it, the new agony coursed through his shoulder and made the legionary bite his tongue. Chonos somehow rose up, but, unable to focus, he took a wild swing at whatever lurked directly in front of him and had the satisfaction of hearing at least one ogre grunt in mortal pain.

Then a spear caught him in the side. The minotaur felt blood coursing from the wound. He shattered the spear with the axe and tried to pluck the broken half from his body. Unfortunately, his shattered shoulder would not cooperate.

Then, to his dismay, Ulthar's axe was torn from his feeble grip. Chonos suddenly imagined it wielded by an ogre against the legionary's own kind. Not only had he failed in his vow, but the legacy of his blood brother might serve the enemy.

"No-o-o!" Lowering his head, the minotaur hurled himself forward. His two-foot-long horns met soft resistance that quickly gave way. A moistness spread over his skull.

A sucking sound accompanied the freeing of his horns from the bleeding tissue. Chonos reached out, seeking the axe.

Another club battered his outstretched arm near the wrist. As the legionary cried out, a second club caught him at the back of his head. With a moan, Chonos collapsed to his knees.

A slew of club blows and spear jabs followed . . . but most of them Chonos never felt.

****

The ogres howled and grunted in triumph as, in their frenzy, they all but tore the defeated minotaur's body apart. Several raised their bloody weapons high in the air to show them to those in the latter ranks who had been unable to take part in the carnage. Some began to fight over the limited spoils, such as the breastplate and the still-intact horns of the enemy.

A particularly huge and ugly ogre with one cracked tusk and scars all across his squat face tore the axe from the hands of a smaller comrade. There was a brief baring of teeth; then the shorter ogre reluctantly backed away. The victor dropped his own, well-worn club and brandished the axe wildly over his head. Others in the patrol roared lustily at sight of the minotaur weapon—

The area was suddenly immersed in shadow.

One of the ogres let out a cry of consternation, followed by a single word. "Tryaldrach! Tryaldrach!"

As one, the heads of the rest turned skyward and beheld the terrible glittering form.

The brass dragon let out a bellow, then shot a stream of fire right in the midst of the ogres. The ogres fled from the area as if each had the huge beast nipping at his heels. The "great victory" became an utter rout. The ogres in command could not keep order and, in fact, concerned themselves only with saving their own flea-infested hides.

Within less than a minute, the region was empty, save for the dragon and what had once been a proud legionary of the empire.

****

The brass alighted near the remains, eyeing them with scorn. The ogres had not had enough time to strip and gut the body entirely. It lay on its stomach, the head twisted to the side at an awkward angle.

With a snort, the dragon turned from the minotaur, instead heading back to Skorios's last resting place. Peering around, the metallic leviathan finally located the thing he had returned for. A small, golden disk, once bound by a chain around the dragon's throat, lay propped against a nearby rock. It had been torn off during the red's wild strikes. He had forgotten the disk, come back for it, and watched the minotaur's demise.

With a surprising delicacy, the brass plucked up the disk with his claws. As he turned the dented piece over, elven markings became evident.

"It is the symbol of an honored friend of my line,"

Skorios had told him. "It is the greatest sign I can give to one who has done so much for my cause."

The winged behemoth clutched the disk tight. He would see to it that another chain was forged, a stronger one this time.

The brass started to spread his wings, then hesitated. Twisting his long, sinewy neck, he gazed back at the sorry corpse of the horned one.

"Stupid minotaur," the dragon said with a snort of smoke.

Yet, instead of taking off, he headed over toward Chonos. The dragon blinked, then, with an expression of exasperation, inhaled sharply.

A moment later, he unleashed a stream of flame that utterly devoured the legionary's corpse.

An object shone in the light of the fire. The brass wrinkled his nose, and finally took it up in his other claw.

The axe—abandoned in the rush to escape the dragon—bore markings in the minotaur script, which the dragon could read. They were names. The last one was *Ulthar.*

"Stupid, stupid minotaurs," he rumbled. The brass dragon paused and turned in the direction of overrun Silvanost. He knew the location of the fort. It would not be a long detour, even with his wounds. A simple shout for Kylus, son of Ulthar, then all he had to do was drop the axe within the walls. Surely the bulls could deal with the matter from there.

After that, the brass could return to his own, more important concerns. Not only was there healing which he needed, but there were also those who would want to know about Skorios's fate and what it meant for the elven efforts.

He tested his wings, already impatient to reach the fort. After the infernal axe was dropped off, that would be the end of this foolishness, the brass thought. No longer would he have to concern himself with mad minotaurs and insane vows of honor.

The metallic leviathan glanced one last time at the axe. His nostrils wrinkled and he snorted derisively, that time at himself.

"Stupid *dragon,*" the brass muttered, then took off to the southeast.

Song Of The Mother

Lucien Soulban

Lucien Soulban is a Montreal novelist and videogame scriptwriter. He's written the novels: Dragonlance: The Alien Sea; Vampire: Blood In, Blood Out; and Necromunda: Fleshworks. He's also written short stories for various anthologies, including the acclaimed The Book of Final Flesh, Horrors Beyond II, and Dragonlance: The Search for Power. He has scripted Relic Entertainment's Dawn of War and Winter Assault, as well as A2M's Chicken Little, Kim Possible 3, and Kim Possible: Kimmunicator. Soulban is the Rainbow Six: Vegas scriptwriter for electronic giant Ubisoft Montreal, and you can learn about him at www.luciensoulban.com.

Song of the Mother

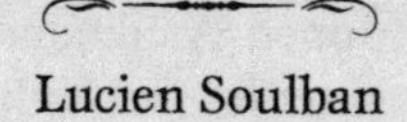

Lucien Soulban

Age of Mortals, 424–426 AC

The storm drove thick nails of rainwater into the ocean and filled its belly with a hungry rumble. The pod of obsidian-colored dolphins swam faster, threading their path in and out of the water. As they struck air, they chirped and nipped at Ashkoom's heels before diving back under. That Ashkoom ran atop the ocean's surface as though it were a cobblestone road did not bother the pod, nor did the fact that Ashkoom was an ocean strider, a rare humanoid creature that measured twenty feet in height and possessed the skin color and patterns of a killer whale.

As far as the dolphins cared, if the sea elf hanging on Ashkoom's back was laughing, they might as well join in.

The young sea elf in question called herself Brysis,

and she clung to the collar of Ashkoom's stitched leather jerkin. Brysis hailed from a branch of deepwater elves called Dargonesti. Like them, her skin radiated the blue of the most indigo of deep oceans, but her short-cropped hair possessed the rarest luster of candlelit gold. She wore a seaweed and chain poncho and loincloth, while an old wicked cut carved its scar over her left cheek and jaw. And indeed she was doing a rare thing—laughing with abandon.

The air that whipped Ashkoom's hair about felt exhilarating. She seldom ran beneath the open sky, for the weight of her body was a crushing hindrance while the air constricted and dried the shrinking net of her flesh. But there, under the storm shower, the rainwater kept her skin moist and the air felt delightfully cool.

Ashkoom shouted something against the peals of thunder, pointing down.

Brysis peered over Ashkoom's meaty shoulder and saw the darting form of something long and slim just beneath the agitated surface. Whatever it was, Ashkoom's long stride drew her closer to it.

With practiced ease, Ashkoom pulled the large falchion blade from her belt and flipped it in her grip as though holding a dagger.

"Now!" she said and dived through the air, her weapon drawn high.

Quickly, Brysis exhaled the air in her lungs to soften the impact.

The road of water beneath Ashkoom's feet turned soft again, and both ocean strider and sea elf smacked the surface in a great splash atop the fleeing creature.

For a moment all Brysis could see were bubbles

and flaying tentacles. She kicked off and down, past Ashkoom and the giant squid. Brysis darted away, a safe distance from the thrashing limbs, and turned in time to see the squid's great ink cloud eclipse the ocean above her head.

In the jet-black cloud, tentacles billowed out, as did the arc of ocean strider arm and blade.

Within moments, it was over.

****

"Does it hurt?" Brysis asked, motioning to the ring-shaped blisters on Ashkoom's arm and thigh. She took another bite from the chunk of squid meat impaled on her dagger.

The ocean strider shrugged. "No more than life," she replied.

Brysis chuckled and shook her head. "And my people call me grim."

"You have your people, at least," Ashkoom said.

Brysis winced. She should have known better than to remind Ashkoom of her lot. The ocean striders were rare and few, and none but a handful of sea dwellers even knew they existed. Even so, they were a race lonely by choice, lonely through sacrifice, lest their combined appetites thin the waters. They believed that only in death could they rejoin loved ones in the afterlife of the Spawning Deeps.

Brysis opened her mouth to apologize, but Ashkoom waved away her concern. "You are my people now," she said with a grin, and added, "And your appetite is small."

Brysis laughed and once again stared at the gloom of the surrounding ocean. Their kill had drawn sharks into the area, but Ashkoom's size kept them at bay. They remained indistinct ghosts in the murk, silhouettes of the awaiting danger.

The oceans seemingly had conspired against its denizens the past few years. The three moons had vanished, taking magic along with them and altering the world's currents and tides. The three moons eventually returned to familiar skies, but the oceans beneath them were no longer the same. The war of great dragons contaminated entire peninsulas and islands; in turn, they poisoned the oceans.

The greatest such disaster was the World Gash, a region where active volcanoes undercut the ocean floor for hundreds of miles and poisoned the waters for thousands more. The animals of those affected domains migrated on whichever currents carried them farthest. This added to the displacement of all of the ocean's children, throwing the once-familiar seas into turmoil.

Brysis continued watching the vague forms swim in wide arcs around them. One such ghost, however, approached with bold swiftness. Ashkoom reached for her falchion, but Brysis quickly laid her tiny hand across her friend's great wrist.

A moment later, a dolphin emerged from the murk. Unlike the playful ebon dolphins that chased Ashkoom and Brysis earlier, plates of metal and toughened seal leather covered this creature. It wore bladelike sheaths on its fins, and a ram-plate helmet protected its head. The creature bore many battle scars, befitting its role as a war dolphin.

"Echo Fury," Brysis exclaimed, glad to see her companion.

Echo Fury uttered a series of chirping barks, to which Brysis nodded. He'd found something worth seeing.

****

The storm had passed, leaving behind a quieter ocean. The sunlight drove shafts of light several dozen feet deep, creating a surface layer of crystal blue waters. Below that, the world dissolved into a greenish haze.

Brysis had seen a crest-breaker only once before. They were reputedly intelligent and very aloof. They measured the size of killer whales, with sea-green skin and thick bone ridges along their crown and flanks. And where they passed, they commanded other whales with a strange majesty that marked them as alpha of any pod.

Ashkoom and Brysis watched as the crest-breaker led three other whales. The companion whales were of different species—a krill-eating jester whale with its teardrop head and wide grin, a small fox whale with its reddish skin and hooklike snout, and a fast-moving gull-wing whale with its long, elegant flippers.

"The crest-breaker is old," Ashkoom said, pointing to its bone crests, which grew more intricate with patterns and whorls as the whale aged. The one in front of them possessed natural molding to shame the most experienced dwarf engraver.

"They all are," Brysis said after a moment's examination. All the whales possessed signs of long lives, from the wrinkles around their wise eyes to the discoloration and grooves of old wounds.

Ashkoom slowly approached the unusual pod of whales, careful not to startle them. Brysis swam a short distance behind, Echo Fury at her side. The crest-breaker, however, turned about and charged straight for Ashkoom. Brysis could barely react, the speed of their attacker startling. Ashkoom drew her falchion without hesitation.

Suddenly, the crest-breaker opened its mouth and gave a cry unlike any Brysis had ever heard—or rather, felt. The song bounced against the back of her skull; it reached through her ears and twisted her senses. Suddenly the ocean itself seemed to flip, and the entire depth of the ocean below pressed down upon her. Brysis tried swimming, but her perceptions were dislodged. She spun, twisting upon herself while trying to swim away. She barely noticed Ashkoom contorting herself under the same affliction.

Brysis vomited, her throat seared by the scouring acids of her stomach.

Finally, after a moment, she recovered enough to stop moving, to wait out the vertigo. It proved difficult; Brysis felt the ocean's every nudge, its every wild motion. She floated there, breathing hard through her gills, trying to settle her stomach, settle the world around her.

"That was unpleasant," Ashkoom said. She floated nearby, her skin pale, her breathing rapid. Likewise, Echo Fury turned and twisted, his senses reeling.

Brysis managed to turn her head, despite the swoon that threatened to overwhelm her. The crest-breaker had rejoined its compatriots and was swimming away. "Good riddance," Brysis muttered.

Ashkoom moved sluggishly, struggling against the strange dizziness. Brysis discovered her faculties returning and her senses anchored again. Her mind and body finally understood up from down once more.

"The whales swim south of the setting sun," Ashkoom noted.

Brysis inhaled sharply, the realization a knife thrust to her chest. Southwest of them rested the last expanse of so-called virgin sea before the World Gash thoroughly tainted the waters. Southwest of them was an area where the predators grew fierce and large, all the better to compete for the dwindling supplies of food. Southwest of them was the domain of . . .

"The dragon turtle Stone-Splitter," Ashkoom said, finishing the sea elf's thoughts.

Brysis stared after the whales, their great bodies almost invisible in the gloom. "They must be lost. We have to stop them," Brysis said. "If the king-titan sharks don't kill them, Stone-Splitter surely will."

Echo Fury snapped out a series of sharp, disapproving clicks. Brysis did not understand Echo Fury perfectly, but well enough. Despite appearances, he was part sea elf and a member of the Dargonesti called the Land Shorn; they'd abandoned their elf bodies to live exclusively as dolphins. His voice came from articulate thought.

"I know they attacked us," Brysis said for Ashkoom's benefit. "But we can't leave them to their fate. They'll be slaughtered."

For a moment Echo Fury said nothing. Brysis knew

she asked much of him; the attack had wounded his pride. Finally, he exhaled a plume of bubbles from his blowhole and grunted in a low tone.

Brysis kissed him on his snout and thanked him.

****

The three companions trailed behind, far enough that the whales vanished in and out of the murk. But their course remained steady. Occasionally, the crest-breaker deviated in its course long enough to stare back at them with its lilac-flared eyes, to remind them it knew they were there.

There was nothing to say, however. The three companions knew what needed doing.

Brysis closed her eyes and allowed the warmth of change to overtake her, to flush through her limbs and wash away the fatigue. The heat melted and resculpted her muscles. Her sinews tightened, and her ears tucked themselves into her elongated skull. Suddenly, the ocean sang with a different voice, one that hummed with vibration. Brysis felt as though she'd been cupping her hands over her ears for far too long. She could finally hear the ocean clearly; Ashkoom's heartbeat became a steady thunder in rhythm with the gull-wing's beating flippers. And Brysis felt stronger, sleeker. She became a porpoise, her change bringing short-lived warmth to the surrounding waters.

She and Echo Fury swam slightly ahead of Ashkoom, their dolphin and porpoise chirps and barks painting their surroundings in echoes. They cried out to the whales, trying their best to emulate the calls of danger.

The red-hued fox-whale hesitated, but the crest-breaker opened its mouth and unleashed a creaking dirge, the wooden groan of a restless forest. It filled the water and silenced Brysis's and Echo Fury's voices. All noise in the ocean seemed to die upon hearing the majesty of the crest-breaker's call.

The whales continued on their path.

Brysis looked back at Ashkoom. They needed to take this to the next step, even though it might be interpreted as an attack. The ocean striders could make allies of animals; the fox-whale was small enough and a friendly enough species. If they could warn the fox-whale, it could warn its friends.

Brysis sighed a small plume of bubbles and watched as Ashkoom swam forward. Brysis joined her as they prepared to warn the whales once more.

****

Brysis floated there, trying desperately to ignore the cloud of vomit that floated around her—her cloud of vomit. She sensed Ashkoom and Echo Fury floating nearby as well, all three of them waiting for the nauseating vertigo to vanish.

"That could have gone better." Brysis said.

****

The argument took some time, longer than anticipated. Brysis and Ashkoom argued over the whales; Brysis wanted to leave them to their foolishness, Ashkoom wanted to help them somehow. Echo Fury, his pride twice wounded by the effects of the crest-breaker's cry, sided with Brysis.

While the three companions prized the lives of the whales, they also understood the nature of the wild: animals died, animals killed, animals prospered. Who were they to interfere? Brysis demanded. As protectors of the wilderness and as trackers, they well understood that simple law.

"Besides," Brysis said, "the crest-breaker seems capable of defending its pod."

Ashkoom, while not denying the crest-breaker's abilities, argued that the recent upheavals had changed the oceans forever. The disasters had uprooted entire species and, by altering ocean temperatures and spreading the World Gash's toxins, killed vast swaths of vital krill and plankton. The very food chain itself seemed on the verge of epic upheaval, if not collapse. And while there seemed little they could do to counter that disaster, it was in their power to help as best they could. Better warn than watch the whales die; better that than feeling helpless, Ashkoom said.

"But they refuse to be warned," Brysis said finally. "The crest-breaker is unusually hostile," she added.

"Yes. But the crest-breaker must listen to reason, or . . ." Ashkoom trailed off.

Brysis nodded. "It's the 'or' that worries me."

****

The course of the four whales remained steady and straight for more than a day, and the three companions found themselves on the edge of dangerous waters, a handful of hours ahead of the whales. A few days' travel away rested a sea range with mountain caps that nearly broke the ocean's surface to form islands. The mountains created a bulwark against the poisons of the World Gash, protecting the pocket of life beyond, even though the poisons slowly trickled through. Still, the region provided sanctuary for refugee species that desperately needed its untouched coral, krill, and plankton. And where the fish and whales came to feed, so too did the region's massive predators.

"Problem is not Stone-Splitter," Ashkoom said, in reference to the dragon turtle. The ocean strider hovered just above a sea floor covered in coral beds and bright orange algae plumes. "The dragon only feeds upon large animals. Whales, king-titan sharks, galleon squids, monster crabs . . . it keeps their numbers low. Fish are not hunted to extinction. The dragon serves nature in its own way."

With that, the three entered the treacherous domains, instantly aware of their surroundings. They swam clear of the blue surface where their bodies would stand out against the sky and the light above. They skimmed well above the coral fields and watched the schools of silver fish for any sudden changes in their swimming patterns. In the distance, to their right, a giant thorn-crab the size of a dolphin scuttled over the coral and vanished into a hole. To their left, a family of ribbon-eels hovered in place and fluttered like banners in the currents.

The companions continued swimming for another hour before Echo Fury bleated and dived down to the coral canopy. Brysis and Ashkoom followed without question.

A moment later, a king-titan shark sailed above their heads. The tan beast was massive, larger than anything natural Brysis ever remembered seeing. Although a dozen yards above them, the king-titan shark eclipsed their sky; it easily measured the span of a minotaur's war galleon, its mouth hooked into a sneer that revealed its thicket of teeth. Spiked cartilage scales also covered its snout.

Behind the languid king-titan followed a fleet of carrion-feeders. Brysis counted at least a dozen different sharks of varying size. She held her breath. The king-titan shark vanished into the turbid mist, its entourage following in its wake. Brysis sighed in relief.

How do we protect the whales from that? she wondered, but did not voice her concern.

****

The whales arrived in their due time, swimming slowly through the water, groaning a soft requiem that echoed in the marrow of Brysis's soul.

"They sing a dirge," Ashkoom said.

"Yes, well, it will surely be a dirge if they continue," Brysis replied. "They'll attract the attention of every hungry mouth for miles!"

Ashkoom agreed; the trio would have to remain extra vigilant. Thankfully, the first few hours of the journey passed without interruption or worry. The whale song attracted the attention of smaller sharks but none of their large brethren. Brysis knew better than to relax, however.

The first sign of danger came with Echo Fury's trumpet cry. It carried no shred of panic, as Echo Fury was a seasoned fighter, but the whales reacted as well; they broke formation and scattered. That caught Brysis off guard. There was safety in numbers, which all animals understood with instinctual precision. She hesitated, uncertain which whale to follow. Ashkoom, however, pursued the crest-breaker and swiftly vanished into the gloom.

A heartbeat later, Brysis found herself alone and immediately aware of the displacement ripple of something approaching. She concentrated, willing herself to become part of the waters around her; she invoked the gift of her people to camouflage themselves; her outline blurred into a soft mist. Although Brysis did not vanish completely, she grew more difficult to see in the turbid green water.

The blue beast that slithered into view shared much in appearance with a giant eel, but with the girth of a redwood's trunk. Yellow undulating frills ran the length of its spine, and it possessed no eyes. Instead its seemingly featureless and long, tapered snout split open into three equal folds that curved back like a blossoming flower, exposing flaps covered with rows of shredding teeth.

Brysis swam away with a curse on her lips, for the beast was heading straight for her. It didn't need to see her to know she was there. The young sea elf looked back in time to see five tentaclelike tongues unravel from its mouth. She dived down and swam harder.

The coral-covered bottom materialized into view, but the beast gained on her. Brysis darted for an opening in the coral's canopy, a gap laced with skeletal ridges. She didn't know how deep in it went, but she couldn't outrace the beast in open water. Brysis squeezed through the opening, screaming in pain. The coral fingers lining the hole sliced open her flanks with thin, deep cuts. Despite the pain that spit fire on her nerves, Brysis squirmed into the widening hole, deeper by a dozen feet at best.

The hole was barely wide enough to maneuver inside, and her blood clouded the water. She turned around in time to see the thorny maw of the beast cover the hole. The bramble of snaking tongues unfurled, two of them finding their way inside her sanctuary.

Brysis pulled her rapier blade and slashed at the tentacles. She cut deep into them, exposing fatty brown membrane. Brackish blue blood flowed from the wounds, and Brysis gagged at the pungent taste in her mouth. The tentacles lashed out blindly, slapping her once against the sharp wall that cut into her back. Another tongue found her foot and coiled around her leg. She cut at it until it released her.

The tentacles suddenly withdrew back inside the beast's mouth still covering the hole. Brysis looked around for escape, but the situation grew worse by the minute. Not only was she trapped, but her blood would likely draw ever-hungry sharks.

Brysis heard the strange gurgling sound first before feeling the pull of water. The beast inhaled, sucking water through its gills and Brysis toward its mouth. The pull strengthened; Brysis dropped her rapier and grabbed for the hole's sharp walls. She screamed again, the coral flaying the flesh from her palms and fingers. Her bloodied grip slipped, and she tumbled.

The beast's teeth were a forest surrounding her, its breath fetid with lodged chunks of carrion meat. She begged for a quick death; instead something shook the water hard. Brysis opened her eyes in time to see her foe pushed to the side. Brysis kicked away and clutched her bleeding hands under her armpits to staunch the flow of blood. She swam free and chanced a glance back. A small red whale battered the flanks of the creature again, dislodging it further from its perch.

It was the fox-whale, Brysis realized.

The beast shrieked in anger and turned on the fox-whale.

Brysis screamed at it to run, but the fox-whale rammed into the creature again.

The beast bit into the fox-whale; its mouth folds wrapped around the whale's flanks, its teeth hooked into its flesh. The fox-whale cried out and struggled in its foe's maw, tearing itself upon the thornlike thicket.

A primal scream ripped past Brysis's lips; a blood-red haze settled over her senses. She could no longer think; she only wanted to hurt, to kill this terrible thing. She launched herself back at her pursuer, to tear at it with her teeth if need be. Suddenly, something tackled her, sweeping its massive black and white arms around her and pinning her to its chest.

"Let me go!" Brysis shrieked, her throat torn by rage. She could barely hear Ashkoom's sad voice; it could not drown out the roar of blood in her ears, could not silence her own rabid cries. But the grip persisted, strong and gentle, and it pulled Brysis away from the fox-whale's death.

****

"How are your hands?"

Brysis barely registered the pain anymore; she had managed to wrap them in treated strips of seaweed, and a seaweed binding also covered her ribs and back.

"They're fine," Brysis said, trying to focus through her misery. The fox-whale's cry still echoed in her ears and hid in the shadows of her thoughts.

Ashkoom sat on a plateau, her back resting against the slope of the small butte. Brysis sat next to her, staring out across the darkening coral plains. The water grew chillier without the sun's warmth.

"Where's Echo Fury?" Brysis asked.

"Following the whales. They joined together again and grieved their friend's death. They are deep in swimming sleep now."

Brysis nodded. The whales could sleep for short bursts while swimming, as long as they were in the company of one another. "They're acting strangely. We better follow them. They'll swim slower now that they're asleep, but they're still ahead of us."

Ashkoom smiled. "My daughter is bright."

"I have a good teacher," Brysis said.

****

After retrieving the sea elf's rapier from where it lay in the hole, Brysis and Ashkoom swam through most of the night to reach the whales; the ocean strider carried her exhausted companion on her back for part of the journey. An hour before reaching the pod, they discovered a caravan of sharks and two king-titans heading in the same direction. The two companions took a wide berth around them and hurried forward. Later they understood the reason for the sharks. The water tasted of blood. Something had been badly wounded. The companions raced ahead.

Echo Fury remained behind the three whales, at a safe distance. The jester-whale was bleeding openly from long, straight gashes that ran from its head and flanks to its fluke. It appeared weak and drained. What Brysis understood from Echo Fury's excited chirps was that the jester-whale had done that to itself. The whale deliberately had charged into a thick coral grove, slicing itself open.

"Are they trying to kill themselves? Brysis asked Ashkoom as they swam after the whales. "Whales do beach themselves occasionally."

"But they do not provoke predators," Ashkoom said.

"The sharks will be upon them shortly. And they're still heading straight for Stone-Splitter's domains," Brysis said.

"In two days. Or if the dragon comes to them . . . less."

"What do we do?"

Ashkoom smiled and turned in the direction of the sharks. "Turn them into the bait." With that, the ocean strider spread her arms and swept them in wide circles. Her fingertips glowed, and her black eyes sparkled. Something pushed Brysis and an indignant Echo Fury back, the displacement of an emerging presence. Five kernels of turbulence-white water appeared around Ashkoom and expanded with surprising speed. Twin green orbs for eyes manifested within each, and in moments the waters churned and roiled to become sixteen-foot high elementals. Their eyes wavered but remained steady inside their wavelike bodies.

"Follow the whales," Ashkoom told Brysis. "More elementals will arrive to assist me. I will turn away the sharks!"

Brysis thought better of arguing. While the ocean striders rarely used their size to intimidate others, they remained fiercely stubborn. Brysis nodded and patted Echo Fury. A moment later, they charged after the whales.

****

Brysis blew a bleat of exasperation; Echo Fury studied his porpoise companion before offering her a soft chirp in reply. He understood her pain, the frustration that spilled over the lip of her thoughts. They continued swimming, however, following the whales through the dark waters.

Thankfully, thick drifts of invisible firefly motes filled the waters. The whales agitated the motes as they swam through the clouds, surrounding themselves in a soft green halo. From their distance, Brysis could easily see the gull-wing whale by the curls of dying light that spun off from her long flippers and elegant fluke.

Movement to the left of Brysis caught her eye. She turned in time to see the dying wisps of light fade away in the distant darkness, like catching the rainfall at its abrupt end; then there was nothing—nothing to disturb the firefly motes, or perhaps something smart enough to avoid them. She hissed to Echo Fury. Something swam abreast of them in the distance.

Echo Fury returned her worry; something else swam parallel to them on their right. Whatever they were, Brysis realized, they were smart enough to avoid the mote clouds and flank the whales.

Brysis and Echo Fury hurried forward, drawing closer to the pod while keeping a watchful eye all around them. They could finally see the crest-breaker whale clearly; it, too, looked left and right, knowing something followed them.

The crest-breaker uttered a low, creaking groan. The gull-wing whale moved closer to its compatriot; the jester-whale drifted farther out.

"What are they doing now?" Brysis cried, her voice a series of clicks.

Echo Fury uttered a bewildered chirp before charging forward.

"What are *you* doing?" Brysis screamed before racing after him.

Echo Fury paid her no heed. Instead he cried out, his voice caught between warning the whales and chastising them. The crest-breaker turned enough to see the war dolphin dashing forth from the murk, but it kept its gaze focused on the unseen threats. It appeared indecisive, uncertain who to deal with first. Echo Fury, however, veered away and swam after the wounded jester-whale. Brysis followed.

Everything unraveled at once. The crest-breaker called out a warning song. The gull-wing swam faster, barreling straight past its compatriot. The crest-breaker appeared ready to follow, but hesitated. The jester-whale veered farther away, toward danger, with a strangled cry on its lips. From the darkness ahead of the jester-whale, an abyss lurker appeared.

At first glance, the abyss lurker looked like a large squid, with multiple tentacles and an elongated head. But its thin white skin was translucent enough for them to see the veins and muscles beneath. It possessed one large eye, like a pool of blood, and at the spadelike head of each tentacle was a ring of needle teeth surrounding a suction mouth.

The abyss lurker's tentacles blossomed outward like a net, revealing its beaklike mouth; its limbs wrapped around the jester-whale's body. The whale cried in pain as the tentacles latched onto its skin and began pulsing. To Brysis's horror, the tentacles turned crimson as they fed off the thrashing whale. Crimson threads spread through the abyss lurker's body as stolen blood fed the different organs.

Brysis returned to her elf form and drew her rapier. Her hand screamed at the pain; her cuts were reopened, but she kept her grip. Echo Fury darted for the abyss lurker, and Brysis followed. She reached a large tentacle that easily measured twice her waist in size and stabbed it with her blade. After cutting several deep gashes into its rubbery flesh, the tentacle unraveled itself from the whale.

Brysis barely dodged the flaying tentacle that sought to swipe her aside. She swam up toward its head. She'd drawn in close when Echo Fury swam past and drove his bladed fin into the creature's eye. His passage popped open a long, deep gash across the eye; blood poured from the wound and filled the water with thick crimson rivulets. The abyss lurker shrieked in agony and released the limp jester-whale. As quickly as it had appeared, the creature vanished back into the darkness.

The jester-whale, its eyes glazed and with no brilliance, dropped away into the darkness. Its wounds no longer wept.

Brysis was about to swim after it when the crest-breaker let loose a trumpet cry.

A second abyss lurker appeared and rushed toward the crest-breaker. Unlike the weakened jester-whale, however, the crest-breaker fought fiercely. It jerked and swayed, staying clear of the groping tentacles. The second abyss lurker, however, had three blood-pool eyes and far more tentacles. It was certainly larger than its cousin.

The crest-breaker pivoted away from the tentacles and unleashed a discordant howl, a bladelike keening that cut through the water; slash wounds appeared across the abyss lurker's body. It severed one tentacle completely and cut an eye open. The abyss lurker shrieked in pain and lunged for the crest-breaker in sudden fury. A half-dozen mouth tentacles latched onto the whale, which immediately turned crimson from feeding.

The crest-breaker bucked and thrashed, only entangling itself further in its opponent's grasp. It cried out in pain, its voice shifting through a horizon's range of chords. Brysis and Echo Fury started forward, wanting to help, but nausea overcame them. The waters around the crest-breaker and abyss lurker shimmered with the whale's powerful voice and clouded with its spilled blood.

Brysis reached out to grab something to steady herself, but there was nothing but open water. Instead, she and Echo Fury tumbled and fought to regain their equilibrium. The crest-breaker, blinded by panic, had unleashed its songs without reserve, catching the sea elf and war dolphin in the wash of its voice.

Despite the vertigo, Brysis swam a drunken path toward the weakening crest-breaker and prevailing abyss lurker.

"No!" someone cried.

Suddenly Ashkoom swam past Brysis, her turbulent passage rattling the sea elf. But the scattered effects of the crest-breaker's song were already fading, and Brysis felt strong enough to chase after her friend.

The ocean strider swam for the abyss lurker, with Brysis feeling useless as she followed. Ashkoom cut at its tentacles. Brysis and Echo Fury also charged, intent on blinding the monster.

Three tentacles dislodged themselves from the whale's flesh with sickening pops; the abyss lurker batted at Ashkoom, trying to keep her at bay, but the ocean strider swung back with equal determination.

Brysis and Echo Fury had targeted the head, but the abyss lurker constantly twisted and jerked away, trying to keep its diminutive opponents away from its two remaining eyes. Brysis lunged and jabbed at an eye, but she caught the abyss lurker's rubbery skin. Her rapier stuck in its flesh, and the creature twisted away, tearing the blade from her wounded hands. She pulled her serrated dagger from its sheath and continued stabbing.

The abyss lurker swung its head into Brysis and Echo Fury, slamming them both with a moving wall of flesh. A stunned Brysis spun away and caught a glimpse of Ashkoom severing another tentacle with her falchion.

"Away!" Ashkoom cried. "Move!"

Brysis hesitated for a split second, long enough to clear her head. She grabbed Echo Fury's dorsal fin and pulled at him to follow. He regained his senses and sped away, Brysis barely holding on. A few seconds later, they swam clear of the combatants; Brysis turned in time to watch Ashkoom stretch out one hand toward the abyss lurker's head. Her hand shimmered, and the monster screamed. Its skin grew tight and burst in places where beads of viscous white liquid appeared. The three eyes bled red globules of blood that instantly diffused in the water before the eyes themselves shriveled.

The abyss lurker shrieked once before letting go of the crest-breaker. It tried to swim away, but its tentacles had also withered; it gurgled, stopped, and floated there, dead.

Brysis and Echo Fury swam up to Ashkoom as she checked the crest-breaker's injuries. The whale appeared severely weakened, but alive. It watched them carefully but did not impede their approach.

"What was that spell?" Brysis asked.

"A spell to steal moisture," Ashkoom replied. "But indiscriminate. Could not risk hurting the crest-breaker. Or you, my daughter."

Brysis nodded. "Thank you," she said. "What of the sharks?"

"I give them pause. But more come . . . many more."

Brysis swam up to one of the crest-breaker's lilac eyes. The whale studied her, almost as though sizing her up. The eye flared with inner light and glowed. A heavy, creaking groan filled Brysis's thoughts with words.

Leave, the female voice said. *We have come to die . . .*

****

They couldn't very well remain; the battle had spilled its share of blood, and already carrion-eating giant crabs and sharks fought over the corpses of the jester-whale and the abyss lurker.

The crest-breaker swam, her strength diminished, but her course steady; the three companions accompanied the whale and the surviving gull-wing deeper into predator-filled water, to the domains of Stone-Splitter.

"Why did you attack us earlier?" Brysis asked.

The crest-breaker paused before an image filled their thoughts . . . Ashkoom's image. Ocean striders were rare creatures; the whale had not understood what or who she was. She'd never seen Ashkoom's like before.

"Yet you swim in dangerous waters—endanger yourselves. Two have died, and neither to me," Ashkoom said, indignant.

It is necessary, the whale responded in a voice that filled Brysis's and Ashkoom's thoughts. *We couldn't die too early.*

"Why are you doing this?" Brysis asked.

The world melted away as the thought in the crest breaker's mind superseded their own reality. The ocean grew clearer. Light suffused every particle of water, and the song of whales filled the seas. Brysis, Ashkoom, and Echo Fury floated there, all of them seeing the same thing. The image was elsewhere, an ocean far away, one that was strange and wondrous to them. Brysis stopped breathing, afraid she might somehow shatter the vision given to them by the crest-breaker. They could see for miles, the water of breathtaking crystalline clarity, the sky above a brilliant azure roof with soft, white clouds.

In the distant waters, spots of blue, green, and white light approached. They numbered in the dozens. As they neared, the lights took form, becoming whales wreathed in shimmering auras. The dozens grew into a hundred, then two hundred, perhaps more. They represented every species of whale—gull-wings, blade-tips, jesters, crest-breakers, tusk-maws, fox-whales, and a score of others—and like a great fleet, they were sailing past the companions. Their songs echoed through the vast blue.

Seeing it through the crest-breaker's eyes, Brysis understood with unequaled clarity. It was a great migration of many pods to safer waters.

It will take them two seasons to reach new oceans. Many will die in the journey, but fewer because of our sacrifice.

Brysis watched the passage in awe. She understood more. The great migration would pass near the waters they swam in soon, near to where the great predators hunted. Brysis shivered, her realization chilling her to the bone. "Unless you distract the predators. You're deliberately leading the predators elsewhere," Brysis said. "That's why the jester-whale injured itself? To draw the them away with its blood."

"You journey for the dragon Stone-Splitter," Ashkoom said.

One of us must reach him, the crest-breaker said in her deep voice. *The predators will fight for our remains and perhaps sate their hunger on each other. They will never know a greater meal has passed them by.*

"Surely there is another way?" Brysis asked.

The vision of the whales faded, and the companions found themselves back in the familiar surroundings. The gull-wing and crest-breaker continued swimming.

Without death, memories are meaningless, the crest-breaker said. *We are committed to this course.*

Brysis, Echo Fury, and Ashkoom remained silent a moment. They studied one another. They shared the same thought.

"We will help," Brysis said. "And we aren't asking."

"My daughter," Ashkoom said with a smile. "She is stubborn."

Very well.

"What is your name?" Brysis asked.

My name? the whale responded. *My name is one hundred summers long and it grows longer with each song I sing. All whales have names that span their lives; it changes as we do. But my name begins...* and with that, the crest-breaker unleashed a rumbling moan that danced in pitch. Brysis closed her eyes and repeated the song so she might never forget.

****

The friends swam for another day, but the crest-breaker grew steadily weaker from blood loss. Her wounds continued to seep with crimson ribbons. Her sea-green skin had turned dull green, and she swam as though dazed. The gull-wing had to bump into her to prevent her from veering from their course.

Ashkoom returned from scouting behind them, but she swam at top speed.

"They come!" Ashkoom said, gasping. "Four king-titan sharks. More maybe. I saw two giant galleon-crusher crabs. And abyss lurkers. Sharks, sea lions—all gathering for the feast."

Brysis turned toward the crest-breaker and nodded.

The crest-breaker opened her tooth-lined maw. A slow distress keen escaped her lips. At first it emerged weakly, pitiful, but it rose in pitch. Brysis and her friends winced at the wailing cry that sounded like two notes grating against one another, then three, then a chorus. So many notes from the same throat, each a different octave; it would carry across long distances, through Stone-Splitter's domain.

And it would draw the predators in for the kill.

"Protect the whales until Stone-Splitter arrives . . . or for as long as we can!" Brysis shouted.

Ashkoom nodded and prepared her spells, the ones natural to her species.

Echo Fury cried out a warning. The predators were drawing near.

****

The two galleon-crusher crabs arrived first, scuttling across the seafloor and skittering below the whales. The normally predatory creatures waited patiently for whatever meal ventured too close to their claws. Next followed several species of large sharks, some of which fell prey to the galleon-crushers. Then the true assault followed with the appearance of three king-titans, each more than sixty feet in length. Their strategy, from what Brysis remembered, would consist of brushing up against their prey and drawing blood into the water to taste it. Then they would attack.

Ashkoom, however, had summoned more water elementals to buffer the whales. When the king-titans approached, the water elementals attempted to repulse them. This only served to agitate the monstrous sharks, which grew more frenzied with the smell of whale blood in the water. Two of the king-titans turned on the smaller predators, devouring great whites and a small abyss lurker in a single bite. More blood touched the senses, and larger abyss lurkers arrived.

Brysis, Ashkoom, and Echo Fury remained close to the whales, the open water growing far too dangerous. Sharks savaged one another in feeding frenzies, two abyss lurkers latched onto a king-titan shark and struggled to bring it down, while the other two king-titans swam in tighter circles around the whales, in preparation for the final attack.

"Here they come," Brysis shouted.

Ashkoom extended her hand toward the nearest king-titan as it abruptly altered course and headed straight for them. The water around the shark grew opaque with frost and echoed with cracking ice. Frost blisters appeared on the king-titan's snout, and it veered away.

The crest-breaker faced the other king-titan as it passed and unleashed her lacerating cry. The effort seemed to drain her further, but her foe veered away with deep-grooved cuts along its flanks.

More predators made darting runs at the whales, but the elementals kept the smaller ones at bay. Several of the large abyss lurkers and king-titans rammed through one or more elementals, ripping them apart or sending them reeling. For those, Ashkoom reserved her strongest abilities—her withering spell that drained the target of water, her crippling ice cone, or the kiss of her falchion. And when too many elementals fell to the predators, Ashkoom summoned a handful more.

Brysis cursed. She felt helpless—a gnat among giants. She possessed no spells to help their cause, and her rapier, which she'd retrieved from the dead abyss lurker, was a poor stinger at best. Even Echo Fury proved useful, making darting runs against the abyss lurkers and king-titans with his bladed fins before retreating to the elementals.

She could no longer abide watching her friends fight without her. Brysis allowed the warmth of change to rush through her and melt her features; she turned into a porpoise. If she could not fight, she would help distract. She bolted away from the safety of the elementals. Ashkoom called out after her, but Brysis paid little heed. She had to assist somehow. She could not wait and watch as a bystander alone.

Within seconds, Echo Fury had joined her, but

rather than chastise her, he bleated joyfully. Happiness and combat were intertwined for war dolphins; regardless of the cost, all that mattered to him was the fight.

Brysis and Echo Fury tore through the water, darting above large sharks and below the grasping tentacles of abyss lurkers. The ocean reeked of blood and ichor, and Brysis gagged on the hard stench. Echo Fury, however, seemed to revel in it. He dashed by a sleek harrow-chaser shark, cutting it with a bladed fin; as the shark whipped around to chase Echo Fury, Brysis barreled into its wound, stunning the shark with a ramming blow. Bleeding and senseless from the pain, it made for easy prey to its companions.

The pair continued in that manner for what seemed like hours, racing and weaving, covering one another and wounding sharks and lurkers alike. They also saw the occasional sea lion with its webbed lion's forepaws and head and its seal-like tail; the waters grew thicker with enemies. It was a feeding frenzy unlike any Brysis had ever seen, one that stretched from gloomy horizon to gloomy horizon.

At long last, the pair swept past the whales. Ashkoom continued fighting alongside a handful of surviving elementals, but she relied on her blade. She appeared exhausted, her repertoire of natural spellcraft almost depleted. The crest-breaker was likewise bereft, though some of her wounds continued to bleed in faint trickles. The gull-wing whale bore several gashes and bites from opponents, but he fought with surprising determination and battered anything that tried approaching.

Brysis was unsure how long they could persevere, but they continued fighting long after the last elemental had fallen and long after a king-titan had managed to shear away part of the gull-wing's elegant flipper.

And still they battled. Their only saving grace was that the predators fought one another as well. The whales seemed to be a prize for only a few monsters of the deep. All others devoured the easier meals around them.

****

Brysis fought, even though her muscles had tightened into bundles of heavy iron. A roar, loud and relentless, carried across the water, waking Brysis from her near reverie of fighting. For a moment, the battlefield paused, predator and prey alike turning in the direction of the newcomer.

Stone-Splitter had arrived, its voice unmistakable.

The smaller beasts reacted quickly, bolting in dozens of directions.

Ashkoom, her body lacerated with dozens of small wounds, motioned outward, to where the thickest swarms of predators swam. That ability she held in check until the last possible moment—the power to control water levels. She furrowed her brows in concentration before an enormous swath of water, more than two hundred feet wide and long, and more than forty feet deep, simply dropped away from the ocean above. After the barest of pauses, the ocean above suddenly collapsed into the gap with a thunderous clap that sent shock waves through the water. Most beasts caught within it were crushed by the falling weight. Others were rendered senseless.

Ashkoom was not done. Again she unleashed her spell, targeting a different group of predators to stop as many of them as possible from fleeing.

Thunder rocked and pitched the ocean three more times.

Another roar wracked the waters. Brysis could see Stone-Splitter. Although it measured smaller than the king-titans in length, almost nothing could equal this brutal dragon's ferocity. Sharp ridges lined its turtle-shell back from which emerged a dragon's head, two gigantic webbed foreclaws, and a long finned tail. Gold and silver highlights on its green scales and shell glittered. It cried once more with its beaklike mouth before unleashing a gout of steam on a nearby king-titan. All creatures caught in that scalding column died instantly.

"Leave," Ashkoom cried, "now!"

As rehearsed, the three companions rose to the surface, swimming as fast as they could. Brysis glanced back once at the scene of carnage below and cried her farewell.

Thank you, a voice said, barely casting a ripple in her thoughts. It was so faint that a moment later Brysis wondered if she'd heard it at all.

Brysis looked skyward again until the ocean above lightened with the sunlit sky. Nothing followed them up from the roars and cries of the darkness.

****

Apoletta, Steward of Istar, was a beautiful sea elf with pearl-white skin, long silver hair that floated gently, and almond-shaped eyes the color of clear emeralds. She wore a long pearl-covered green gown that was slit along its length to permit freedom of movement.

"Ashkoom?" Apoletta asked. "She is well?"

Brysis nodded. "Yes . . . and she is a good teacher."

"What does she make of this?"

"It isn't good, that's certain. Many whales are leaving the Courrain oceans for safer waters. That will throw the local wildlife into disarray. We lost some significant companions. And soon, when the World Gash poisons the waters we just left, the predators will flock elsewhere. Some will come here."

"I know," Apoletta said. "I must consult with the other stewards to decide on a course of action."

Brysis nodded. "Ashkoom and I will try to find more crest-breakers. They seem to be the ones leading the great migration. Now that we've helped them, maybe they'll be willing to talk with us."

"I hope so, for all our sakes."

"I better go. Ashkoom is waiting for me beyond the Sea of Istar."

Apoletta smiled and pulled Brysis into her embrace. Brysis stiffened at first, then returned the warm hug. Apoletta pulled away and gently held Brysis's wrists, bringing her hands up to examine the wounds.

"You should see a priest," Apoletta said.

"It's all right," Brysis replied. "I don't want to easily forget what happened."

"Don't they hurt?"

Brysis smiled. They did sting, but her thoughts seemed to linger more upon a melody than the pain.

The opening chords of the crest-breaker's name resounded in her thoughts with a strange clarity. And hearing it brought her peace.

"They don't hurt," Brysis replied. "At least . . . no more than life."

Apoletta smiled, and though obviously bewildered by the comment, she nodded. "Fair journey, Brysis."

Brysis smiled and allowed the flush of change to overtake her. She left the steward's palace as a porpoise, singing out loud the crest-breaker's name. And the whales that served Istar returned her voice with their own melodies, each of them sharing a part of their history, each incorporating the crest-breaker's song into their own lifelong name.

The Eight

Miranda Horner

Some people suspect that Mary H. Herbert has a split personality. By day she is a mild-mannered paraprofessional working with special-ed students at a middle school, but by night she turns into a free-lance writer who has written fourteen novels, three Forgotten Realms stories, and several stories, reports, and bits for Dragonlance guides. She is very familiar with sleep deprivation. She still lives near Atlanta, has the same husband, the same two kids, and a dog. Why change a good thing? Her latest Dragonlance work is the *Linsha* Trilogy. She is currently working on her seventh book in her own Dark Horse series.

The Eight

Mary H. Herbert

Age of Mortals, 425 AC

Linsha lay on her back, staring at the ceiling and counting the cracks. She reached the same number: five. Five large cracks split the stone above her head. In truth, it wasn't the number of cracks that held her attention so much as the fact the cracks were getting bigger. A little while ago, those cracks hadn't been there at all. The large pieces of stone that lay around Linsha and on top of her had been a part of the ceiling. Then the mountain had hiccupped, an earthquake shook the tunnels, and there she lay, trapped in a cave-in where she wasn't supposed to be, and no one knew she was there.

One creature might know where she was, but she didn't have much faith in that one going for help, even if he realized what had happened. He was worse than a kender, sometimes. He'd get distracted by something or someone, and by the time he remembered to tell Crucible, the cracks probably would have joined together and another section of the fragile roof would have collapsed and that would be all. Her soul would join that of the guard who had pushed her back up the tunnel and now lay somewhere near her legs. He had not been so lucky.

Linsha tried to breathe slowly and carefully. She *had* been lucky in that first fall of rocks because the dropping slabs had pinned her legs and hips without crushing her. She had a broken thigh—she knew that—a few cracked ribs, and a multitude of bruises, but so far her lungs and heart and head still functioned. She had used her mystic powers of the heart, the one little hint of magic ability she possessed, to ease the pain in her legs and chest, but she did not have enough strength left or real talent to heal the bones, lift the stones, and get herself out.

Holding very still, she extended her senses outward to try to touch the aura of anyone close by. Anyone! But the caverns and tunnels around her were empty. And why not? No one in their right mind came down there. Even the shadowpeople avoided the place.

"Children!" The word rose like an annoyed hiss from the back of her throat.

Gods of all, if she heard anyone—servants, townsfolk, officers, knights, merchants, sailors, anyone—complain about *their* children, she would lock them in the dungeon of the palace with *her* children, all eight of them. People just didn't have an inkling of what it was like to be a human mother to eight four-year-old brass wyrmlings. Who else had children that were four to five feet long, flew, ate everything in sight, breathed flame, were endlessly curious, and were so gregarious they could talk the sun out of the sky?

Oh, they each had their own personality traits and quirks, but unlike many dragon nestlings, they were almost inseparable. Where one went, they all went . . . usually.

Linsha turned her head to avoid looking at the cracks above her. A pounding headache made her temples throb and interfered with her ability to think. From the hot stink of sulfur that wafted through the cracks and openings in the rockfall, she suspected her small prison was filling with gases from the volcano. Her lamp had miraculously survived the fall and sat only an arm's length away from her head. Its flame had an odd bluish tinge, but as long as it still burned, Linsha hoped that meant there was enough air to keep her alive.

Her vision wavered out of focus and she shut her eyes. *Crucible, please come!* her soul cried.

"He's not here. He's at the mines," she told herself fiercely. Desperate to keep a grip on her thoughts, she opened her eyes again and saw a glint of reddish light and heard what sounded like a grinding. She squinted hard to see what it was. "Eight? Is that you? Go get Crucible, please!"

Whatever it was, it was gone. She heard only silence. Darkness gathered around her in dense shadows. Somewhere, far away, the mountain rumbled again, and Linsha felt the slight tremble in the stone. Small pieces of rock pattered down around her, and dust filled the air.

She groaned. Her head felt as heavy as lead; her skin was cold and clammy in spite of the hot air. How ironic, she thought, that she survived plague, war, slavery, attacks, betrayal, a duel, a death sentence, and a sea voyage only to die in an abandoned tunnel near the ruins of the Temple of Luerkhisis on Mount Thunderhorn. All because a rambunctious wyrmling decided . . .

"But Lady Linsha, it wasn't my fault!"

She could hear his high, childish voice as clearly as she had that morning. Her eyes drifted closed, and she heard herself reply, "Yes, it was! I saw you chase Ashfall down the hall. You know you're not supposed to fly in the palace! You're too big. You have an entire valley and three mountains to fly around. Why do you have to do it inside?" Even to herself, Linsha knew she sounded aggravated and peevish.

"But it's raining outside, and Sir Hugh promised us a visit," Eight pointed out, as if the answer were perfectly obvious.

Linsha silently cursed her friend, Sir Hugh Bronan. The wyrmlings loved the knight's visits because he told them tales of the War of Souls, of Crucible, and of the great brass dragon Iyesta. They would sit quietly for him when he talked, but if he were late or had to cancel his visit, they would take their disappointment out on everyone in the palace.

Linsha looked down at Eight's unrepentant expression, then down to the torn mess on the floor that had once been a priceless Ergothian tapestry. After a violent tug-of-war performed in midair through the huge assembly hall and several corridors of the palace, the irreplaceable tapestry was a total loss. Ashfall, the other perpetrator, was nowhere to be seen.

"This tapestry was a favorite of Lord Bight's. He is not going to be happy." Linsha saw Eight cringe, and she knew she had said the wrong thing. Hogan Bight was the human name of the bronze dragon Crucible, who served as lord governor of Sanction and mentor to the eight baby brasses. As such, he commanded their utmost respect and obedience.

Linsha was a nondragon, and although she had forged an unusually strong bond with the brasses, every once in a while, they would reveal to her an attitude of arrogance and smug disdain. She knew she should never defer to Crucible's authority if she ever wanted to keep the wyrmlings' respect. She would have to handle the situation herself.

"I want you to take this tapestry to the weavers' guild and ask if anyone can fix it. Then you and Ashfall will apologize to the guards you knocked over and clean up the glass you broke in the window in the north wall of the hall."

The baby dragon tilted his plated head away from her and grumbled something. The only word Linsha caught was *pothoc,* the Draconic word for *stupid.* She'd learned enough of the ancient dragon language from Crucible to know that and many others.

She thrust the ruined tapestry at the small dragon and snapped, *"Gethrisj!"* Go!

His yellow-brown eyes rolled as if he wanted to argue, but he flipped his wings, snatched the tapestry in his mouth, and turned his back on her.

She watched him carry the tapestry out the door, heading—she hoped—for the front doors. The big weaving was bigger than he was and dragged on either side of his body. It would be a muddy mess by the time he carried it through the rain to the weavers, not that it mattered. It was ruined already. The point was, Eight had to make an effort to repair the damage he had done.

She shook her head as she went to check on the other wyrmlings. Since young dragons chose their own names, she and Crucible had simply called them One to Eight for simplicity's sake. Only Eight still clung to his hatchling name, while the others had chosen names taken from the Lords of Doom, the three volcanoes where they liked to explore. Ashfall was the oldest and usually the most reliable. Linsha intended to have a word with him, too.

Linsha stirred slightly, and her awareness returned to her stone prison. She could feel more pain in her hips and back, along her side, and into her neck. Her skin was cold and numb where the rocks pressed her down; her throat and mouth were parched. She tried to ignore the sensation of hundreds of pounds of rocks lying on top of her and blessed the god Kiri-Jolith that one of those rocks had landed beside her in such a way as to protect her from the worst of the crushing weight. It was unfortunate that the rock wasn't big enough to protect all of her if more of the tunnel's ceiling collapsed.

She tried to focus her mind on her mystic power, so by channeling the power to her broken leg and ribs, she could numb the pain for a little while longer, but she knew she was getting weaker. Shock was setting in. Before long, she would not be able to summon any magic, her body would shut down, and she would drift into unconsciousness—if the ceiling didn't crash first or the air didn't go foul or . . .

Linsha veered away from such thoughts. She had to stay alert in case Eight came back or Varia found her, or perhaps Crucible would return.

She sighed. Crucible would not return, at least not in time. He had gone to the mines on the southern edge of Sanction Vale to investigate several new veins of silver. He would be furious about the tapestry. It had been one of his treasured possessions.

Her eyes closed again, and her thoughts slid back to that morning. It had taken her a while to look for the wyrmlings. There were so many places just around the palace where they liked to go. They were not in their favorite sandpile in the courtyard, nor were they exploring the lower levels where the stores and the wine vats were kept. After a frustrated search, she finally found one of the governor's guards coming off duty who reported he'd seen Eight go down the hill toward the north postern gate.

The north gate, Linsha noted, not the road into Sanction. She also noted that the day was waning and the weather worsening. What would possess Eight to go out of the city in that weather, and where was he going? She thought about wakening Varia to fetch Crucible and finally decided to let the bird sleep. The storm was getting too rough for a small owl.

Fuming, she ordered a horse to be saddled. She could just let Eight go and wait for him to come back, but she was not going to allow him to ignore her. It was the principle of the thing.

Two governor's guards joined her and escorted her

out into the pouring rain. The wyrmling's trail was easy to follow in the soft, wet ground, and as she had been told, he had made a straight path toward the northern postern gate that led through the city walls to a path over the north pass. At the small gate, the guard showed Linsha the wet, muddy ruin of the tapestry that Eight had abandoned by the wall.

"He went out that way, Lady," the guard said, and pointed east toward Mount Thunderhorn. "He dropped that rag and took off like an arrow for the peak."

Thunderhorn, Linsha pondered. A chill of foreboding frosted her thoughts. The wyrmlings often played and explored on the flanks of the great volcano, but Crucible had forbidden them from entering the secret passages. Why would Eight go there alone?

She cantered her horse around the eastern walls, her escorts close on her heels, and entered the fortified camp where the city guards trained and the garrison of the Knights of Solamnia maintained a constant watch on the passes. The threat of invasion from the Knights of Neraka had lifted at the end of the War of Souls, but Sanction was a prize that still had her share of enemies, prompting Lord Bight to keep a close watch on the mountain roads. At the main fortifications, other soldiers and guards confirmed they had seen Eight fly by, cross the lava moat, and head up the mountain's flank.

Linsha glanced up the mountainside where the clouds and steam crowned the towering summit. The wyrmling was nowhere in sight. She muttered several words she had learned as an alley basher; then, leaving the horses at the main fortifications, she and the two guards hurried over the lava moat where the heavy rain hissed and turned into instant vapor on the slow-moving stream of lava.

They hiked up the rough trail toward the ledge on the side of the mountain where a cavern opened into the volcano's interior and Crucible made his own private lair. He seldom used the cave for anything more than a work space to wield the powerful forces of magic he used to control the three Lords of Doom, but he had forbidden the brasses from entering and considered it to be his domain. The cave, Linsha knew, led into the bowels of the volcano and delved into the labyrinth of caves, tunnels, passages, and secret places that ran like woodworm holes under the entire city and vale.

By the time they reached the ledge, the three humans were soaked and weary. Linsha looked gloomily into the interior of the cave, and there, on the dry floor, were the damp, muddy tracks of a young dragon. In the back she could see the glow from the deep crevice where an underground stream of magma flowed. It radiated just enough light to prove the cave was empty of small dragons.

"Send word to Lord Bight," she ordered. "I'm going after Eight."

"My lady, wouldn't it be better to wait for the Lord Governor?" suggested one of the guards.

"Probably. But it will take too long to reach him. I don't know where Eight is going, but he has no reason to go down there. It's too dangerous."

The guards exchanged exasperated glances. They knew if the caverns were too dangerous for a young dragon, they would certainly be too dangerous for humans. But they did not say as much. They knew

Linsha too well to waste the breath. One guard bowed to the lady knight and hurried back the way they had come to retrieve his horse. The remaining guard loosened his sword and nodded his readiness.

Linsha took a deep breath of cool, rain-soaked air and strode into the cave. On the summit above, Thunderhorn grumbled and hissed steam into the storm-wracked afternoon.

****

Less than a mile from Linsha's stone prison, Eight lifted his head suspiciously. Something had moved in the black corridor behind him. He listened for a moment, then turned away and headed for the passage that he hoped would lead him to the cave entrance. He had to get out, get help. He never imagined Linsha would follow him, never. Why had she done that? Now she was trapped, and he had to find help before the mountain caved in on her. If something happened to Linsha, he dreaded to think how Crucible would react.

He kept moving, unaware of his own danger, for besides Crucible's possible reactions, there was a dreadful, hot terror in his own heart that Linsha could die. That prospect burned away his original plans, consumed his attention, and clouded his sense of self-preservation. He sped on through the dark caves until he finally spotted the dull glow of red from the open crevice in Crucible's cave. He hurried out into the rain, unaware that he had been followed.

****

In the highest room of the tallest tower of the governor's palace, seven baby brasses lay curled in various poses of sleep, lulled by the sound of the wind and the pounding rain outside.

One wyrmling, a dark-greenish-brown brass, lifted his chunky head and stared worriedly at a point vaguely east. His amber eyes closed and abruptly popped open in consternation.

"Eight is in trouble," Ashfall said.

"Again?" Caldera yawned.

"Where is he?" grumbled Smoke.

Ashfall stared fixedly at a window. "Thunderhorn. I sense danger."

"Of course. It's Eight. What's he doing out there in this weather?" Fumarole sighed, knowing she was going to have to go outside.

While the other six wyrmlings uncurled and rolled to their feet, Ashfall clawed open the barred shutters in a narrow window and stared out into the storm and gloom. He spotted a small, dark spot that struggled toward the palace through the winds and blowing rain. The nestlings waited impatiently until Eight flopped wearily through the window and dropped to the floor in a puddle of water.

"What have you done now?" Fumarole asked with haughty exasperation.

Eight ignored her. His dark yellow eyes were filled with alarm and worry. He told his nestmates everything that had happened. "I knew she was following! I just didn't want to stop. Then the mountain shook and the roof collapsed!"

Firestream snorted. "*Why* did you go in that mountain? Why didn't you just—"

"Because," Eight cut him off and went on in a rushed voice, "I remembered Sir Hugh's tale of the temple and the red dragon that used to live in the cave and I thought, maybe, there was some treasure down there that Crucible hadn't found. I just wanted to find something to replace the tapestry. He's going to be furious."

Ashfall looked abashed, and the others nodded with sympathetic understanding. Crucible's temper was known all too well.

"And now you've made it worse," Smoke pointed out with the smugness of someone who is very glad she is not in the same position.

Windstone looked worried as a streak of lightning seared across the clouds and thunder shook the tower. "Are you sure she's alive?"

"Yes, I heard her," Eight cried. "I never thought she'd follow me!"

"Should we find Crucible?" asked Caldera.

Eight shook himself off and went back to the window. "There's no time. We don't know where he is. We have to get her out now."

"But the Temple of Luerkhisis and Crucible's lair?" said Fumarole. "We're not supposed to go within. There's *things* in there."

"Linsha went after him," Ashfall pointed out in a voice that brooked no more argument. Without waiting for the others, he slid over the window ledge and launched himself into the wind. Eight and Caldera followed close behind. The remaining five scrambled to the window. They tangled, necks, wings, and legs in their enthusiasm to push through the narrow window at once. Finally they sorted themselves out, took wing into the heart of the storm, and followed Ashfall toward the massive peak of Mount Thunderhorn.

****

Linsha blinked and stared blearily at the ceiling again. Was that a sixth crack? There had been five before. Or was it six? She couldn't remember. She could barely focus on the cracks anymore. Her light had dwindled to a dull flame, and when it went out, she would be cast into a shroud of impenetrable darkness. The darkness was already there, just beyond the feeble edges of her lantern. It brooded, waiting to move back and claim its rightful place.

Something else waited, too. Linsha hadn't paid much attention to the noises at first because the creatures had kept their distance while the lantern burned, but as the flame faded, she could hear them move closer over the rocks. They made a dry, whispery clacking sound that stirred bitter memories. Unbidden and unwanted, the image of the corpse of Iyesta, the huge, magnificent brass dragon, returned to her thoughts. The dead dragon had been reduced to tattered bones and piles of scales in just a few days by the same kind of creature that rustled and skittered among the rocks only a few feet away from her body . . .

Carrion beetles. She had already felt a few crawl by her legs under the tumbled stones as they drew in to feed on the dead guard at her feet. Linsha shuddered.

She pulled the lantern a little closer to her head and adjusted the wick, which brightened the light from a firefly glow to a candle's gleam. But the adjustment would burn the fuel and wick faster, and there wasn't much left. She was debating turning the wick down again when a beetle scurried over her face. With a half-strangled scream, she batted frantically at the large insect. It dropped off and vanished into a crack. The chittering noise grew louder.

"Eight!" Linsha shouted. "Are you there?" Her voice dropped to a mournful murmur. "Where are you?"

Gods above, she thought, listening to her heart pound in her chest. She had always understood that in her chosen service as a Knight of Solamnia, she would have to face death, probably sooner than later. In her twenty-seven years in the Solamnic Order she had escaped death more times than she could remember. But each time there had been others around her. They might have been trying to kill her, but at least there were faces to look at, dangers to avoid, friends to watch her back, or living beings she cared about to keep her company. Never had she been so close to death and so utterly alone.

Tears welled up in her eyes. *Crucible.* Her thoughts beat outward into the empty passages and caves. He had found her on the open Courrain Ocean. Couldn't he find her in his own mountain?

Not if he did not know to look, she thought. Her heart ached for him, for the man he chose to be with the strong hands and the deep golden eyes like wellsprings of wisdom and love. She could imagine him striding into the tunnel where she lay, moving aside the heavy stones with ease, lifting her in his arms, and carrying her out of the cave to safety.

Her eyes slid closed again. "Crucible," she whispered.

The carrion beetles scuttled closer.

****

Weary and wet, the eight wyrmlings landed on the ledge before Crucible's cavern and ran thankfully out of the tempestuous rain into the hot cave. In front of them, the cave stretched back about a hundred paces into the flank of the mountain to a deep crevice that glowed from the magma's reddish orange light. Just to the right of the open crack was the tunnel Eight had taken to leave the mountain, the tunnel they needed to reach Linsha.

Eight hurried forward, the dull red light reflecting in his large eyes, while the others came behind. So determined was he to reach the lower levels, he did not see the strange, fiery creature that rose from the magma stream and reared out of the crevice beside him.

The others did. Crying a warning, Ashfall and Firestream lunged after their nestmate and slammed him forward just as the large fire dragon swung its head toward him, its mouth gaping open to snatch him. The fire dragon's teeth missed Eight's body and closed instead on the tip of Ashfall's membranous wing. Before the fire dragon could swing the terrified wyrmling up out of reach, Firestream twisted around and grabbed Ashfall's tail. Eight snatched a leg, and both wyrmlings pulled desperately. Ashfall squealed in pain and terror.

For a moment, Ashfall was caught between the two brasses and the fire dragon in a terrible tug-of-war for his life. Then the fire dragon's searing mouth burned through the wyrmling's wing, and Ashfall tumbled back to his brothers' feet. They wrenched him backward into the momentary safety of the tunnel as the creature subsided back into the crevice and studied them malevolently.

The other wyrmlings scrambled back to the mouth of the cave and huddled in the rain. Five heads craned around the edge of the opening.

"Did you *see* that thing?" breathed Windstone.

A tense silence hovered in the cavern while the wyrmlings stared at the fire dragon and at each other and tried to decide what to do. Fire dragons lived and thrived in the searing heat of places such as the Lords of Doom, and although they were rare and wary of Crucible, they were rapacious, vicious, and a menace to dragons as small as the baby brasses. They also were extremely hard to kill.

Ashfall panted in pain. The burns on his wings were agonizing. "Where did that beast come from?" he hissed. "Did you know it was there?"

"No!" Eight wailed. "The fire dragons usually stay away from Crucible's lair. It wasn't here when I left." He hesitated, mulling a thought that came to him. Had something been following him earlier? Fire dragons could bore through solid rock, or follow the flows of magma through a mountain. Had that one been the source of the noise behind him in the dark? But if so, why was it still there?

The creature, lurking in the crevice, glared at them

through eyes that flared like embers. It was a strange-looking beast, even to the brasses, for while it resembled a living dragon, fire dragons had been created from molten rock by Chaos, the Father of All and Nothing. Their wings were charred leather; their scales were formed by the cooled volcanic magma where its surface touched the air. Between the scales that shifted and bumped as the dragon moved could be seen the faint reddish glow of its internal heat. Spikes like shards of stone ran up its back and crowned its head with stony horns. Long, wicked talons, as black and shining as obsidian, curved over the edge of the rock crevice where the dragon crouched.

"How do we get past that thing?" Caldera called to the three in the passage.

Ashfall closed his eyes. Although some adult dragons could communicate telepathically when they wanted to, Ashfall was the first of the eight nestlings to be able to do so. While he could not read another's mind, he could sense powerful emotions in his nestmates, transfer his thoughts to them, and often knew when they needed help. Ignoring his pain, he focused his thoughts on his sister and reached out to her with a silent message. *Do not try. We will go to Linsha. You get help.*

"Get help where?" she shouted back. "And how do we find you again?"

I don't know! You think of something.

"He said what?" Smoke hissed. Caldera repeated the message from Ashfall.

"But we have to get past that dragon," Smoke insisted. "They need us!"

"We can't fight it," Fumarole said, pressing back out

of the sight of those fiery eyes. "It's at least twenty-five feet long, and the passage is too narrow to squeeze by. We should do as he says and get help."

Caldera crouched, fuming with indecision. "From whom? Who is out here that can fight a fire dragon?"

"The shadowpeople?" Sulfur suggested.

A brief thoughtful silence followed.

All at once the other four burst out in loud comment.

"Is that supposed to be a joke?"

"They won't talk to us."

"We're not allowed!"

"Crucible forbade—"

"Linsha is under a cave-in," Sulfur pointed out. "If we don't get her out soon, she will die. We can go down through the ruins of the old temple of Duerghast."

The wyrmlings looked at one another again.

"How do you know about an entrance in the ruin?" Smoke demanded.

Sulfur shrugged his wings. "Linsha told us. In a story about her journey with Crucible to meet Sable."

"She did not," snorted Smoke.

"Yes, she did!"

A fireball suddenly seared through the wet air in a brilliant blaze of gold and exploded on the rock ledge behind them. A second firebomb blasted out of the dark and struck the stone entry close to where the wyrmlings huddled. The sudden boom shook them. The fire dragon howled like a gas vent.

We have to get out of here, Ashfall sent the message to Caldera. *Come soon.*

As one, the five baby brasses turned and launched themselves into the stormy sky. They dropped south and east and followed the curve of the mountains until they reached a tumbledown grass-grown ruin barely visible in the growing gloom. One by one, they landed and squeezed into the crumbling entrance. Led by Sulfur, they found the passage leading down into the maze of tunnels beneath the city and began their hunt for the shadowpeople.

****

"Come, this way," Eight cried, ducking down another passage barely wider than a crack. Firestream followed, but Ashfall hesitated. He looked over his shoulder at the darkness behind them. Was that a glow he saw reflecting on the rocks or merely his imagination? Where was the fire dragon? He tucked his burned wing closer to his side and squeezed through the crack after the others.

Ashfall was breathing heavily from the pain, and he realized the air had the strong smell of sulfurous gases. There had been a minor earthquake, Eight had said, which caused the cave-in where Linsha had been searching. Was it possible the quake had opened a new magma crack somewhere near the old temple, which invited the fire dragon to trespass into areas where the beasts did not usually go?

Eight and Firestream were waiting for him at the end of the narrow crack. The passage opened into a wider tunnel that sloped gently downhill. The path appeared to have been used, for its floor was smooth and its walls showed signs of tool marks.

"Are you able to keep going?" Firestream asked.

Ashfall managed a nod. "The wing membrane is

burned. Not the bone. I will keep up."

"Ah, good," said Eight in a tight, strained voice, "because the wall is starting to melt behind you."

The three wyrmlings cast one frantic look at the yellow and orange circle of molten rock that slowly dropped to the floor in large globules, and they bolted down the tunnel. The fire dragon's head pushed through the hot spot. It spotted them and roared its anger; then it shoved its body all the way into the tunnel and lumbered after them.

The wyrmlings plunged into the darkness. Their highly tuned senses—hearing, sight, smell, taste, and touch—worked together to give each dragon a refined knowledge of the cave system around them: the subtle currents of air; the changing depths; the presence of walls, cracks, and cave formations; and the distant movement of magma. That information allowed them to move quickly through the passages, so in just a few moments, they had left the fire dragon behind . . . at least for the moment. But each wyrmling could sense an ominous quiver in the stone beneath their feet and knew without question the fire dragon was still following.

"What are we going to do?" Eight growled. "We cannot lead that thing to Linsha."

Even in his pain, Ashfall took charge. "We will have to lose it," he said.

****

The five small brasses had run into a problem. They had raced through the tunnels and corridors of stone deeper and deeper under Sanction Vale until, with little warning, a wall suddenly appeared before them, blocking their way. It was not a natural formation, for the wall had been polished smooth and until very recently, it had had a lintel carved from a lighter stone that formed an arch of grace and beauty. However, only remnants of the arch remained, framing a large hole that had been blasted through the door. Scorch marks radiated from the hole, and blobs of cooled stone lay on the floor.

"There were magic wards in that stone," Sulfur said in horror.

Warily they crawled through the ruined door and entered a cavern that echoed with the whispers of a vast space. A reek of ash and smoke and hot stone struck their nostrils. A few heaps of molten stone still glowed with an inner heat and slowly cooled in the smoky air. The brasses walked together in a tight group across the floor toward the center of the huge chamber.

"I think this is the shadowhall where the clan gathers," said Sulfur, peering upward toward the lofty ceiling.

"Is anyone here?" Caldera called. "Please, we just want to talk. We need your help."

Silence.

"Do you think they're dead?" she whispered to the others.

Windstone cocked his head, his nostrils flared to catch the smells in the air. "I think some are here."

"They don't like strangers," Sulfur observed. "And they're angry. Here, let me try it." He pushed forward and raised his voice. "Elders, we are the wards of

Crucible, dragonlord and governor of Sanction. We beg your advice. A fire dragon attacked us while we were attempting to rescue the Rose Knight, Lady Majere, who is trapped in a cave-in. Please, we mean you no harm."

You could not harm us, wyrmlings. The voice came boring into all five minds with forcefulness fueled by anger. Scratching noises like claws on stone came from overhead as several dark shadows flitted across the walls. Something growled close by; then a strange figure coalesced out of the darkness before them.

The wyrmlings drew together, their heads bowed respectfully. To them, the shadowpeople were creatures of tales. They had known a clan of the elusive, strange folk lived under Sanction in a mutual agreement with Crucible, but they had never been allowed to see them or meet them.

Almost manlike in shape, the shadowman standing before them was barely Linsha's height, yet beneath the smooth, dark fur that covered his body, powerful muscles bulged on his limbs and torso. A thick membrane connected his arms to his legs, and a pair of fangs protruded over his lower lip. He stared at the wyrmlings with huge eyes that glowed with a fierce green luminescence.

We have seen the fire dragon. The storm drove it down through a new vent in the side of the mountain. It did much damage to our hall and tunnels. Several of our clan are dead.

"We are sorry to hear of your plight," Caldera said.

We cannot help you.

Sulfur lifted his head and met the shadowman's angry gaze. "Please! We just need one or two of you to help us free Lady Linsha before the fire dragon finds her."

The male looked them all over carefully and replied, *There are eight of you. That is sufficient for your needs.*

"That's it? That is all you can say?" Windstone demanded.

The shadowman took a step back. *I will tell you this: The storm has sent much runoff into an underground pool near the collapsed tunnel. There is only a weak dam of debris holding it back. If you release it . . .*

"We know fire dragons hate water," Sulfur said. "But how is that supposed to help?"

He received no answer. The elder vanished between one breath and the next, leaving only silence.

"How did he know there are eight of us?" Fumarole asked.

"This is their realm. They probably knew when Eight came in."

Smoke snorted in irritation. "They should have thrown him out. What do we do now?"

"Find the others," said Windstone. "Free Lady Linsha. Get back to the palace before Crucible returns."

"But we don't know where she is."

"Eight said he was somewhere near the old remains of the Temple of Luerkhisis when the cave-in happened. We could start there," Sulfur suggested.

Feeling disgruntled and disappointed by their lack of success with the shadowpeople, the five brasses hurried northeast again through the maze of tunnels toward the roots of Thunderhorn and the buried ruins of the dark goddess's temple that lay beneath the flanks of the mountain.

****

Four years before, during the wyrmlings' traumatic hatching, another event took place in the old Temple of Luerkhisis that changed the destiny of Krynn. Gods had returned, a goddess had been vanquished, and many of the old ways had been irrevocably changed in the monumental upheaval that took place in the temple. Shortly after his return, Crucible had done what he could to obliterate the remains of the blood-soaked arena, the chambers, and the halls of the temple. Only a few walls, some minor tunnels, and a chamber or two remained.

There was no ancient treasure hoard as Eight had hoped, not even a jeweled brooch, a gilded cup, or coin left behind. There were only some unsteady passages, an ancient taint of evil, and carrion beetles.

It was Ashfall who saw the first small stream of carrion beetles scuttling down a narrow passage. During their flight from the fire dragon, the three wyrmlings had become lost from the path Eight remembered. Frantic, they had searched through the black fastness of the labyrinth for any sign of Linsha and found nothing, not even her scent. The earthquake that had brought down the tunnel on Linsha and her guard had damaged other sections as well, making the search much more difficult. Nor were they helped by the persistent fire dragon who dogged their every step. They could hear it roar close by.

"Eight, follow those beetles," Ashfall ordered. "We will distract the fire dragon."

The smallest wyrmling stared down the passage,

where the beetles were moving with obvious intent. He hated carrion beetles. They tasted nasty and were fit only as targets for his fiery breath weapon. But if they would lead him to Linsha . . . "How will I let you know if I find her?"

"Use your head," snapped Firestream. "It has to be good for something."

Eight watched his two nestmates go before he ducked down the passage beside the line of beetles. A furious roar and a glare of reddish light made him freeze in place while the fire dragon stamped by after the other two brasses. When the dragon was past, Eight hurried on. Following the insects, he finally squeezed into the remains of a passageway that looked familiar. He looked around in dismay. Heaps of debris littered the floor around him, and the ceiling looked dangerously fragile. He lifted his head. On the slightest drift of air, he caught the smell of blood and a very familiar scent. The beetles moved toward those scents with determined purpose. Relief and terror flooded through the small brass. He ran down the passage until he was brought to a stop by a pile of rock and debris from the collapse of the roof, and there he spied a feeble bluish glow from a lantern. The lantern was hers, but he could not see or hear her. The tunnel was silent except for the rustle of carrion beetles.

"Linsha?" he dared whisper. He moved forward and found her lying in her stone prison, unconscious but still alive. "Linsha, I am here," he told her softly. "Please stay awake. I am here and help is coming."

At least he hoped help was coming. He realized after studying the rocks lying over Linsha that he could not move them alone. He needed his nestmates. But how would they know where to find him? There weren't that many carrion beetles to follow in the caves.

Use your head, Firestream had said. He was a fine one to talk. He usually used his muscles first and his head later. But he had a point. Eight hadn't learned yet to use his head the way Ashfall could to send telepathic messages, yet he had something all brasses had and used often: his voice.

He didn't want to shout, that would not be effective in that place. He needed a sound that would penetrate the darkness and carry through the nearby tunnels and corridors of the labyrinth. If one wyrmling heard his call, the message would be passed on. Crouching by Linsha's head, he tried to think. What other creatures did he know—besides brass dragons and Varia—that could make much noise? Then he remembered Grayback.

Many brass dragons have an affinity for dogs, and the palace had its share of dogs for hunting, tracking, and guarding. Eight knew every sound they made, but he remembered one dog named Grayback who was part wolf. That dog had a particularly penetrating howl that could be heard for miles on a still night. It was worth a try. Lifting his nose, Eight began at the low register of notes that shivered the bones and swiftly slid up the scales to the high, slightly sharp sounds that rose into the farthest reaches of the darkness.

****

The odd cry spread outward like ripples into the tunnels and caves, the crumbled spaces, and the passageways. In a dank tunnel above and not far from Linsha's position, the five wyrmlings heard the cry and recognized it for what it was. They found a passage leading downward and raced toward the source of the call.

Ashfall and Firestream heard it too, but they could not respond so quickly. The fire dragon had plunged deeper into the mountain, found a magma stream, and followed the molten rock to another section of the tunnels where it emerged and appeared in front of the baby dragons, cutting them off from the others. The two nestmates were forced to turn around and flee, while the fire dragon roared its hunger. They did not see the fire dragon stop and turn its head to listen, and they did not realize immediately that the dragon no longer tracked them. It had turned another way and followed its instincts toward a sound that signaled a creature in distress.

****

Eight continued to howl in the hope that someone would hear him. After a while a faint sound interrupted him and something light brushed Eight's leg. He stopped abruptly.

Linsha blinked up at him, a ghost of a smile on her lips. "You came back," she whispered.

He dipped his head to see her expression. "We came to get you out."

She nodded, her eyes already sliding closed again. "Just don't leave me. Don't leave me alone."

The small dragon gazed down at her, too full of

roiling thoughts to find a word. He had expected blame, recrimination, anger—not pleasure and relief. Had she doubted he would return?

"Eight! Where are you?" Faint voices called to him from the far side of the rockfall.

He leaped to his feet, his eyes glowing with relief. "On this side!" he shouted. "We're over here."

Scrabbling sounds came through the pile of stone and dirt. "Linsha? Is she still alive?" Caldera called.

"Yes! Hurry."

Eight crouched again close to Linsha to protect her from rolling debris and dust and listened as his nest-mates dug through the heap from the other side. Stones clashed and rolled on the far side; gravel shivered down the heap; a few rocks fell to the floor.

Eight looked up at a louder sound, and a wyrmling's head poked through a gap near the ceiling: slender, gray-toned Smoke. She peered down at Eight and Linsha; then with a heave of her powerful hind legs, she pushed through and clambered down the slope of the rocks and slabs. A little more of the debris was pushed aside, and the other four wyrmlings climbed through and down to join the others.

Fumarole shook off the dust. "I'm going to need a bath after this."

"Was that you making that racket?" Windstone asked Eight. "Sounded just like Grayback."

Caldera, always the nurturer, peered carefully at Linsha, studying her pale face and the flicker of pulse in her neck. "She is close to death," the wyrmling told her nestmates. "We must get her out and warmed, or the shock of her injuries will soon kill her."

"What did you do with Ashfall and Firestream?" asked Sulfur.

Eight explained about the fire dragon and the carrion beetles while they worked to move the stones and slabs that trapped Linsha. "Where did you go?" he asked.

They told him about the shadowpeople and the damage to the shadowhall. "The elder said there is a trapped pool of water near here. We think we found where it might be, but you called and we came here first," Sulfur said.

Six now, the wyrmlings concentrated their efforts on moving enough of the collapsed stone to extricate Linsha. Although small, they were stronger than humans, and working together, they were able to yank, wrench, shift, and pull enough rocks out of the way to lever the big slab up and carefully pull Linsha out from under her prison. She cried out once in pain and woke long enough to smile a welcome at the babies; then she lapsed into unconsciousness again and lay unmoving at their feet.

Caldera checked her again. "This is not good. Her thigh is broken. Some ribs, too. She's in shock."

"How are we going to move her?" Eight asked, the worry raw in his voice.

Caldera cocked her head and thought. "She is wearing a cloak; that will help. And she still has her short sword. We can use that to splint her thigh. Does the guard have anything on him that could help?"

Smoke looked down sadly. "Sergeant Samuals is buried too deep. We can't get to him."

"Sergeant Samuals?" Eight repeated. He had not realized who the guard was who had followed Linsha into the caves. He hung his head, feeling grief and remorse for the death of a guard he had liked.

Eight? Where are you? Ashfall's telepathic call rang in the wyrmling's head, causing him to squawk in surprise. The two wyrmlings must be very close.

"We're here!" he shouted, startling the other brasses; then he stopped himself, lifted his nose, and howled the peculiar howl that had drawn the others.

Instead of Ashfall, the roar of the fire dragon answered his call, and to their horror, the bellow came from down the open passage in front of them. With a frantic burst of activity, the baby brasses pulled Linsha's sword out of its scabbard and made a makeshift splint on her broken leg. Then they wrapped her tightly in her cloak, and four of them carefully carried her up the heap of stone and rubble to the gap at the top and pushed her through to the other side.

The last one scrambled through just as the fiery dragon appeared in the tunnel, its body outlined by the glowing cracks between its scales. It snarled at them and blew a fireball at the gap just as the last wyrmling disappeared. The brasses heard a rumble and a crash, and a storm of dust blew through the gap before it was sealed off. What was left of the tunnel's ceiling collapsed, blocking the tunnel behind them.

The six looked at one another in relief. They could hear the fire dragon rumbling around on the far side and knew it would not stay there for long. But for the moment, they were safe.

"Now how do we get out of here?" asked Windstone.

Sulfur took the lead and Windstone stayed in the rear while the others picked up Linsha in her cloak and carried her up the passage. The wyrmlings had no clear-cut idea of where to find an exit out of the mountain, so they retraced their steps back the way they had come from the upper level. Eight continued to send an occasional call down the few corridors they passed in the hope that Ashfall and Firestream were close.

"We can't be too far from Crucible's cave," Smoke managed to say through the fabric of the cloak in her mouth.

"No, but the fire dragon might go back there," Caldera pointed out. "And we don't know how to get there from here."

Something dark and indistinct flitted across their path. An odd, rumbling voice echoed in their thoughts.

Take the woman to the tunnel on your right. Follow the path. You will pass the pool of water and cross a stream. Once across, go up the first tunnel. You will find your way from there.

"What was that?" Eight cried, almost dropping his corner of Linsha's cloak.

Sulfur stared hard into the darkness, but he saw nothing more. "A shadowman. At least one of them must have followed us." He raised his voice and called their gratitude to the invisible watcher.

Accepting the shadowman's directions, they trotted hastily into a rough-hewn tunnel on their right and climbed up a steep slope. There was a path of sorts, which they followed through a shallow crevice, along a black, echoing cavern and into another narrow, winding cavern with a low roof hung with stalactites. Water dripped endlessly from the roof onto the cavern floor. During rainstorms on the mountains, most of the water ran off the mountainsides in streams and freshets that rushed down the slopes into Sanction Bay. Occasionally, if the storms were particularly heavy, some of the runoff seeped down into the depths of mountains to fill the underground streams and pools used by the shadowpeople. The wyrmlings could see a stream usually flowed through the cavern, but the volcano's earlier tremor had broken off a weak section of the ceiling and several stalactites that had crashed down into the channel, forming a low dam just upstream from the wyrmlings. The water backed up behind the dam into a deep pool that was growing deeper by the moment.

The wyrmlings studied the new lake with wide, thoughtful eyes for a moment before they gathered up Linsha's cloak again and hurried across the wet floor in the shadow of the dam.

"You might want to move faster," Firestream's voice shouted behind them.

The six turned and saw their missing two burst out of the tunnel, galloping as fast as their short legs could carry them. A dim glow illuminated the depths of the tunnel behind them.

The eight came together just as the fire dragon erupted from the tunnel. The beast roared its pleasure to see its prey and charged after them.

"Take the cloak, Firestream." Eight gave his brother no choice but thrust the corner of the cloak at him and let go, forcing him to take the fabric or drop Linsha's shoulder.

"Eight! You fool, where are you going?" Ashfall shouted.

"Go! Take her out! I'll catch up," Eight called as he

sprang upward and brought his wings snapping down to catch the air.

The others carrying Linsha hesitated only a moment before they realized there was little they could do as long as they were responsible for the injured woman, and Ashfall could not fly with his injured wing. They moved hurriedly on toward the opening they could see on the far side of the cavern. That left only Smoke and Caldera.

Like a brace of quail, the two brasses threw themselves upward after their nestmate and caught up with him circling above the jammed rocks and eroded sand that formed the crude dam.

He looked as if he wanted to say something, but the two females glared at him, daring him to send them away, and he flicked his tail in greeting instead. The three tucked their wings close to their bodies and dived down toward the fire dragon.

The creature, intent on the group that fled across the cavern floor, did not see them until they swooped by, clapping their wings close to its face. It roared and snapped at them, but the brasses were agile in the air and twisted away, calling insults to the ponderous creature. They rose and dipped again, their wings dangerously close to the fire dragon's head.

Do it now, Ashfall's voice spoke in Eight's mind to let him know the others were out of the way. He called to his sisters and led them to the top of the dam, where they perched and peered over at the enraged fire dragon. They were counting very heavily on the temper of the fiery beast and its lack of serious intelligence.

The fire dragon did not disappoint them. It reared

back and released a fireball from its mouth that seared across the damp air and slammed into the unstable dam where the brass babies had been sitting. The entire structure shuddered. Steam rose from the water where the fireball struck.

Smoke and Caldera backed away from the dam and flew close to the roof to watch, but Eight wanted to be certain. He circled down again and sent a stream of white-hot fire into the dragon's face. The wyrmling's breath weapon certainly did not have enough strength to harm a fire dragon, but it was enough to fuel the beast's rage. The dragon retaliated with another fireball. Eight tried to dart out of the way and banged his wing on the rocks of the dam. He tumbled backward over the edge and into the water. The missile struck the dam with a low thud and buried itself in the depths of the rock and sand.

Suddenly steam shot out of the hole, followed by a powerful geyser of water that hid Eight from view. The rocks began to shift and shudder. More water shot through, weakening the walls even further. All at once, the dam collapsed.

"Eight!" shouted Caldera. She and Smoke dived toward the turbulent water.

The fire dragon saw its mistake too late. It turned to flee the water and was caught by the deluge that broke loose from the shattered dam. The two wyrmlings were lost to sight in a huge cloud of steam that rolled off its hot body. The wave of flood water wasn't a big one, but it was enough to knock the fire dragon off its feet and wash it, squirming and raging, out of the cavern. It fell into the depths of the underground stream and was carried for nearly a mile before it could escape.

The other wyrmlings stared from the mouth of the tunnel in stunned silence.

"There they are!" Ashfall cried, and they all saw the two females rise slowly out of the steam and mist, carrying in their talons a wing and a tail attached to a very bedraggled and muddy Eight. They flew to the tunnel's opening and dropped him by the others. He looked up at them, his eyes bright with laughter, and belched up a bellyful of muddy water.

Fumarole rolled her eyes in distaste.

Pleased with their success, the three joined the others, and all eight helped carry Linsha to Crucible's cave and the surface. If they were lucky, they thought, they could get Linsha back to the palace and to the healer before Crucible came home. They knew the truth would come out eventually, but if she were safely back and healing nicely in bed, they hoped Crucible's wrath would not be so severe.

Night had settled over the vale while they were in the cave, and the ledge outside was barely visible in the dense, stormy darkness. They left the cave and walked out onto the ledge before they realized they were not alone.

A large, bulky figure landed heavily on the stone path before them and glared down with eyes that glowed like fire in the dark. Lightning flared and reflected off shining bronze scales. All eight brasses cowered down before him. The big bronze dragon said nothing, which was almost worse than a tirade, in the wyrmlings' minds. He scooped Linsha into his arms and launched himself off the ledge, leaving the brasses behind.

****

It was past midnight when the eight finally walked wearily into the gates of the palace. Seven of them could have risked the storm and flown back much quicker, but none of them would leave Ashfall to come back alone. Tired and full of trepidation, they cleaned the mud and water off their feet and bodies and trooped silently into the palace. In a tight group, they climbed the stairs to the governor's personal quarters.

Lord Bight was sitting in a padded chair near the large canopied bed he shared with Linsha. A single lamp burned on the bedside table. Varia stood watchfully on her perch, her great dark eyes scanning the room. She hooted softly when she saw the wyrmlings at the door.

Eight peered around the doorframe and saw the man sitting in the chair. His eyes went to the bed, and he almost cried out in relief when he spotted Linsha asleep under several blankets.

"She will live," a stern voice addressed them.

The eight came nervously into the room and gathered around the bed and the chair. Eight bowed his head. With help from Ashfall, he told his story of the events of the afternoon, and with deep remorse, he accepted the blame for everything that had happened, including the death of the guard.

Lord Bight said nothing, but let him talk without interruption. When the wyrmling was finished, the dragonlord nodded once, rose to his feet, and opened the door to indicate the meeting was over. As the wyrmlings walked out, he said, "You have much to think about from this day, but I want you to remember one thing: there was only one treasure for me under the mountain, and you brought her out. I thank you for that." And he quietly shut the door behind them.

He turned and saw Linsha watching him from the bed. She smiled sleepily and winked at him.

No Strings Attached

Miranda Horner And Margaret Weis

Miranda Horner continues to keep herself busy by editing game material for the Wizards of the Coast Web site, writing the occasional short story, and playing games. She lives in the Kansas City area with her game-loving husband and dice-loving cats.

Margaret Weis collaborated with Tracy Hickman to create the setting of Dragonlance; the Chronicles has sold over twenty million copies worldwide. Weis is the solo author of many bestselling series as well, including the Deathgate Cycle, the Sovereign Stone series, and Dragonlance's Dark Disciple series.

No Strings Attached

Miranda Horner and Margaret Weis

Age of Mortals, 430 AC

"That wizard's back again tonight," muttered Philip, wiping his cloth over the bar.

Tansy rolled her eyes. "Well, if nothing else, he's persistent," she said, adding the last tankard of ale to her tray.

"Like your admirer over there." Philip nodded at the large, chestnut-haired man who was smiling at Tansy from a table in the corner.

"Trent? He's all gentlemanly brawn, that one," she said with a smile and a blush. "Keeps his hands to himself like a gentleman, too. Not like that nasty old wizard."

She cast a glance at the man who had just come down from his room above the tavern. He had to be sixty years old if he was a day. He was slovenly and unkempt. His loose-fitting black robes could not conceal his blubbery gut. His thinning, gray hair was slicked back with goose grease. He leered at Tansy as he sat down and made a motion for her to come to him. She sniffed and turned away.

Philip frowned. "You take care, girl. You don't want to go fooling with mages, especially those who wear the black robes."

"He's been the one fooling with me. But we'll soon fix that," she added under her breath. She grinned at Philip. "Don't fret. The wizard won't give me any trouble. I know how to handle him."

"Looks like he's the one handling you," the tavern keeper retorted.

Tansy recalled the previous night. Every time she came near the old man, he managed to get his filthy hands on her. The thought of the wizard's groping made her almost physically ill. She glanced at the handsome Trent again and, recalling their plan, she felt better. "Don't worry, Philip. I'm sure the wizard's evil ways will come back to haunt him."

Philip grunted and shook his head in doubt. "Just get out there and do your job, girl. You should be used to the occasional bottom-pincher by now."

"We'll see who pinches who," Tansy muttered, grinning.

After delivering drinks to her first few tables, Tansy stopped by to give Trent his ale. Her lover was a big, strapping man with chestnut hair that fell across his face in an engagingly boyish manner. He smiled at her and took a pull at his ale. Then, lowering his mug, he leaned near her and said softly, "Do we go through with it?"

"After what he put me through last night, you can

count on it," Tansy said grimly. "Mind you don't go overboard on the ale, though," she added as he lifted the tankard and drained it.

"I do my best work when I've had a few," Trent stated.

Tansy snatched away the empty tankard. "You do your best work before you have too much."

Trent grinned. "One more to keep my nerve up."

Tansy shook her head, but promised another mug of ale. As she turned away, she saw Philip motioning toward the mage. He may have been a repellant man, but he was a good customer. Heaving a sigh, Tansy walked slowly over to the black-robed man.

He licked his fat lips. His eyes wolfishly devoured her. "At last! The evening can get no better now that you're here, my girl."

Tansy forced a smile. "You're fast on your way to becoming a regular, sir," she said, sidling out of his way as he tried to fondle her. "What business keeps you in town?"

"Oh, nothing worth talking about, though it is quite lucrative. Very lucrative," he boasted, and he patted a bulging purse he wore on his belt.

Tansy eyed the purse, and stole a glance at Trent to see if he noticed. She had only looked away for an instant, but the mage took advantage of her lapse to reach out his hand, grab hold of her rump, and give it a squeeze. Then he smacked her hard on the backside and laughed when she winced.

"Sir, please!" Tansy scolded, forcing a giggle. "The other customers will be jealous if I give you all the attention."

The wizard smiled broadly and shifted back in his chair. His eyes roved up and down her body. "So, what does a man have to do to get a drink around here this evening?"

"Yes, sir. What would you like?" An idea struck her. "Might I recommend the house specialty?"

He quirked an eyebrow at her. "What would that be?"

"A flaming dragon," she said.

"What's in it?"

"Ah, that's our secret," said Tansy and she flounced away, deliberately letting her thigh touch his knee as she passed him.

Once at the bar, Tansy was pleased to see that Philip had gone into the kitchen to fetch an order. That left her to make the flaming dragon herself. She stole a quick gulp of dwarf spirits to give herself courage, then mixed together the strong liqueurs and other ingredients that went into the drink. The result was a thick, viscous beverage that had a sweet, cloying, licorice taste. The drink sparked into a subtle, blue-limned fire when she added the last dash of powder.

With an ingratiating smile, Tansy placed the drink in front of the mage, leaning over to treat him to a good view of her full breasts. He stared and again licked his fat lips.

"Buy a girl a drink?" She indicated another mug of spirits on her tray.

The wizard fumbled at his pouch and threw out a coin.

"Here's to good ale and pleasant company." She tossed off her drink, and he gulped down the flaming dragon.

The mage's eyes bulged. He coughed and gasped a bit, drawing in a deep breath.

"Another, sir?" she asked, once more leaning over the table to take his empty glass.

He smiled at her, and his smile was most unpleasant. "I will if you will," he said.

Tansy felt a qualm of fear. Maybe Philip was right. Maybe they should leave the Black Robe alone. She was just thinking that when she felt his hand try to slide up her blouse.

Anger stirred in her, roused by the dwarf spirits. He deserved what he got. He'd treated her like a whore all week. He would pay for his groping.

"Rest assured, sir, I'll take care of you," she said softly.

The mage placed a bright steel coin down on the table. "And there's more where that came from."

Tansy took up the coin and placed it in the small pouch she kept inside her bodice. "Many thanks, kind sir! I'll be back as quick as a hare."

It didn't take long to return to the mage with the next drinks. She gulped down the dwarf spirits and felt even more courageous. She glanced at Trent and gave him a nod. He winked at her and rose slowly to his feet and ambled toward the stairs.

"Oof, sir, these drinks are quite strong." Tansy fanned herself. "Is it warm in here? Good thing it's almost time for my break."

She gazed at him provocatively.

He placed another steel coin down on the table. That time, Tansy took her time when placing it in her hidden pouch.

The mage's heavy-lidded eyes glistened with lust, and Tansy felt another qualm. She had the feeling, suddenly, that he was shamming, only pretending to be drunk.

"I will show you where I store my coins if you show me where you stow yours," he said, leering.

Tansy giggled. "Oh, sir, I'd be happy to show you where I stow my coins."

He pushed himself from the table and rose unsteadily to his feet. He could barely walk, and Tansy decided that he wasn't playacting. He draped his arm around her, insisting that she help him. She almost gagged at the noxious smell coming from some of the bags tied to his belt. He rubbed his fat body lasciviously against hers, and she gagged again, then nearly fell over as he leaned heavily on her.

"What room number, sir?" she gasped as they reached the stairs.

Trent stood there, leaning on the railing. He stepped aside to let them pass.

"Roomthree," the mage mumbled.

"Room three?" Tansy repeated loudly.

The mage nodded. Trent nodded.

Tansy led the mage to the door of his room. "Whoa, there," she said as he stood swaying and fumbling with the key. "Don't pass out on me until after we've had some fun," she said as she opened the door.

"Fun," the mage repeated. "Muss . . . have fun."

Tansy gave Trent a moment to get into the room unseen and shoved the man into the darkened room. He staggered halfway across the floor and came up against a chair. Tansy slammed shut the door, leaning her body against it.

"Trent?" she called in a loud whisper.

"Here!" he said grimly, jumping out of the shadows. Making a fist, he slammed it into the mage's jaw.

The mage fell to the floor, taking down the chair with a crash.

"Quiet!" Tansy warned, cringing. "We don't want Philip up here spoiling our fun!"

The mage groaned.

"The lady said to keep quiet," Trent told the mage and kicked him in the ribs.

The mage groaned again, but he managed to snarl out, "You'll pay for this."

"No, you're paying, old man!" Tansy said.

Seizing hold of his purse, she ripped it off his belt. Then, grabbing the poker that stood next to the fireplace, she thwacked the mage across the shoulders. "That's for putting your nasty hands on me!" she told him and thwacked him again, that time on the rump.

Tansy laughed. "This is just like a Punch-and-Judy show!" she said, and she thwacked him again and again. "Only I'm Punch!"

The mage lifted his head. Blood dribbled down his chin. He stared at her and there was something about the look in his eyes that made her shiver.

"C'mon, you've got his money, let's get out of here," said Trent nervously.

Tansy gave the mage one last strike, then flung the poker aside. She took hold of Trent's arm, and the two started toward the door.

The last thing Tansy heard was the mage muttering strange-sounding words . . .

****

"That wizard's back again tonight," muttered Philip, wiping his cloth over the bar.

Tansy rolled her eyes. "Well, if nothing else, he's persistent," she said, adding the last tankard of ale to her tray.

Someone tittered with laughter, and someone else giggled. Tansy looked around the bar but couldn't see anyone. The bar was empty except for her, Trent, Philip, and the mage.

Philip was frowning. "You take care, girl. You don't want to go fooling with mages, especially those who wear the black robes."

"Let that be a lesson to you, Johnny," said a woman's stern voice. "Never trust a Black Robe."

Tansy glanced around, bewildered. What was going on?

"He's been the one fooling with me," she said. "But we'll soon fix that." She grinned at Philip. "Don't fret. The wizard won't give me any trouble. I know how to handle him."

"Looks like he's the one handling you," the tavern keeper retorted.

Guffaws of laughter and some clapping of hands erupted.

Tansy couldn't understand what was happening, and she was suddenly terrified. She tried to turn and flee, but found herself walking over to the black-robed man.

"At last!" he said. "The evening can get no better now that you're here, my girl."

Tansy forced a smile. "You're fast on your way to becoming a regular, sir," she said, sidling out of his way as he tried to fondle her.

There was more laughter as she darted and dodged and the mage kept trying to grab her.

"What business keeps you in town?" she said desperately.

"Oh, nothing worth talking about, though it is quite lucrative. Very lucrative," he boasted, and he patted a bulging purse he wore on his belt.

"Oh ho!" said someone. "He's made a big mistake now!"

Tansy was feeling dizzy, and she put her hand to her head. She knew what was going to happen next. She was going to glance over to Trent. The mage was going to reach out his hand, grab hold of her rump, and give it a squeeze. Then he would smack her hard on the backside. She knew it was going to happen, and she didn't want it to happen, but it did, just as she'd pictured it.

Gales of laughter erupted as Tansy jumped and yelped. She looked frantically at Trent, who was sitting at his table. He only winked and nodded his head.

A voice said, "Uh oh! You better watch out, old man!"

"Get to the good part!" called out someone else.

"I will show you where I store my coins if you show me where you stow yours," the mage said, leering.

Tansy jiggled her breasts. "Oh, sir, I'd be happy to show you where I stow my coins."

"Woohoo!" voices shouted, and there was clapping. Feet stomped on the floor.

Tansy was truly frightened. She tried to run, but she

kept getting tangled up in the strings, and every time she turned and twisted there was more laughter.

"Trent?" she cried, panicked.

"Here!" he said grimly, jumping out of the shadows. Making a fist, he slammed it into the mage's jaw.

The mage fell to the floor, taking down the chair with a crash to hoots and howls of merriment.

The mage snarled out, "You'll pay for this."

"No, you're paying, old man!" Tansy said, and there was a round of applause.

Seizing hold of his purse, she ripped it off his belt. Then, grabbing the poker that stood next to the fireplace, she thwacked the mage across the shoulders. "That's for putting your nasty hands on me!" she told him, and she thwacked him again, that time on the rump.

"Hit him again!" voices shouted.

Tansy laughed. "This is just like a Punch-and-Judy show!" she said, and she thwacked him again and again. "Only I'm Punch!"

At that, there was a standing ovation.

****

"That wizard's back again tonight," said Philip.

Tansy moaned as everyone else clapped. The show was starting at last.

She felt a string jerk, and she jiggled her breasts. Another string tugged, and her right hand lifted and she brought the poker down, thwack, on the back of a black-robed mage.

Children laughed and their parents clapped. Tansy looked up in terror to see fat lips grinning down at her and heavy-lidded eyes glitter with cruel pleasure. A pudgy hand encased in a black sleeve hovered above her.

"You're Judy, my dear," said the mage, and he twitched a string and Tansy danced.

An excerpt

The Stonetellers
Volume One

The Rebellion

Jean Rabe

One

The ground shuddered and a rumbling began—the sound had no direction, seemingly coming from nowhere and everywhere deep in the Neraka mine. It was a soft sound at first, almost comforting. But it quickly grew in intensity, becoming hurtful and blotting out the clang of pick-axes being dropped and miners calling to one another in panic. A great breath accompanied the quake, the earth exhaling in a thunderous whoosh that belched up from its depths centuries-old dust the color of cinnamon.

Moon-eye's throat grew painfully tight as he clung to a support timber. The lantern hanging from a spike directly overhead jiggled. Its light sent shadows careening frantically along the shaft walls. The young goblin peered through the dust, falling like a steady rain now, and flinched when fist-sized chunks of the ceiling came loose and struck him. He fought the urge to run toward the surface, instead edging away from the timber and making his way deeper into the collapsing mine.

Fleeing goblins brushed by him as he went, some begging him to turn around and leave with them. A few carried guttering torches, which helped Moon-eye make out the jagged tunnel walls and avoid the largest pieces of stone littering the floor. Some struggled with bulging sacks—fearing their whip-wielding taskmasters more than the quake, and therefore not willing to abandon the precious ore they'd mined. One dragged a diminutive goblin with a crushed skull.

"Feyrh!" Moon-eye heard a large goblin holler at him. *Run. Escape. Flee.* The single shouted word was almost lost amidst the continuing tremor and the slapping of the swarm of goblin feet against the floor.

Twice he fell when the mine shook violently. Both times he got back up and pressed deeper, only to fall again when a burly hobgoblin running in the opposite direction pushed him out of the way. "Feyrh!" the hobgoblin spat at him. "Feyrh, dard!"

Flee, fool!

Moon-eye shook his head, then got up slowly in relief as the ground grew still and the rumbling quieted.

"Feyrh!" the hobgoblin called a last time before lumbering out of view.

"Cannot leave," Moon-eye said to himself. "Not without Graytoes." Broken shards of rock cut into his bare feet as he continued on. Then another tremor struck and more falling debris bombarded his back and shoulders and set his small body to bleeding and aching fiercely. At a side tunnel he waited for another group of fleeing miners to pass, then sniffed the dust-choked air.

Moon-eye's sense of smell rivaled the finest hunting dog's. He sorted through the tang of the goblins' sweat and terror; the scent of the old bracing timbers, which were threatening to split at any moment; and the odor the very stone gave off. He sniffed the sweet traces of water; rivulets always trickled down walls in parts of the mine from some hidden stream. He also picked up the disagreeable stench of waste. Permeating everything, blood was heavy in the air, and Moon-eye knew this was not just his, that many other miners had been injured.

How many injured?

How many dead?

"Graytoes!" He called twice more, then inhaled deeper and smelled the fetid odor of something rotting, a hint of sulfur, and the stink of a Dark Knight. One of the taskmasters was down this side passage, and he hoped the vile man didn't make it out alive.

Moon-eye disregarded all those scents and continued probing. He drew as much of the fusty air into his lungs as he could, over and over, finally finding the familiar scent he'd been searching for.

"Graytoes." His quest led him farther down the main tunnel. He started off at a careful lope just as the ground bucked even more strongly, once more sending him to his knees. This time the rumbling was like the sustained growl of some maddened beast, and this time it came from a specific direction.

Moon-eye looked over his shoulder and picked

through the shadows to see a wall of earth and rocks rushing at him. Broken goblin limbs and a helmet that must have belonged to a Dark Knight roiled in the churning mix. The mass moved with torrential speed, forcing the dank, dry air of the mine howling before it, bludgeoning the support timbers and shattering them, and gathering the falling ceiling into itself before rushing on.

Moon-eye sped deeper down the main shaft, forcing himself to ignore the rocks biting at his feet and trying unsuccessfully to shut out the roaring cacophony so close behind him. He concentrated on the familiar scent; it came from yards distant. He turned at a side passage, then another, this last one angling upward and well away from the racing wall of earth. He leapt into the passage just as the ceiling gave way in the tunnel behind him.

"Graytoes!" Moon-eye thought he heard a reply to his call, though a part of him feared it was his imagination.

The ground shook again, and the odors all around intensified, settling in his mouth and threatening to overwhelm him. The dust filtering down was as thick as a curtain now, and all Moon-eye could see were bands of black and gray. This tunnel was a more recent excavation, he realized, and the timbers were strong and fresh and holding so far.

"Graytoes!" Moon-eye was crawling ahead now, focusing on the remembered scent, constantly wiping his left eye with one hand, while the fingers of his other hand felt along the wall to guide him. His right eye was a solid milky orb, oddly large and protruding from his leathery orange face. It was wholly worthless. The feature inspired his name, his father telling him that the eye reminded him of a full moon. Moon-eye had been born on a night when Krynn had only one moon, before the War of Souls. On the very night that Solinari, Lunitari, and Nuitari mysteriously returned, his family was captured by ogres and sold to the Dark Knights. When he was old enough to work, he had been sent to these mines, where he'd been toiling for the past years. He had no idea what had happened to his parents and siblings, lost like the single, large moon.

He passed a fissure in the stone and through it came muted screams and the sound of rocks falling. He pressed his face into the crack and inhaled, registering and discarding one horrid odor after the next before continuing down the passage.

It felt like an eternity, though he guessed it was only seconds, before the quaking paused again and he stopped to catch his breath and steady his nerves. Moments later he reached a chamber filled with mounds of ore, buckets, picks, and crumpled bodies under chunks of stone. The nearest form was the only one breathing, a young female goblin whose legs were pinned by a fallen beam. A lantern that hung precariously from a crooked spike cast a soft glow on the scene.

"Graytoes." His voice caught as he moved toward his mate. Her skin was the color of sunflower leaves, but it looked dead and ashen from the stone dust. Her once-delicate features were marred by deep welts. "Moon-eye's Heart," he whispered as he knelt by her, smoothing at her cheeks with his calloused fingers, his gaze darting from her face to her trapped legs.

The blood he smelled in this place was not hers, so perhaps she was not too badly hurt. He gently touched her slightly rounded stomach, covered only by a canvas rag of a shift; she carried their first child.

"Moon," she sighed. Her eyes fluttered open, filled with pain and fear, and her thin, shaking fingers grabbed at him.

"Moon-eye's Heart," he said. "Must escape this place."

Steel Town

One Day Earlier

Grallik rose before dawn and stared across Steel Town. The buildings and the men blended in shades of gray and brown, as if someone painting the scene had used so much water that everything ran together to create a drab spectacle. The air was colored dully, too, from the dust swirling thick. And it was heavy with sweat and waste and dirt. No amount of spitting could rid Gralllik of the foul taste.

The Dark Knight mines were an extensive labyrinth, and piles of debris from the excavated tunnels lay everywhere, including just outside Grallik's door. The largest piles formed the northern and western boundaries of the camp, one the size of a hill, rising nearly a hundred feet and occasionally luring goats from the eastern mountains.

Grallik breathed shallowly and kept his eyes on the debris hills as he strolled to the center of the camp. He passed neatly maintained residences of wood and stone with colorful curtains at the windows, dingy shops that looked like a strong wind would blow them over, and men and women scurrying from one place to the next . . . all of them haggard-looking because of the dust and grime and stink that blew everywhere and stuck to them.

Grallik coughed and held a hand to his mouth. The cough he'd developed a year ago came more frequently in recent weeks; he sometimes worried that it signaled a serious malady.

He did not have to be up at this early hour. He could stay in what passed for his home and wait until perhaps the breeze stilled and at least some of the dust settled. But long months ago it became his habit to rise early and watch the men, a mix of Dark Knights and paid laborers. The latter worked in hot, dry, and desolate Steel Town because the coin was good; the knights were posted here. Long before sunrise, the knights and workers were swinging heavy mallets at mounds of ore, smashing the rocks in a perfect, ceaseless cadence. The smaller chunks were easier for Grallik to deal with.

Grallik was Steel Town's resident sorcerer. A Knight of the Thorn, or a 'gray robe' as some called him, he would have preferred a posting in the capital of Neraka, or with an army in a more hospitable clime. But he'd taken the Blood Oath decades past, and recited it again every morning: "Submit or die." Obey the will of his superiors and put all personal goals behind the aims of the Order. He accepted his duty in Steel Town because he believed in the words, and in The Code, the strict set of rules by which all the Dark Knights lived. He just wasn't as fervent about them as he had been in his younger days.

Grallik's ash-gray robe was always spotless, save for its hem, which was permanently colored brown by the clay and dust that spread from one end of Steel Town to the other. He wore his blond hair cropped so short that the faint points of his half-elven ears showed conspicuously, and he allowed not the faintest hint of stubble on an angular face that would have been handsome were half of it not horribly scarred. Not only was the left side of Grallik's face disfigured, so was the entire left side of his body, his left hand twisted, and the skin on that hand oddly shiny and forever looking wet.

There were scars elsewhere, but none so bad or noticeable—especially with his robe covering most of his features. All of them were the result of a fire that took his home and his parents and twin sister when he was little more than a child. His magic couldn't heal him. Not even prayer to Takhisis and Zeboim helped. And in all his years with the Dark Knights, serving alongside their priestly Knights of the Skull, and before that with the Wizards of High Sorcery, no one had been able to provide any relief.

Grallik no longer entertained any thoughts of improving his appearance. He was intent merely on bettering his arcane knowledge and on doing his job, which at Steel Town entailed heating the rocks the Dark Knights and laborers were breaking up, and forcing the iron out of them. The same fire that had taken his family and forever marred his appearance was now part of his job; fire fascinated him and served him well.

The sorcerer, using spells and charcoal, melted off the impurities and turned the ore into carbon steel so that blacksmiths—some of the best in this part of the country—could pound it out and fashion swords and armor for the Order.

Never any halt in the work, and never a change to the routine . . . not in the thirty-eight months he'd been here.

In the years before Grallik's arrival at Steel Town

the Dark Knights had used wagons to haul the ore to Jelek and the capital of Neraka, where the ore was processed in forges with flues as tall as three men. Later the knights grew to rely on a smelter built at the camp to cull the iron ingots that were transported to weaponsmiths in the north and east. The smelter was in disrepair now, serving only to provide shade for one of the slave pens. It was likely never be used again, and that was because of Grallik and his skills.

One of the knights Grallik observed this morning acted sluggish, raising his mallet once for every two times his fellows did. The sorcerer noted the knight looked pale; perhaps had acquired some ailment. Grallik took a few steps back to distance himself. He did not want to catch something in this desolate place where there were only four Skull Knights available for healing, and none of them able to mend his scars or stop his cough.

Grallik dug his slippered foot into the earth as he continued to watch the Dark Knights and workers labor to turn large rocks into small ones. Sweat plastered their tunics and tabards against their bodies and slicked their hair against their faces. It was hot already, though the sun was not yet up. But it was not nearly so hot as Grallik would soon make the stone.

The rocks and stone had to be very hot indeed in order for him to leech the precious iron from it.

"Look," a knight said between swings. He pointed to a small volcano to the north of the camp, its cap glowing bright orange. "One of these days it's going to bury this place."

"The gods won't let that happen," another knight said. "Steel Town's too valuable to gods and men."

"Hell Town," Grallik muttered, thinking that was a better name for this camp. "Aye, Hell Town is far, far too valuable."

The commander currently in charge of Steel Town, a decorated veteran of the Chaos War, Marshal Denu Montrill of Solace, approached and stopped at Grallik's side. Montrill also rose early to supervise the knights and laborers.

"Marshal Montrill," Grallik said, greeting him. "The slaves have been collecting richer ore from the deep part of the mountain, and I pull more iron from those rocks. But I do not believe all of our efforts should be spent on that shaft. There is still iron in the older sections, and it would be a waste to leave it there. We should mine the older sections until they are dry. Leave nothing useful behind."

Montrill nodded. "True enough. Still, I've had the youngest and strongest slaves assigned to the new shaft. And I've sent word to the Lord of the Night that we need more blacksmiths. They cannot keep up with you regardless, Guardian Grallik. They can't forge the swords fast enough."

Montrill's eyes sparkled darkly as he added: "More blacksmiths and armorers for the fine, fine steel you provide."

The knights and laborers backed away from the rubble they'd created, took several deep breaths, then started shoveling it into a cart, mindful not to splash any stone or dust on the commander and Grallik.

"Thank you. And now I think I must go about my business, Marshal Montrill, rather than waste too much time. If you will excuse me." Grallik respectfully withdrew to his workshop, mentally preparing himself for the spells he was going to cast upon the rocks. He hoped to finish at least one cart before the sun came up and the daily ritual began again.

****

Grallik participated in the ritual this morning. He recited the words perfectly, though merely by rote on this occasion. His mind was elsewhere—on the second mound of ore waiting for him in his workshop; on his talon, which had been grumbling about the lack of water and being assigned a shift of digging the new well; on the mine, which he feared would be rich with ore for an eternity; on being trapped by his usefulness, here in Steel Town.

He did not eat breakfast with the officers, instead heading straight to his workshop after the ritual and starting work on the ore. He had no appetite, and he ignored his thirst. He concentrated on the fire he summoned to swirl around the damnable rocks.

The furnace made the workshop impossibly hot and drenched the sorcerer in sweat. His eyes, pale blue under the sun, shone as he worked, and his scarred skin glistened as the iron began to drip from the rocks and pool beneath them. It was not terrible work, he had to admit. Playing with the fire pleased him.

Grallik did not leave his workshop until the horn was blown for the evening meal, his empty stomach convincing him that it was finally time to eat. The light had gone out of his eyes, giving his angular face a forlorn cast, an expression that told the others in the crude hall to give him a wide berth. He was exhausted, but not physically in the way the knights were who also sat at the tables. His muscles didn't ache from pounding rocks as theirs did, though his chest ached from his coughing bouts. Still, he was fatigued to the point of collapse. Fire magic drained him. Grallik demanded too much of himself and the magic. It was a point of pride with him that he nurtured the flames until he could scarcely stand or breathe.

He sat at the end of a long table, two lengths of his arm separating him from the nearest knight. He caught the glance of a young man, the tavern owner's son, who desired to be a squire to the Dark Knights, and who often worked the hall. The boy immediately filled a plate for him, bringing it steaming. A half-filled mug of water, which was rationed even for officers, quickly followed. Dinner was some sort of meat pie, served in an appealing golden-brown crust. Grallik savored the smell of it before cutting it open. He suspected the recipe had been intended for venison or beef, but there were no deer in this part of the country, and the Dark Knights did not keep cattle at the camp.

So mutton had been used instead, and not liberally. The pie was mostly made of chopped prunes and dates, with raisins lining the bottom. These fruits were readily available at Steel Town, as knights coming in for rotations brought wagons of supplies with them. There was a small side of a spinach pudding, and though it was reasonably tasty, Grallik thought the cook had used too much fennel. Dessert consisted of pears poached in wine and covered with a sweet syrup. All of it passable, he decided, though he'd had better at the camp. The food was not bad for the knights, at Steel Town.

When he was sated, he returned to the ore and went back to work until he nearly passed out, emerging before midnight in search of a bit of welcome coolness. But there was none. Despite the lateness, it was still uncomfortably hot.

It was darker than he expected, as the clouds had grown thick since dinner and stretched in all directions like they were sealing Steel Town and the mine in from the stars. Lightning flickered through the thunderheads, and Grallik could see curtains fluttering in open windows. He heard the pine trees shaking—no doubt shedding their needles.

He was irritable for a reason he couldn't define and blamed his foul mood on the starless sky. He lifted his head until he was staring straight up, feeling dizzy as he continued to watch the lightning fingers. Grallik breathed deep, hoping to find the scent of water in the clouds, something to cut the heat and override the odors of the knights and the stable and nearest livestock pen, and the worse stench that wafted from the slave pens.

Grallik faintly smelled the pine trees, this the most pleasant thing, and woodsmoke coming from the chimney of the tavern, even the iron nuggets in his workshop. He could always detect the smell the iron. The air that stirred the scents around him seemed trapped under the clouds, however, and made the world feel suffocating and cloying.

The thunderheads continued to pulse with lightning, and faint booms chased each other. The ground shuddered slightly under Grallik's feet, but not a single drop of rain. His scarred flesh tingled with anger and anticipation.

There must be a storm! Grallik prayed. Something to relieve the hell of hellish Steel Town, to drown out the stench that swelled under the cloud dome, to turn the damnable dust into damnable mud, to clear the air, however briefly, so that he could breathe easier and stop coughing.

If he had the right magic, he'd try something to coax the clouds into giving up the rain. But he didn't, and his magic was all but spent tonight anyway.

He heard the crack of thick lightning, and the rumble that followed it. He heard the guttural conversation of goblin and hobgoblin slaves; the whinny of horses; the laughter of someone in the tavern, the clink of mugs; the growl of the massive hatori—the huge digging beast kept near the base of the southern mine. He wished to hear the drumming of rain.

Water might be at a premium now, but the proprietor across the way had wine and ale and liquor aplenty. He dropped his gaze to the warm glow that spilled from the tavern window. He would buy something strong with the coins in his pocket, and he would sit in a corner by himself.

JEAN RABE

THE STONETELLERS

"Jean Rabe is adept at weaving a web of deceit and lies, mixed with adventure, magic, and mystery."
—sffworld.com on *Betrayal*

Jean Rabe returns to the DRAGONLANCE® world with a tale of slavery, rebellion, and the struggle for freedom.

VOLUME ONE

THE REBELLION

After decades of service, nature has dealt the goblins a stroke of luck. Earthquakes strike the Dark Knights' camp and mines, crippling the Knights and giving the goblins their best chance to escape. But their freedom will not be easy to win.

August 2007

VOLUME TWO

DEATH MARCH

The escaped slaves—led by the hobgoblin Direfang—embark on a journey fraught with danger as they leave Neraka to cross the ocean and enter the Qualinesti Forest, where they believe themselves free. . . .

August 2008

VOLUME THREE

GOBLIN NATION

A goblin nation rises in the old forest, building fortresses and fighting to hold onto their new homeland, while the sorcerers among them search for powerful magic cradled far beneath the trees.

August 2009

MARGARET WEIS
&
TRACY HICKMAN

The co-creators of the DRAGONLANCE® world return to the epic tale that introduced Krynn to a generation of fans!

THE LOST CHRONICLES

VOLUME ONE
DRAGONS OF THE DWARVEN DEPTHS

As Tanis and Flint bargain for refuge in Thorbardin, Raistlin and Caramon go to Neraka to search for one of the spellbooks of Fistandantilus. The refugees in Thorbardin are trapped when the draconian army marches, and Flint undertakes a quest to find the Hammer of Kharas to free them all, while Sturm becomes a key of a different sort.

VOLUME TWO
DRAGONS OF THE HIGHLORD SKIES

Dragon Highlord Ariakas assigns the recovery of the dragon orb taken to Ice Wall to Kitiara Uth-Matar, who is rising up the ranks of both the dark forces and of Ariakas's esteem. Finding the orb proves easy, but getting it from Laurana proves more difficult. Difficult enough to attract the attention of Lord Soth.

July 2007

VOLUME THREE
DRAGONS OF THE HOURGLASS MAGE

The wizard Raistlin Majere takes the black robes and travels to the capital city of the evil empire, Neraka, to serve the Queen of Darkness.

July 2008

RICHARD A. KNAAK

THE OGRE TITANS

The Grand Lord Golgren has been savagely crushing all opposition to his control of the harsh ogre lands of Kern and Blöde, first sweeping away rival chieftains, then rebuilding the capital in his image. For this he has had to deal with the ogre titans, dark, sorcerous giants who have contempt for his leadership.

VOLUME ONE
THE BLACK TALON

Among the ogres, where every ritual demands blood and every ally can become a deadly foe, Golgren seeks whatever advantage he can obtain, even if it means a possible alliance with the Knights of Solamnia, a questionable pact with a mysterious wizard, and trusting an elven slave who might wish him dead.

December 2007

VOLUME TWO
THE FIRE ROSE

With his other enemies beginning to converge on him from all sides, Golgren, now Grand Khan of all his kind, must battle with the Ogre Titans for mastery of a mysterious artifact capable of ultimate transformation and power.

December 2008

VOLUME THREE
THE GARGOYLE KING

Forced from the throne he has so long coveted, Golgren makes a final stand for control of the ogre lands against the Titans . . . against an enemy as ancient and powerful as a god.

December 2009

EXPERIENCE THE MAGIC

Return to Dominaria!

Time Spiral

Scott McGough

Teferi Planeswalker returns to his home plane of Dominaria to right the wrongs of the last war—only to find the plane in the throes of a temporal chaos that threatens to destroy reality.

Planar Chaos

Scott McGough and Timothy Sanders

Teferi Planeswalker sacrificed everything to save the world—and it only served to delay the inevitable. He needs allies, but who would ally with Teferi the traitor, who ran away during the last war?

Future Sight

Scott McGough and John Delaney

Teferi Planeswalker is out of friends, out of luck, and out of time. For the sacrifices of his friends to be worth it, he must get help to stop the temporal chaos before it stops everything.

RAVENLOFT™
THE COVENANT

RAVENLOFT'S LORDS OF DARKNESS HAVE ALWAYS WAITED FOR THE UNWARY TO FIND THEM.

Six classic tales of horror set in the RAVENLOFT world have returned to print in all-new editions.

From the autocratic vampire who wrote the memoirs found in *I, Strahd* to the demon lord and his son whose story is told in *Tapestry of Dark Souls*, some of the finest horror characters created by some of the most influential authors of horror and dark fantasy have found their way to RAVENLOFT, to be trapped there forever.

LAURELL K. HAMILTON

Death Of A Darklord

CHRISTIE GOLDEN

Vampire Of The Mists

P.N. ELROD

I, Strahd: The Memoirs Of A Vampire

ANDRIA CARDARELLE

To Sleep With Evil

ELAINE BERGSTROM

Tapestry of Dark Souls

June 2007

TANYA HUFF

Scholar of Decay

October 2007

LISA SMEDMAN

The New York Times best-selling author of *Extinction* follows up on the War of the Spider Queen with a new trilogy that brings the Chosen of Lolth out of the Demonweb Pits and on a bloody rampage across Faerûn.

THE LADY PENITENT

BOOK I

SACRIFICE OF THE WIDOW

Halisstra Melarn has been a priestess of Lolth, a repentant follower of Eilistraee, and a would-be killer of gods, but now she's been transformed into the monstrous Lady Penitent, and those she once called friends will feel the sting of her venom.

BOOK II

STORM OF THE DEAD

As the followers of Eilistraee fall one by one to Halisstra's wrath, Lolth turns her attention to the other gods.

September 2007

BOOK III

ASCENDANCY OF THE LAST

The dark elves of Faerûn must finally choose between a goddess that offers redemption and peace, or a goddess that demands sacrifice and blood. We know what a human would choose, but what about a drow?

June 2008

THOMAS M. REID

The author of *Insurrection* and The Scions of Arrabar Trilogy rescues Aliisza and Kaanyr Vhok from the tattered remnants of their assault on Menzoberranzan, and sends them off on a quest across the multiverse that will leave FORGOTTEN REALMS fans reeling!

THE EMPYREAN ODYSSEY

BOOK I

THE GOSSAMER PLAIN

Kaanyr Vhok, fresh from his defeat against the drow, turns to hated Sundabar for the victory his demonic forces demand, but there's more to his ambitions than just one human city. In his quest for arcane power, he sends the alu-fiend Aliisza on a mission that will challenge her in ways she never dreamed of.

May 2007

BOOK II

THE FRACTURED SKY

A demon surrounded by angels in a universe of righteousness? How did that become Aliisza's life?

November 2008

BOOK III

THE CRYSTAL MOUNTAIN

What Aliisza has witnessed has changed her forever, but that's nothing compared to what has happened to the multiverse itself. The startling climax will change the nature of the cosmos forever.

Mid-2009

"Reid is proving himself to be one of the best up and coming authors in the FORGOTTEN REALMS universe."

—fantasy-fan.org